WHOLESOME HOPES

Becky's Prayers

Karen Mallory

PublishAmerica
Baltimore

ISBN: 1-60672-946-2
PUBLISHED BY PUBLISHAMERICA, LLLP
www.publishamerica.com
Baltimore

Printed in the United States of America

Dedication

Above all, I cannot say or write this enough! Thank you for loving me, for extending your mercy and grace beyond what I deserve. My Father, my Savior, my friend. I love you and will praise you always.

To my dear sweet husband, I give my dedication as well. Your love and friendship along with your support in all ways, helped tremendously throughout this journey. Again, I thank God. If it were not for Him, I would never have had the honor and privilege of knowing my fabulous, adorable, loving and giving husband. Thank you, my love for all you do.

I also want to include my family and friends. All their encouragement, I believe, God exquisitely planned. To be where I am is where He placed me to learn and do this work. It is also, where I finally realized our God is who He says He is and where I became a believer, taking Jesus as my Lord and Savior. He gives my family strength so He could work this in me and they have loved and supported my journey with patience beyond my expectations. I pray they know in their hearts, just how much I love them. I know God does. Thank you again, God! My parents, family, and friends are fantastic!

Prologue

Rebecca Stanley, an only child of William and Elizabeth Stanley, was born November 13, 1943 in San Diego, California. She was a very happy child and loved the companionship with other children. Being an only child, her parents never spoiled her to the point of having everything she wanted. Both, her parents believed in moderation when it came to material possessions. She was never in need or left feeling she went without. Her home was quiet, peaceful and full of love. Family vacations were amusement parks and exploring different beachfronts along the coast. William kept their spiritual bible studies mainly at home, with the occasional Church Sundays in the community. They believed in God and read from the Bible every evening.

Elizabeth, from the day she brought Rebecca home from the hospital, called her, "Becky", and she went by this name always. She was a tomboy, which started in her early childhood. She wore jeans and played cowboys and Indians with the neighborhood children. School was a struggle for Becky, as her attention was always on playing with her friends. Her favorite subjects in school were recess and physical education. Having many friends in grade school, things changed when she entered her first year of high school. Most of her friends were in different classes and they seemed to lose the closeness they had once shared together as children. Her freshman, sophomore and junior years were uneventful. She had one very special friend, Dusty Green, and the two girls spent their time together doing homework and playing tag football with the other kids at the high school field.

Dusty, much like Becky was a tomboy too. At the end of their junior year, they had started attending the basketball games and going to the dances. Their maturing process was now edging its way into a full bloom. Dusty met a boy soon after the dances became more enticing, sort of an anticipation of the unexpected. She met a boy named Richard Brooks there and fell head over heels in no time at all. That left Becky alone the summer before their senior year. She spent the majority of her time listening to music and wondering if she would ever fall in love like Dusty. Elizabeth tried to get her to change her hairstyle that summer and even encouraged her to start wearing light make-up.

However, Becky always thought she was plain and did not think all that would do her any good. When Elizabeth took her shopping for new school clothes, even pointing out to her the latest styles all the other girls were wearing, had no effect. Once again, Becky refused and was determined to wear what she liked and did not care what anyone else thought. Dusty tried too, but Becky was her own person and going to stay that way. Dusty and Richard decided to spend time getting Becky to go out with them to movies, games and dances.

She would go, but refused to go all the time, saying, "The two of you need to be together by yourselves too."

It was now November into her senior year. Becky began to feel herself changing. Her hair was blonde and hung down to her waist. She wore her dresses loosely around her now shapely figure. The days of her childhood were transforming and blossoming into a completely new person. What were changing were her emotions. She dreamed of romantic scenes; dancing a waltz in a long gown, her hand being held by a boy and falling in love. Dusty would tell her; that words could not describe what your heart is capable of feeling when you are truly in love. Becky would sigh and dream on once again.

Chapter One

Dusty, after falling in love with Richard, would talk about how they would marry, live in the same neighborhood and raise their children together.

Becky would always come back with, "Dusty will marry and have lots of terrific kids, and plain old Becky will become an old maid."

For she had no interest in the boys she had met in school and was convinced that her destiny would be to become, "the old maid", she had told Dusty on several occasions.

Christmas break was now upon them and Dusty had talked her into attending the dance with her and Richard. Becky, stubborn as always, she wore her usual everyday dress, her hair in a ponytail, tennis shoes with white socks, and completely unaware how her life would change forever on this evening.

Instead of the usual records played by the music department, the school booked a local band. Everyone was full of excitement, with the exception of Becky. Richard surprised the girls by taking them out to dinner before the dance, at a very exclusive restaurant, where he gave Dusty her Christmas gift, a beautiful engagement ring. Dusty was extremely overwhelmed with joy and Becky was excited and pleased to share this moment of joy with her dearest friend. She listened to their plans for the future and was so very happy for the both of them. Engulfed with their plans of marriage after Richard finished boot camp, that coming summer, they did not notice anything different in the gymnasium. After finally settling down, Richard took Dusty to the dance floor. Becky stood at the back of the gym as she always did and watched. As she gazed about the floor, her sights kept returning to Richard and Dusty, she saw how happy and in love they were, by the deep staring into each others eyes, as if they were the only two people in the room. Sighing with a peaceful smile, she viewed on around the room and stopped when she spotted the band. She didn't realize they were there until that very moment. Looking further, her eye came upon a boy playing the guitar. Her eyes fixed as she watched every move he made. The song they were playing was a slow easy song. Mesmerized, she started moving closer to the stage. With the dance floor crowded, she moved through as if no one else were even there. Capturing Dusty's attention, she nudged Richard; they both stopped dancing to see what was drawing her. Becky stopped just behind a crowd of girls, dancing and trying to get the attention of different members of the band. When she realized where she was, she quickly moved to the back of the room, but never taking her eyes off this boy. She thought to herself how soft his eyes were, as he sang the most beautiful song she had ever heard.

Her mind went on and on, with such tremendous speed, she could not stop and did not want to either. Dusty went up to Becky and had to shake her to get her attention. Not knowing what was happening to her, she felt she was having some kind of spell or even a seizure. Back to herself again, Becky told her about the boy she was watching. Explaining in the same detail, that she had going through her mind. Dusty just sighed with relief.

As Becky went on describing this boy, Dusty realized she was finally attracted to someone. Becky went on to say, what an idiot she must be, for thinking he would ever have anything to do with the likes of her. Dusty tried to argue that point, but Becky's face projected the disappointment unlike any expression she had ever seen. She could find no words of comfort for what Becky was feeling. Her eyes now filled with tears, she hurried through the crowd to the girl's room.

Richard had already figured out what to do next. He stood by Becky before she ran off, just listening. Dusty quickly followed behind her and Richard went back stage to wait for the band to take a break. While on their break, Richard talked to some of the members of the band. He, himself played guitar and was readily accepted into their discussions. By the time the break was over, Richard received an invitation to a jam session and permission to bring the girls along. Then he returned to the back of the room and waited for them.

Through her sobbing, she told Dusty she wanted to go home. She told Becky she would find Richard and be back for her. Before Dusty could say anything to Richard, he told her what he had been doing and of his plan to get Becky to meet the boy, she had been watching. Dusty was just in "awe!" how Richard had managed to read Becky to a "tee". She hurried back through the crowd and found Becky in the bathroom stall, still crying. Again, she shook her, and then told her what Richard had done.

Becky dried her tears from her face and said emotionally, "I would have to become someone else for that boy to notice me. Paint my face, dress in tight fitting showy clothes, lots of curls in my hair and tons of make-up, all those things I don't believe in doing."

Dusty encouraged, "Just give it a try, and see what happens. Then, one way or the other, you will know. If you let him pass by, you will never know and always wonder. "Please Becky!" just try, and if he is truly for you, it will happen to him, just as it did to you."

Becky agreed, hesitantly, and then stated, "What do I have to lose!"

As the evening ended and everyone was leaving, Becky watched the boy as he untangled the wires to all the equipment.

Dusty's thoughts flowed aloud; "what would happen if this boy were not attracted to her? Would this ruin Becky, forever? What could she do to help her dearest friend through such deep devastation?" Turning quickly to Richard for his advice, she only found his thoughts were the same.

Becky trailed behind on the way to Richard's car, so not to interrupt their conversation. She looked through the parking lot and watched as the band loaded the instruments into their van. Not seeing the boy she watched for so long, she looked further. Out of the building, with arms full of cords and carrying two guitar cases, he came. She watched, thinking how she would like to help him carry some of his load. As she watched, he dropped one of the cords. Not realizing what he had done, and without thought, she ran across the parking lot, picked up the cord and ran straight to him. Just as she came up upon him, she suddenly realized how she must look. "Too late now!" she said to herself.

Her face fully flushed with embarrassment and almost totally out of breath, he turned with a smile. Her eyes beaming as she told him what he had done. His eyes met hers and he could not say a word. His thoughts ran wild of her unpainted beauty. He had never met a girl before, besides his sisters, without tons of make-up and fancy little other things. As he tried to find the words to thank her, he also wanted to ask many questions about this find of a lifetime. A prayer, quickly came to mind, "Please God, don't let me mess this up, she's too special."

Still waiting, she straightened her dress, as if she had

taken a tumble in the dirt, and then said, "I like your music."

He looked deeper into her big brown eyes and said, "I know I've never met you before, but I feel I've known you a long time. I hope it's not too much of me to ask, if we could go out sometime and talk? And if you would agree, I'd like to make it a date."

Becky's heart was now pounding even harder. Trying not to show just how excited she really was, she could not because her face could tell no lies. With a deep breath, she composed herself and enthusiastically accepted his date.

He asked if the following night would be too soon and she quickly replied, "No that would be fine." She then said, "Goodnight", and went to Richard's car.

Still full of wonder and her heart calming to normal she proceeded to tell Dusty and Richard all the details. They were very happy to see Becky experiencing this exciting new change that she would hold dear, the rest of her life.

Becky, very quiet on the drive home, and Dusty not knowing what to say, they all sat in silence. The thoughts going through Becky's mind were once again endless. One thought following another, leaving her numb. Trying to answer or even reason out these thoughts only brought more to perplex her even further.

All she could manage to decipher among those thoughts were the words Dusty had said earlier that evening, "To just try to see."

Then Becky added to herself, "And a lot of prayers."

When Richard pulled into Becky's drive, Dusty told her she would be over first thing in the morning to help her get an outfit together. Becky, in a quiet voice just said, "O.k."

She thanked them for dinner and helping her through the rough spots of the evening then went inside. As she walked through the front room, she noticed her mother was in the study reading. She went in and sat down by her on the couch. Elizabeth asked if she had had a nice time at the dance.

Becky hastily volunteered, "I met a boy and he asked me out on a date."

"What did you say?" asked Elizabeth.

"I accepted," Becky simply answered. Elizabeth laid down her book on the coffee table and turned to Becky.

Then she asked, "What's wrong, honey? You look so sad."

Becky hesitated again for a few moments, and then told her everything that had happened that night.

Elizabeth's first thought was of this boy; "no one knew his name, where he lived or anything about him," but she kept quiet while Becky went on through the evening events.

When she had finished, she told her mother she was tired and went off to bed. Elizabeth's mind was now filling with even more questions and concerns.

At the breakfast table the next morning, Elizabeth told William about Becky's night out. He was very concerned that this boy could hurt Becky and even possibly mark her reputation as well.

After finishing his coffee, he stood up from the table and said," We will continue this discussion at dinner."

Elizabeth reminded him that Becky was to go out that evening on her date.

He replied, "I will take care of this myself! Let her go tonight and we'll take it from there."

This was a side of William, Elizabeth had never seen before and the tone of his voice was not one to be provoked.

Dusty arrived at Becky's by eight a.m that morning to find her still fast asleep.

"Get up sleepy head, we have some work to do!" she said.

Becky pulled herself up, looked at the clock, and grouch fully said, "Are you crazy!" its only eight. Is it going to take all day to do the impossible? Why bother! He is going to run the first chance he gets. He's probably sorry already."

Dusty ignored her statements and went to the closet, saying, "Let's see what we have in here to work with."

Becky moaned, threw off the covers and groaned, "Can I at least brush my teeth and wash my face, thank you!"

"Not a morning person." whispered Dusty under her breath.

Looking through the closet, she found a nice stylish dress way in the back, hidden behind an old overcoat.

She pulled it out and when Becky came back to the room, Dusty was holding it up with a big grin on her face.

Becky looked at it and said, "I've never worn that dress. I didn't even remember it being in there."

"What do you think?" asked Dusty.

"It will do if it fits, I guess." replied Becky.

Dusty sat down on the bed and folded the dress on her lap, asking her, "Why, are you so down in the dumps and what happened to all the excitement?"

Becky sat down beside her and said, "I'm not sure, I feel like something is going to go wrong. And I don't know what or why, it's just a feeling."

Dusty put her arm around Becky's shoulder and said, "There's only one way to make that feeling go away! You have to think positive and be tough. Go out tonight, have the best time and get to know Sam."

Becky jumped up! "You know his name!"

"Richard told me last night," replied Dusty.

"What else did he tell you?" she asked.

Dusty went on, "His name is Sam Frankie Malloy, he is eighteen and graduated last year. Oh, and get this! He joined the army and goes to boot camp the same day Richard leaves. They may be stationed together."

Becky just sat repeating his name. After a while, she asked Dusty what she was going to do while Richard was gone.

Dusty answered, "I'll be very busy with our wedding plans and thinking about college, too."

Becky apologized for letting Dusty's plans completely skip her mind.

Dusty smiled, then said, "There's no need to apologize, we are friends and friends never forget. You just have so many things on your mind that the future is too far off to think about."

Becky looked so pretty that night. Dusty had curled her hair and convinced her to wear stockings with her dress shoes to finish off the perfect look for the evening. No make-up, but Dusty did put around her neck a dainty heart necklace, she had found in the dresser. Becky laughed!

Dusty asked, "What's so funny?"

"He doesn't know where I live." She said.

Dusty replied, "Yes he does!"

With that, at the same time, both girls said, "Richard!"

That day they had talked about how their lives could be as perfect as any fairy tale. Both finding true loves, settling down, and being happier than they had ever dreamed. Behind all the fun and talking the two shared, Becky was still feeling the same in her thoughts about something going wrong. It was too good to be true. There was going to be something to take all her joy now in her heart and toss it away. She tried so hard to reason what it might be, but she could not find anything. She would have to wait and see what it would be that would break her heart. Dusty knew her part was finished for the day and said her goodbyes with a hug with a kiss on the cheek for good luck. Becky thanked her for the wonderful day and all the help. Then she told Dusty, she could not have done it without her.

Dusty responded, "We are good together and I am so happy you are my best friend." Then, saying she would be over sometime the next day to hear all about her date, and left to meet Richard.

Right at seven p.m., the doorbell rang. Elizabeth answered and there stood Sam. Not a hair out of place, clean cut, dressed in a sharp black suit.

Very politely, he gave his name, and then said, "I'm here to pick up Becky."

Elizabeth asked him in and took him to the living room, then had him take a seat while she went to get Becky. William came in just as they were leaving and Sam introduced himself with a firm handshake. William gave his name and told both Becky and Sam to have a nice evening. Becky was nervous, as would have been expected on any ones first date, but managed not to show it at all. Sam did most of the talking to break the ice at first, which didn't take too long, as Becky could be a real chatterbox! Throughout the evening, he kept noticing her staring at him, as if she was in a trance. He finally asked her if there was something wrong.

She smiled and answered, "No, I just like your eyes; they seem to say so much about you, that's all."

"I know what you mean; when I look into your eyes I feel the same thing. But I also feel there is something you are worried about." said Sam.

She assured him there was nothing worrying her and said she was just a bit nervous.

Then added, "I am more at ease, the more you talk".

Sam had taken Becky to a quiet café, to spend time talking and just getting to know each other. They took turns asking questions and soon it became somewhat of a game between them. She could ask a lot more personal questions than he could, as she knew he played the guitar, sang and wrote his own music. He, on the other hand, had no clue as to what she liked to do. Once Becky started talking, it was completely obvious that she was capable of extensive conversation. She told him her likes and dislikes without holding anything back. He found in Becky, an honesty and directness, unlike anyone he had ever met. This was a pleasure that both of them would come to share.

After a long while, Sam looked into her eyes and told her how beautiful she looked.

Making it clear, that she did not have to make any fuss for him, he said, "Becky," you have a beauty all your own and I wouldn't want to see you change."

She blushed, and then told him, "I can't be anyone else but who I am and it makes me happy to hear that you appreciate that."

Then went on to tell him how handsome he looked in his suit. Adding, she would make a guess, that he would have been more at ease in jeans. He laughed and told her she was very good at reading him.

"But", he said, I do like to dress up for special occasions and if you would admit it, you do too."

As the evening ended, both Sam and Becky had had the best time they could have ever imagined, exchanging to each other the joy they had found and making plans to go different places together. All her fears seemed to be gone, with all her prayers so far, been answered. Sam had her home that night by eleven, so not to worry her parents.

He walked her to the door and said, "I'll see you soon."

Both her parents were waiting up for her return that night. She came in smiling ear-to-ear and laughing. Her mother asked her to come in, sit with her and tell them how her evening had gone. Becky could hardly stay in her seat, telling them how much fun it was to just sit and talk for hours. She told them he was from Missouri and was born September 16, 1942, in a small hospital in town. For the last year, he has been traveling with his band and has taken up residency here in San Diego. In June, he will be leaving with Richard for boot camp in the army. She told them that during his time in the service, he plans to go to school and become a doctor. She went on to tell them how he learned to play the guitar, sitting under a tree on the family farm. He has six brothers and two sisters, all,-older then him, still living in Missouri. He said his brother's help run the family farm and his sisters come home to help their mom with the garden and canning. She told them of how he talked about his mother and how very much he loves his family. He is homesick a lot of the time, but he writes and calls every week and plans to visit them soon. Elizabeth told Becky that she thought Sam was a very nice boy, and William agreed.

When she excused herself to go to her room, her father interrupted saying,

"Becky!" we need to have a talk."

All her happiness was about to end. What she had felt when she told Dusty, that something would go wrong, was about to become a reality.

Her father said, "Becky, I don't want you to get upset. There are things I need to say. And I want you to completely hear me out before you say a word."

She asked, "Daddy", what's wrong?"

William came back with, "Nothing is wrong! Please, just listen."

As he spoke, Becky became numb, she clearly understood her fears were not in Sam's acceptance but it was her own parents who were about to break her heart.

Her father told her that he had enrolled her into a private boarding school in Boston and she would be finishing out her senior year there, and then she would begin college in the summer. He had planned to sell the house and move to Boston just as soon as they could get the paperwork in order. Becky grew angry, thinking how they could plan her life without her being involved; they had never done anything like this in all her seventeen years, why now. She let them have their say, but she was so overwhelmed, she had no words to fight for herself. She asked then to be excused, and went to her room. Elizabeth followed her, but Becky turned to her and said she would like to be alone.

After a long night spent crying, Becky started to think. She had no family other than her parents. Her grandparents had long pasted away and no aunts or uncles at all. No one to help her defend or reason with her parents plans. She felt so alone and hurt, that she had completely forgotten what a wonderful time she had the day before with Dusty and Sam on their first date. Now she had her future pre-planned for her with no regard for her own dreams. Before, they had always made it a point to plan everything together as a family.

As she sat on the side of her bed, she began to discuss her thoughts aloud; "why had nothing ever been said before, and it was not until I met a boy that things changed so fast. They are jumping to all sorts of conclusions without any reason whatsoever."

She knew there was absolutely nothing she could say or do to remedy the situation. The Bible, she reflects on, tells her to be obedient to her parents and respect their judgments. The day would come when she would be making choices and decisions for herself and all the guidance her parents had taught her would guide her to the right path through life. However, for now she would have to give into their plans and do as they say, without any argument. Becky being an emotional teenager, this would be the most difficult task she felt she would ever have before her.

For the next three days, she did not leave her room. Torn with the thought of her parents plan to send her so far away from everything and everyone she had ever known.

She refused telephone calls from both Dusty and Sam. Dusty came to the house, but Becky refused to see her. Elizabeth tried to reason with Becky, that it was in her best interest and her father wanted only the best for her. The only way Becky knew to keep from saying things she might regret to her parents, was to stay quiet and not talk at all. The pressure was building inside her. Somehow she would have to let the anger go. So she prayed to the Lord to forgive her, that she needed emotionally somehow to deal with everything. Her father came in from work one night and told her, to stop being a baby that she needed to realize they were right and too tough it out, and no more said, no more moping. He ordered her to start packing and that she would be leaving in six days. That was the end of the conversation.

The next morning, she was up at dawn, dressed to go to the park and run. Her mother called Dusty just as soon as she left the house, telling her how much Becky would need to talk to someone. Dusty rushed over to find Becky in the park with a baseball bat. Hitting trees, the ground, picnic tables, just anything she crossed. Shocked by her behavior, all she could do was watch.

Becky cried crying out, "Why", why now, why not a long time ago! My parents hate me, I just want to die!" As she stopped and stood up straight, she sighed. "I'm already dead. My heart can't take this. "Dusty!" Please tell me I'm just in a bad dream. Wake me up, somebody, wake me up!"

Dusty went up to her and Becky just fell into her arms sobbing.

After Dusty managed to calm her down enough for her to tell her what was going on, Becky proceeded to cover the words her father had said the night she came home from her date. Dusty was horrified, to say the least, as Becky gave her the news of having to go away.

With her eyes full of tears, she looked at Dusty and said, "How am I going to handle this, I can't run away or hurt my parents."

"Why can't you talk to your parents about how you feel?" asked Dusty.

"If you could have heard the tone of my father's voice, you would know there is no way to reason. He has given me his orders and I am to do just as he says," replied Becky.

Dusty told her that Richard and Sam would need to hear this, and that Sam had been very worried by her refusal of his phone calls, saying, "He must have done or said something wrong or that you just were being nice to him and that you are not interested in him."

Becky gave out a strange peculiar laugh then said, "He's everything I've ever dreamed of and everything I am going to loose."

"Let's go to Richard's and then try to find Sam so we can explain to him what's been happening," said Dusty.

When they arrived at Richard's house, he and Sam were standing in the garage. Both boys ran to the car. They could see the girls had been crying even before they reached the doors. Sam could only figure it had something to do with him and that Becky's parents did not approve him suitable for their daughter. Dusty jumped out of the car into Richard's arms, but Becky just sat. Sam opened the door for her, but she did not move. She just stared at the floorboard. He knelt down and took her hand.

Then he asked, "Becky", tell me what's wrong."

She turned her head to him, looked into his eyes through the tears and wrapped her arms around his neck. She held on for the longest time, neither one saying a word. After almost an hour, she took a deep breath and pulled herself away. Again, he asked her what had happened. She told him her father's plans to send her away and she had six days before she had to leave. He stood up, looked up into the sky and pressed his palms to the sides of his face in anguish.

Now Richard was thinking on the lines of finding a place for Becky to go, if she chose to run away. Dusty wanted to ask her parents if Becky could stay with them. And Sam knew he could not help, as he could barely make ends meet for himself. He thought about calling her parents and trying to arrange a time to sit and talk this over, that maybe if they understood his intentions were of the utmost honor, they might, consider a change of heart. From the short time he had spent getting to know Becky, he knew she would have to make the first move.

He was ready to back her up with any decision she made. So he asked, "Becky", what do you want to do?"

She eagerly replied, "Stay here, just like things are. I can't run away, I would hurt them more than they have hurt me. I love them and I will have to do as they say. I will have to leave my friends, miss Dusty's wedding, give up what might be my only chance of knowing the love of my life. And why? Because I cannot hurt them, I do not want to hurt anyone. To do this I must carry all the pain and go on like its nothing."

"Becky? Sam asked, would you write to me and come back for the wedding if I bought you a plane ticket?"

Dusty added, "You are my maid of honor, you have to be here. You can stay here when you come."

"I'm not much of a letter writer, but I will call all the time and learn to be the best writer you ever dreamed of," Sam promised and then, after boot camp, we may have many plans of our own. I haven't known you very long, but I have a feeling your going to be my girl forever."

With all those, heart felt words; Becky smiled, and in a joking response said, "I can live with those plans!"

The last five days for all of them went far too fast. Becky filled them with time alone together with Sam. Dusty understood and gave them their space, but she knew how much she was going to miss her best friend. Sam took her dancing, he played his guitar for her in the park and they took long walks on the beach. The day before she was to fly away, Dusty planned a going away party. The four of them shared the day swimming, visiting and making plans to help long distance with the wedding. Becky had to be home that night by ten. Sam wanted a few hours for the two of them to share their last few moments that would have to last in their hearts and minds for the next five months. They decided to walk the beach and just sit for a while hand in hand.

As they sat watching the surf, Becky said, "Tonight is the last time we will see each other for several months and I want to ask you something. "Please!" don't say anything you do not feel. I know we have not known each other very long, but I am in love with you. And I truly mean this from every fiber of my heart."

Before she could go any further, Sam interrupted and said, "Becky!" I fell in love with you in the parking lot the first night when our eyes met. I looked into those frightened big brown eyes and if you can remember, I was lost for words. I prayed for help to keep from messing up, so that I wouldn't say something totally so unappreciated that I would blow any chance of ever seeing you again. I have been, so blessed by our Lord; he answered my prayer that night beyond my deepest dreams. I continually thank Him every day for bringing you to me. You are the love put on this earth for me and nothing will ever change the way I feel. You may be worried that I could meet someone else after a while, but you are wrong. I have you in my heart and only you for the rest of my days. Now I have a question and you don't have to answer it right away, it may be one you will need to think on for a while." He took her hands into both of his, scrunched and wiggled to get to his knees from sitting in the sand and asked, "Will you marry me, Becky?" Then he took one hand away, pulled a ring from his pocket, and placed it on her finger, saying, "I don't mean to rush you, but I would like to get married when I finish boot camp. I don't know where the army will send me and I need you with me."

Her eyes welled with tears pouring, and with a smile as warm and gentle as could be expressed, she answered, "You were right in the way, our Lord answers our prayers. We are so blessed and, "Yes!" I will marry you."

Sam added, "We can make our plans in our letters and phone calls, so that everything is set by the time you get back." Then he took her in his arms, kissed her, and made her a promise, "I will keep myself only unto you and if any time you need me, I will be there and please never forget just how much your love means to me."

Becky, once again in tears, feeling extremely happy and sad at the same time, could only fall into his arms. Neither could say anymore and held each other in their own way to cherish the moment. Then arm in arm, quietly sitting back, they stared out into the ocean until it was time to leave.

He had Becky at her doorstep just before ten.

She quickly said, "No goodbyes." Because she knew, there would be no holding back her emotions if they did.

Sam smiled and said, "I'll see you soon."

As Becky entered the door, she looked back and he quickly returned to his van. She watched until he was completely out of sight, and then sadly closed the door.

William had gone to bed and Elizabeth had waited for Becky. She made them the special tea that Becky had always enjoyed when they spent times talking. Then she called Becky to the kitchen and they sat at the table, but neither one could find the words to comfort the hurt feelings or awkwardness they both felt. Becky sat reminiscing in her thoughts, a time of love, sharing and all the conversations her family had once shared. How that had changed so suddenly, it just broke her heart. All those things they once strived for were gone and she knew, that time was gone forever. If they had only spent some time with Sam, they would have come to find what a special person he is, they would have grown to love him, too. None of this needless pain for each one of them would have ever occurred. She thought if she could say this out loud to her mother, just maybe they could bring back that closeness, but she was not sure exactly why or even if her meeting Sam was the cause if all this turmoil. So, they sat in silence and finished their tea, then Elizabeth told Becky she had better get some rest as her day would be a long and tiring one ahead.

Elizabeth woke her up at four a.m., as her flight would be leaving on schedule at seven. By five thirty, she had showered and finished the remaining packing. Conversation at the breakfast table was of only instructions of her flight time and who would be meeting her in Boston. William told her to follow all the school protocol and get into no trouble whatsoever.

Elizabeth asked Becky if she would be all right.

William interrupted, sternly telling Elizabeth, "Becky is seventeen, a young lady. We have taught her right from wrong; she will be just fine!"

Elizabeth stood up from the table, walked over to Becky, kissed her on the cheek and quickly left the room. With that, William stood and announced it was time to go. It was a very quiet ride to the airport. William checked in Becky's luggage, and then proceeded to the gate. The flight was announced over the intercom, Becky and William, gave their cold goodbyes and Becky boarded the plane.

Chapter Two

On arriving at the Boston airport, Becky saw a woman holding up a sign with her name. She introduced herself as, Miss. Woodward, the housemother of her dorm at the Boston Academy for girls. The two shook hands and retrieved Becky's luggage.

During the thirty-minute drive from the airport to the academy, Miss. Woodward spelled out the house rules; "At this academy, we have lights out by ten p.m. You are to be in the building no later than seven thirty. We will not tolerate tardiness, loud laughter, angry conversations with others, fowl language or sloppiness. You will be prepared for class with neatly done assignments and no one else is to help neither you, nor you them. There is a pay phone in the hall for everyone's use. No one gets more than five minutes a call. In addition, you may have only two calls per week. Now, all rules have exceptions, but you must earn them and always get my permission as well." After she had finished laying out all her rules, she abruptly asked, "Do you understand?"

Becky was quick in her response with, "I understand

completely, Miss. Woodward, you will have no problems from me."

Then Miss. Woodward ended the conversation with, "We are very pleased to have you and I'm looking forward to see all your fathers expectations fulfilled."

Those words suddenly brought back the angry feelings between her and her father, but with closing her eyes and putting an image of Sam's smiling face in her mind, her anger subsided. She had already decided to keep to herself. Dusty had given her a gift from her and Richard, which was a box filled with writing paper, stamps and envelops.

In one of the envelopes, Sam put in quite a bit of cash, along with a note saying, "To be used for a one way ticket back to me at any time."

He had told her to call collect whenever she felt she needed a pick-up. And so, Becky felt more comfortable knowing her friends and fiancé really were not so far away. She could keep her loneliness with those words and by staying busy.

Even though the drive was full of rules, Becky found pleasure in the beautiful sights. Not congested like California and so many more trees. The weather was cold instead of cool and Miss. Woodward had told her that the weather forecast was calling for at least eight inches of snow overnight. Seeing the sights on the weekends might be a bit more difficult, but Becky looked forward to this new challenge and could not wait to make a snowman.

Surely, there would be some children out, that would show her how and tell her all their own adventures. She asked Miss. Woodward if there was a store near by where she could find a heavier coat. She told Becky she would need more than just a heavy coat, that one of the girls would assist her to find gloves, scarves and snow boots also. Entering thru the tall rod iron gates to one of the most beautiful landscapes of brick buildings and walkways, Becky felt as though she was out of place. The driveways and walkways were all of red brick. With manicured shrubbery guiding the pathways on to join one building to another. Although she felt consumed by it all, there would be plenty of sights to see and peaceful walks to take that would help the next few months go by quickly. The early American décor of the dormitory was elegant, to say the least. It was spotlessly clean and extremely quiet. Her room felt cozy and warm with a privacy all her own. Everyone else in the dorm had a roommate but her. For a while, she thought maybe her father had planned this also, but it was not as she thought. Miss. Woodward left her to rest and put away her belongings.

On her way out the door, she said she would have Mrs. Nelson come to do her uniform fitting. Then said, "You will hear the dinner bell ring at six-o-clock sharp, adding, dresses are required in the dinning room."

Becky wrinkled her face and pointed her nose in the air after Miss. Woodward turned to leave the room. She closed the door and walked over to the bed then knelt down on her knees to pray. Asking for forgiveness for the attitude now developing in her mind, she prayed for patience and acceptance. She had a rough road ahead and needed all the blessings possible; in order to adapt to her new surroundings.

During dinner, Miss Woodward introduced her to all the girls in the dorm. All in their fancy clothes, make-up and all like puppets, taking turns on cue as instructed. There were fifteen meticulously groomed as well as beautiful girls, yet they all seemed the same.

Becky reminded herself, "I am Becky!" Becky is going to be Becky, Becky is not a puppet, and Becky will not become a puppet, not now, not ever!"

The next morning, once again, the loud bell rang. This time it served as an alarm, situated in the hall for the whole group. After dressing, it was down to the dinning room for a fun filled breakfast. No conversations between anyone were shared, just the sounds of everyone eating in their polite little world. Prior of being excused from the table, Miss. Woodward assigned Lenetta, the most beautiful girl in the dorm, to be Becky's guide through her classes for the day.

"Yes, Miss. Woodward, it would be an honor." She stated, exactly as a trained parrot would answer upon request.

Lenetta had no intension of becoming friends with her. After dropping her off at her first class room, she would be waiting when the bell rang to drop her at the next. Becky new she had better make herself a map, so not to have this most pleasant person to follow behind tomorrow.

Most of the instructors seemed cold rooted, with the exception of her biology instructor who was also her swimming coach as well. Her name was Mrs. Miller and Becky could see right from the start that she was not a robot like the others. Somehow, Mrs. Miller knew Becky was different and immediately took her under her wing. She told Becky's housemother that Becky would need special attention after class in order for her to catch up with the rest of the class. Miss. Woodward agreed as long as Becky kept up with all her other studies.

In a short time, not only did Mrs. Miller bring her up in biology, she helped Becky with all her classes. After a few sessions with Mrs. Miller, Becky asked her why she was being so nice to her.

Becky stated, "I'm the only one here after school! Then asked, Am I that far behind the rest of my classmates?"

Mrs. Miller told her of her own experiences going to private academies, provided by her loving stepfather. Then she said, "I know you don't belong here, because I see a lot of myself in you. Moreover, it is so nice to see a change from young people who think they are better than someone else. "But, Becky!" you didn't hear that from me."

Becky laughed and said, "I'm so thankful you are here, I know God is watching out for me now."

Becky and Mrs. Miller had hit it off well and both were glad to have one another. Mrs. Miller had told her, that on weekends she was free to see the sight, take in a movie, shopping, anything her heart desired as long as she was in the dorm by seven thirty. By that weekend, they had made a secret pack to explore some of the sights. In addition, by the first two weekends, they were planning every weekend with something new.

Neither Becky nor Mrs. Miller asked anything to do with the others personal life and both seemed to be comfortable with the unsaid arrangement. After a while, Mrs. Miller managed to get permission for Becky to do her studies at her home. They were so much more comfortable there and could talk more freely. Mrs. Miller even told Becky, she could do her long distance calling while she was there. She knew Becky had no privacy at the dorm and a simple pleasure such as this would lift her spirits.

The first month seemed to fly by because of her new friend. Her grades were now in the top five of her class and Miss. Woodward agreed to let Becky continue her studies with Mrs. Miller. Becky thought it was odd, that she never saw Mr. Miller. With all the times, she had spent at their home and his personal things around the house. Nevertheless, she knew it was none of her business, so she would never ask any questions.

Spring break was upon her and all the girls went in different directions to enjoy their time off. Becky's parents said it would be far too expensive to fly her back and forth for such a short time and they knew she wanted so much to see Sam. They had made tentative plans for this time off and the disappointment crushed her feelings. She could understand all this if she had really done something wrong, but trying to make sense as to why, totally baffled her. When Mrs. Miller found out from Miss. Woodward, that Becky would be the only one left behind at the dorm, she asked a very special favor of her to let Becky stay with her over the break. Ordinarily she would denied her request, but she herself was leaving and Becky would be completely alone which was forbidden. So, and exception for just this circumstance was made and Mrs. Miller was delighted. She had to wait until all the other girls had left before she could surprise Becky when she picked her up for the week.

They spent time lounging around and watching television into the late nights. Eating popcorn, they made in the fireplace and Becky getting Mrs. Miller hooked on herbal teas. Becky wanted so much to ask where her husband was, but knew she had better not. It could upset her and ruin their time together. Therefore, Becky kept still.

One day while they were strolling through the park, Mrs. Miller sat down and started telling Becky about her life.

She said, "First of all, Becky, my name is Sarah. When we are, alone, I would really like it if you would refer to me as Sarah. I grew up in a boarding school all through my life and never went home to visit. They would come to the school, take me out to eat, and then it was right back. After I finished college, I married Brian. The reason you have never seen him is that he died of cancer two years ago. I know I should get rid of all his things, but I guess I have been reluctant to let go. He and I were very much in love and I still love him as much today as ever. It is as if he really is not gone. I don't know how to get past him and I don't want too either."

Becky was surprised that Mrs. Miller, Sarah, would open herself up to her with her most private thoughts, and said, "I think I would feel the same way if something were to happen to Sam."

Sarah asked her if she would like to tell her about her Sam. She was hesitant at first, but she felt she could trust Sarah, so Becky started from the beginning, explaining how they had met and bringing her to up to date of where they are now.

This week off turned out to be a cold one. The weather forecast called for heavy snow, with blizzard conditions. Their walk in the park left them chilled to the bone. Sarah would always start a fire in the fireplace, while Becky made them cups of hot herbal tea. As they sat warming themselves, their conversation continued. Sarah's life was very lonely until she met Brian. After they started dating, they spent all their spare time together. He finished college and was working as a stockbroker in a large firm. They had secretly married two days after her graduation, as her parents had already chosen someone for her to marry. Brian's parents were loving people and opened their hearts to her. She finally felt what it was like to be part of a family. When she told her parents of her marriage to Brian, their anger vowed never to see her again. Moreover, after eighteen years of the most wonderful marital bliss, Brian became ill. That is when he was first given the diagnoses of terminal bone cancer. She had lost three babies do to miscarriages over the years and was told she would never be able to carry a pregnancy to term, so they stopped trying. Both Brian and Sarah spent time with his brother and sister-in-law, as they had four children, which were spoiled by all four of them.

Brian would have good days then bad ones. He worked as long as he could, to try to keep his mind off the pain. When it finally became too much to handle, he was at home with continuous I-V medication. Sarah's hands were full taking care of him the last few months of his life. The pain was so intense at times, he would cry out in the night, waking her in absolute horror. His family stayed with them the last few days before he passed away, taking turns relieving her, to rest and get some fresh air. The day he passed away, was one of his most peaceful days in months. They held hands, kissed and talked about all the special memories they had made together. He went over all his arrangements he requested and the things she would need to do for the insurance company to send the holdings of his policy. She tried to stop him from talking like he was going to die, but he told her his time was near and these things needed to be discussed. Becky's eyes filled with tears as she listened, and as Sarah talked, her eyes stayed fixed into the fire.

Then she paused a moment, and said, "These were his last words; Hold me my darling, I love you so, you have filled me with love, both my heart and my soul." Sarah stopped and started crying and then quickly pulling herself together, finished, "For now we must part, but a time will come, when we will meet in heaven and with a new life begun." Sarah, lowering her face into her hands softly said, "After he said those words, he drifted into a deep sleep and was gone."

Becky, even at her young age could see the heartache Sarah had been living with for those past two years. All she could say to her was how sorry she was, and with that walked over to her and hugged her.

The rest of the day Becky encouraged Sarah to tell her all the good times she and Brian had together. They laughed, they cried, but in all, Sarah was finally healing her heart and feeling the love they shared and lost. She told Becky that she realized now; she truly had a good life with him and was thankful for all those precious memories. She also grew to understand just how important it is to have friends. Becky told her she needed to start getting out and finding people her own age to share new life experiences.

"How does such a young person find the right words in a way to help heal an older person's heart? Asked Sarah, then, especially when that young person, has not experienced a loss of her own perfect love."

Becky replied, "I guess I can only say it was the way you described your feelings with such emotional detail."

Sarah just looked at her and smiled.

First day back after the break was full of homework, as if it were punishment for having fun. Both Sarah and Becky were far too busy to have any time for personal conversations. Becky did manage to stay on top of her workload in order to call Sam. Dusty had wrote her and kept her up on the wedding plans, and Becky was becoming very excited for the school year to end. However, she and Sam still had to plan their own wedding and he had been saying that he would take care of everything on his end. She had asked Sarah for advice concerning what she should do while Sam was gone to boot camp. Sarah told her it would all depend on the army, as to what college she might like to attend. So pretty much, everything was still up in the air.

Becky had not realized that graduation was only six weeks away. She would need plenty of time to study for finals and still get all her plans in order as well. Even though Sam was getting things together on his end, she still had a lot to organize with Dusty's wedding, and the fact of telling her parents her plans, which was something Sarah, told her not to dwell on, because it would interfere with her studying.

42

Unable to reach Sam over the weekend, Dusty called and told Becky, that he and Richard had gone to LosAngeles to play for a private party. Richard was so excited to be a part of the band and he told Dusty that Sam was well and could not wait to be with his Becky again. She said there are times; Sam would get down, so Richard takes him everywhere to keep him busy, working on cars, and writing new songs. She informed Becky that everything was set with the wedding; rehearsal would be June ninth, followed by the wedding on the tenth. Then said, all the dress fittings would need to be done one week before, but she had made special arrangements for her to get hers done on the eighth. With that, she asked Becky if she could be there on or before that date. Becky said she would be there even if she had to use her get away money! They were so excited about getting back together, but neither one of them had mentioned how much they had missed the other with all the plans being made. She told Becky she would send her an agenda by mail as soon as possible, and then Becky said to have Sam call at a certain time to help her with travel plans. Dusty said she would relay the message to him and she would call her again soon.

Five weeks to go and Becky was growing tense. She was afraid she would not do well on her finals with all her thoughts on Sam and the wedding. Sarah had to get firm with her to keep her concentration focused. She explained to Becky that her grades would mean a lot when she applied for college and she could do very well if she could just keep her mind centered for what was happening at this moment. Even though Sarah knew until Becky had, her travel plans made with Sam that she would not be able to concentrate and took it upon her to quiz Becky, just to see how she might score.

Sam finally reached her at Sarah's house. He told her all the things he had done to keep himself occupied and she told him she was happy to hear he was is good spirits. Then Sarah interrupted the conversation, telling Becky she had better write down everything she needed to remember. Becky thought she had her best interest at heart and thanked her as she handed her a pen and note pad.

"I do have one small problem, "Becky", said Sam. Then, I can't make our wedding plans until you are here for us to make them together."

Becky stated; "That will be fun and probably would be the best for both of us. "Sam!," I am getting too stressed with everything all at one time and right now I have to get these studies down to make good grades on my finals. Please forgive me for sounding so selfish."

Then he said, "Honey, you do not have a selfish bone in your body! I know how much you have on your mind right now and I understand. You need to do well on your exams. What we are going to do is, number one, focus on your tests, number two, let me arrange your flight schedule, number three, put yourself in my hands and everything will work out fine."

"You're so good to me!" replied Becky.

Then he asked, "Tell me what day I can schedule your flight?"

She answered, "The day after graduation is the second, so either that day or the next."

"That will work, He agreed and then, I will have your ticket by the end of the day tomorrow and that will be one less worry on your mind. Then ending their conversation, it won't be long until we can look back on this time of our lives and be able to laugh about all the needless worry we put upon ourselves. You hang in there "Babe!"."

Three days before finals, Sarah ran Becky through a series of tests she had made up on her own. Each night after, they would go over what she had missed, until she was satisfied that Becky was ready. Their discussions during supper were mainly study related subject and Sarah at times would even add pertinent information that might be of possible help in the future, not found in their books. Her education in the private school she had attended was much more intense. She wanted Becky well prepared for college knowing she might be far away from any family or friends to help during a time when Sam was away in the service.

The evening before finals began, when Becky returned to the dorm, she found a note taped to her door that said a call had come in several hours earlier and that she was to call her father sometime this evening. His greeting was, as if they had never had any problems. He was happy to hear her voice and wished her well on her finals. Elizabeth even sounded extremely happy to hear her daughter's voice as well, as she took her turn. They talked very quickly as they knew they only had five minutes. William informed her they had sold the house and their plans were to be in Boston by graduation. He told her how very proud he was of her accomplishments and then, elaborated his hope to improve their relationship to where it was before. Asking her to forgive him and apologizing for his behavior. This came as quite a shock, but she wanted things between them back to the loving times and it gave her hope just hearing his words. She felt an instant peace come over her and that feeling was another prayer gracefully answered. She thanked him and expressed how important it was to her that they become close once again. Then, for the first time in her life, she heard her father cry. Becky joining him, he managed to say they would be happy again and the past was now behind them.

Then softly he said, "Becky, we love you, always have, always will. We want only the best and I have come to learn, to trust my daughters judgment. You are a good girl and very capable of finding your way in this world without my interference."

Becky was stunned, she could not think of what to say and blurted out with, "I love you too, Daddy."

He told her he knew she would do her best on the finals and they would see her on June first. Becky said her goodbye and took a big deep sigh of relief as she hung up the phone.

After grading the tests Sarah had made up, she felt very confident Becky would do well. She knew Becky's out look, had improved by the conversation she had had with Sam and her confidence was exactly right on target. Her last instructions for Becky were, no studying tonight; go to bed early and to have a good filling breakfast before she left the dorm. Becky found pride within, for putting in such an effort this past semester and was thankful to have had a wonderful friend and mentor to guide her.

She entered her first class, calm and confident. There would be three more exams after this one today and another four tomorrow before she finished. She was determined to keep her cool, no matter what came up. By the end of the rough two days, she felt she had done her best and was thinking of what to do to keep her mind off the results of the exams. Sarah was busy with grading and completing all her records on her two classes, so Becky took walks on her own and spent time thinking about her parents, Sam, and the wedding of her friend.

It was a good ten days, when the tests results appeared on the bulletin board. Becky's name topped every page. She had risen higher than ever expected and was overwhelmed with joy. Sarah was so proud of her and took her out to eat to celebrate.

Miss. Woodward was now receiving complaints from the other girls and their parents. They knew Becky had done a lot of studying with Mrs. Miller and thought there might have been some cheating going on. The only way, Miss. Woodward would be able to prove the accusations one way or the other was to redo the exams and use the more difficult ones. Sarah's employment, along with her teaching license would now be on the line as well.

While out celebrating, neither Sarah or Becky had any clue as to what they were in store for when they returned. Miss. Woodward was waiting outside the dorm when Sarah drove up to drop off Becky. She walked over to the driver's window and told Mrs. Miller she needed to see her in her office immediately. Looking through the window further, she also told Becky, she was to come in as well. Sarah had immediately thought about the rules of her tutoring Becky and that may be the concern and urgency. Becky had no idea, but by the look on Miss. Woodward's face, she began to fear the worst.

Sitting into the over-stuffed red leather armchairs in front of Miss. Woodward's desk, Sarah sat motionless while Becky fidgeted with confusing thoughts.

Miss. Woodward began speaking in an angry tone, "There are rumors all over the school that Becky was coached into cheating on all her exams. I for one am very skeptical. I let Becky do her studies with you to bring her up to the class, not exceed them. Furthermore, Becky was told on her first day here, not to help anyone else or them her. Therefore, the only way to make a fair decision will be further testing. These next exams will be a bit more difficult than the last. Your alternative is failure, and for you, Mrs. Miller, you will be dismissed from our employment and possibly loose your license. So you need to make a choice right this minute and if you choose retesting, we will begin right now."

Becky took a deep breath, looked Miss. Woodward straight in the eyes, and said, "You can begin the testing whenever you are ready. I did not cheat; and I am appalled with the rich and spoiled, who have nothing better to do than spread rumors. Not one of them has given me the time of day since I stepped foot in this dorm. If I must prove my innocents and Mrs. Miller's, so be it."

Sarah was astounded; by Becky's bluntness to Miss. Woodward, she knew it would only make this situation far more difficult, and then she went on to say, "Miss. Woodward, I asked several of the girls to come in after class for help, but they always refused. The rules on studying together need amended in my opinion. I would have loved to see all the girls doing the best possible."

Miss. Woodward sat back in her chair and replied, "I'll tell you what!" "If Becky passes the exams here tonight, I will change the rules. But if she fails, I will be even harder on all of them in the future." Then looking at Becky said, "I have not informed your parents at this time. If you fail these or even one of these exams, your parents will be extremely disappointed in you and I will have no choice but to expel you immediately. Are you ready for the first exam?"

Miss. Woodward dismissed Sarah and ordered her to be back in her office by six a.m. the following morning.

Becky, once again refused any interference into her mind. In full concentration, with a good meal under her belt, she relaxed and was ready to begin. She focused in her mind that these exams would be no different from any of the others and without anymore thought, she started the first of a series of many. After finishing the first, she would request the next, with no expression whatsoever on her face. She would not even request a break, until she had completed them all. Miss. Woodward was amazed, by the determination Becky held, which started to make her feel that they had been wrong in their accusations of guilt. Then she asked Becky, if there might be anything else, she would like to add, or say in her defense. Becky was exhausted, both mentally and emotionally, nothing came to her mind to add except, that she be able to go to her room. Miss. Woodward excused her and told her the results would be ready by breakfast and her scores read aloud at the dinning room table for everyone to hear. Becky said goodnight and headed for the hall.

Not knowing what lie in store for her that morning, Becky dressed and joined everyone in the dinning room. All eyes were on her; they whispered and shared little giggles behind Miss.Woodwards back. Then they turned with smirking gestures towards Becky, trying to make a spectacle of her. Becky held her head high and did not give them the satisfaction they were looking to achieve.

Miss. Woodward stood and requested everyone's attention. She then said, "First of all before I give you the grades of Becky's exams, I want to thank Becky for making it possible for all the girls here at this academy, that from now on, anyone who needs help with their studies will be helped by whomever they chose. That rule that I bestowed upon you was unfair. It took a bold step for Becky to confront me on this matter. She not only did it in defense for herself, she did it for all of you as well. You should be thanking her for taking this stand. "Now!" here are the results of her scores. In English, 96%, in geometry, 98%, biology 100%, world history 98%, advanced Spanish 94% and sociology 98%. Finally yet importantly, Becky exceeded the overall scores of anyone who ever attended this academy. The exams given to her were second year college exams. I would like Becky to stand at this time, to shake her hand and asked forgiveness for all the rumors and judgments that were placed upon her."

Becky was beaming! She had no idea she could have done so well. She asked for permission to say a few words and Miss. Woodward held out an open hand and guided it across the dining table.

Then Becky said, "I know that none of you have liked me from the start, I'm not sure why that is, except to say you never tried to get to know me. I would like to end this year on a good note with each one of you. I, for one, did keep to myself, not letting anyone near me and I am sorry for that. I must have led you to believe, that I thought I was better than everyone was. "But I'm not!" I am just Becky, plain and simple Becky. And if I am given a chance in the future to become a friend, I would be honored."

Lenetta stood up and said, "Becky, I am sorry for treating you different. I am the snob, not you. Can you forgive me? And, I would like to invite you to my graduation party."

Becky smiled and replied, "I would really like to come."

The rest of the girls got up from the table and moved to Becky, giving hugs with congratulations and welcoming her as one of their own.

Miss.Woodward interrupted and said, "Girls, today is a free day; you can turn in your books tomorrow. All I request from you today is to go out and have some fun."

With that, all the girls left the room, except Becky.

"Miss. Woodward? She asked, what will happen to Mrs. Miller?"

"I gave her a very complete apology and a raise in her salary," she replied.

Becky gave Miss. Woodward a hug and thanked her for being so nice. After walking somewhat briskly out of the building, she ran the rest of the way to Sarah's house.

Sarah was leaning against the front door with her arms folded when Becky ran up. Asking, "What took you so long?"

Becky bending forward with her hands on her knees to catch her breath and grasping for air, asked Sarah, "How long have you known the results?"

Sarah replied, "Six a.m., and she was talking like I have never heard her before. And I now, thanks to you, I have a rather substantial raise and opportunity to teach any class I desire."

Becky, grinning ear to ear, in her most mischievous way said, "Let's go and really celebrate with a large banana split and a scary movie."

Sarah laughed then said, "That sounds like a wild way to celebrate."

The last week was filled with returning books, packing to go home and talking to the other girls as if the had been friends all their lives. They signed each other's yearbooks and visited together about their families. Becky told Lenetta how much she was looking forward to her party and that she wanted to see how the very rich people had fun.

Lennetta laughed and said, "You will be amazed how boring they can be, but I'm in charge of this one and my parents will be in for the time of their lives. I have a band coming to play the kind of music we like, not the old organ music they like. You have given me a wild streak, Becky, and I am having the time of my life."

"Lennetta", said Becky, then, "You should always be exactly who you are and don't let anyone take that away. I think you are a very special person and I'm glad to know the real you."

Lennetta told her she had a dress for her that would really look nice for the party, if she did not have one. Becky took her up on the offer and asked her if she would help her with her hair, too. Lennetta became very excited when she asked for help and told her she would come to her room when she finished dressing.

The day of the party, Lennetta had Becky in curlers just after they had finished breakfast. One by one, the girls in the dorm came to Becky's room to give any assistance she needed. It was like having a large family with all her siblings' sisters. She felt for the first time, that she was really a part of something loving and caring as a family should be. Not regretting her life as an only child, but blessed to experience the comfort of abundance.

When Lennetta did her final additions, Becky looked beautiful! She remembered what Sam had said about liking to dress up at certain times, and it was at that moment when she finally felt and truly understood what he meant. She had called herself, plain old Becky for so long, she really thought she was, but looking in the mirror and feeling so alive, it erased the negative attitude she had bestowed upon herself.

Miss. Woodward stepped into Becky's room to announce that the limo had arrived, but she had to say before she told them, just how nice each one of them looked.

Lennetta led Becky by the hand and then asked, "Are you ready to see the funny expressions on my parent's faces when they hear the rock and roll band?"

Everyone busted out laughing; even Miss. Woodward got a kick out of picturing that.

Heading for the front door, Becky said, "I've never rode in a limo before."

Lennetta replied, "It's about time you did then. You must experience everything in life and if you never do ride in one again, at least you can say you did."

As Becky moved through the crowd, warmth filled her heart, by the genuine friendliness. She had pictured in her mind, people making their rounds, nodding their heads and not saying much at all. The look on Lennetta's mothers face when the band started was as if she had been accustomed to the sound forever. There was no shocking reaction, which they had anticipated. Everyone danced and had a very nice time throughout the entire party. For Becky, the music brought homesick feelings and her excitement grew to be with Sam. The day they would be back together could not come soon enough to comfort her heart. The party ended with an enormous cake rolled out on a cart and Lennetta's father toasted his daughter and all her classmates. After the limo ride back to the dorm, they had a slumber party, filled with all the girl talk one could imagine.

Before leaving for Sarah's house the next morning, Becky thanked Lennetta and all the other girls for a spectacular day and the fun filled evening together. Then told them she wished that every night in the dorm could have been that way. They agreed adding other comments on the lines of things they could have done to make the instructors and Miss. Woodward crazy during the past years.

Arriving at Sarah's early, eager to start the day, Becky asked upon Sarah opening the door, "What's for breakfast?"

Sarah asked, "What do you have in mind for this early breakfast?"

Becky replying, "Whatever you serve will be just dandy!"

They laughed and headed for the kitchen. After a cup of coffee, Sarah made pancakes and fruit cups. Over stuffing themselves, Sarah told Becky she would be good to go for the whole day. After eating a stack of six, Becky felt the same way. They talked about the party and Becky did not leave out even one detail. Sarah was so happy for not only Becky, but for the memories, all the girls had made together.

Becky asked her if she would mind her making a few phone calls.

And her response to Becky was, "You should know by now, you are welcome to use the phone at any time, "Darlin."

Then she told her that her agenda would be a long list of errands to run, which would take her into the mid afternoon. She gave Becky the run of the house for the day. Becky, in her own joking way, informed Sarah she would have the chores done and a whole stalk of pancakes ready for dinner. Sarah just laughed as she walked to the car.

After finishing the dishes and picking up, she grabbed a pen and notepad, and then headed for the phone.

She called Sam, and when he picked up the phone she said, "I'm one day closer to you now!"

He laughed and told her he felt the same way.

"I am busting at my seams for that day, do you feel that way too? She asked.

He replied, "Honey, you have no idea how quiet it's been without you, I can't wait for my bouncy chatterbox to consume all the rest of my days and then some."

She started right in telling him about the party and the limo ride the day before. Then, how there really is no difference between rich and poor people, except you have to coax them on to get them started.

Adding, "Kind of like an old mule that wants to stay in the barn."

He laughed so hard his sides hurt and he had to wipe the floodwaters from his eyes before he asked, "How would you know what an old mule acts like, you've never been on a farm, have you?"

"Nope, just guessing or maybe something I've read somewhere." She stated.

"It's so good to hear you happy and full of spunk again," he said sincerely and softening his tone he asked, "Becky," are you still in love with me?"

She quickly replied, "Are you kidding! I love you everyday. There's not one moment that goes by without your picture in my mind since the day I left San Diego." Then she asked, "Why are you asking me this? Is there something or someone you want to tell me about?"

"No Baby!" It's just my insecurity because you are so far away, that's all," he answered.

Then she stated, "Soon, I promise to mend all that insecurity of your heart and start on our new adventurous life together as one."

Sam was a little ashamed for even asking her such a question, but it had been a long time and if she were to have second thoughts, he needed to be prepared before she came home. Becky asked if Dusty had shown him a copy of the agenda she sent her with all the details for the wedding. He said he had not seen her agenda, but Richard kept him up to date and everything was set. Then she went on to tell him all about the conversation she had with William and how he cried when he asked her to forgive him. Sam was pleased to hear that they had made up and hoped to be able to get to know them. She was so glad he could find it in his heart to start out fresh, without holding a grudge against him. They both felt that with their plans, it would be best to break the news in peace rather than making a bad situation worse. However, for the time being, Becky wanted to keep their plans to themselves as they had agreed on, and take one day at a time. He gave her the flight number that he had booked and when she would be leaving there, the day after graduation. She was excited to be finally putting all the arrangements into place and having a set plan scheduled. Then when they finished with all the plans, they talked on about what they wanted to do the day she returned.

After a while, they ended the conversation and Sam said, before he hung up, "I'll see you soon."

Becky's next call was to Dusty. As soon as she had her on the phone, Dusty was asking questions faster than Becky could answer.

She had to say, "Dusty!" loud, then, "calm down!" I will be there on June second. I just got off the phone with Sam and he gave me my flight number and everything."

Dusty said, "Oh Becky!" I am sorry, I am just so excited and nervous, and well, you know me. I need you here to get me through this."

Becky said, "I'll be there, don't you worry about a thing, everything will be just fine, so calm down."

She told Dusty what had happened with the school, having to take the exams over, and how they turned out to be college tests. Dusty could not believe that they could have done such a thing. Then Becky gave her the results of the exams and Dusty about fainted. It took Becky at least a full minute to get a response back from her.

Then Dusty finally asked, "What did Sam say when you told him?"

"I haven't told him yet," she answered. Then, "I'm waiting to see the reaction on his face when I do."

They went on talking about the wedding and Becky told her about the party and her limo ride. On ending their talk, Dusty told her how very proud she was of how she had endured the past five months and how she came thru shining brighter than the North Star. Becky told her she would probably not call again until she arrived, but stressed to her to stay calm and enjoy the events with the wedding and not let them overwhelm her.

The last thing she said was, "Remember!" cherish all the moments now that you possibly can, you only have one wedding day, and those special pictures in your mind, you will carry the rest of your life."

Graduation now three days away, Becky started closing up all the loose ends of her packing. She wanted to spend these last few days with Sarah. It suddenly dawned on her, that she may never see Sarah again. Not knowing for sure, what plans her and Sam would make, and she promised to stay close and always keep in touch with her. Her true friend had become more like a big sister and she would always have a place in her heart as a part of her family.

The two shared their innermost feeling over those last days. Never leaving the house, they conversed about the future, with neither one having any definite plans. They agreed to write and call often, from wherever life would be taking them. The day before graduation, faculty and students met for commencement rehearsal. Prior to dismissal, the class was instructions to be in line with cap and gown by ten a.m. sharp the next morning. As she walked towards her dorm, enjoying the day, she looked into the distance, too far away to recognize anyone, she noticed a man waving his arms over his head.

At first, she looked around her and found herself alone, wondering who it might be for several minutes, then suddenly whispering, "Sam."

Her walking became a quick stride; until she actually knew, it was her Sam. Now running, her heart was pounding harder with every stride the closer he came. She remembered how his hair would fall to a curl on his forehead when a breeze would come up. His eyes, dark as night would dance and the dimples from his smile so deep in his cheeks, she would just irresistibly have to touch his face. As they met, they melted together like butter on steaming bread. Both saying each other's name, both knowing their love was stronger than ever, was now relieved and affirmed in each other's arms.

Without quite leaving his arms, she started asking, "When did you get here? Is everything o.k.?"

Sam placed his index finger over her lips and answered, "I love you. I wanted to share this time in your life. I just couldn't wait another day. Everything is perfect now."

Becky smiled and kissed him softly, then hugged him again telling him how much she loved him too.

They walked around the campus for the next several hours, bringing each other up to date. Becky asked if it would be all right with him, if they could have dinner with Sarah.

He immediately replied, "I can't wait to meet this wonderful lady. Dinner sounds great; I am starving. The last meal I ate was eight hours ago. That was a small apple and some popcorn. I just can't eat while I'm flying."

Sarah was not home yet when they arrived at the house, so they sat under a tree in the front yard and continued to visit. Becky decided she had better tell Sam about what had happened over the final exams before he heard it from someone else. He was shocked not only as to how well she had done, but also why anyone who knew Becky would have ever thought she could cheat. He had no idea that she had been under this kind of pressure. For her to excel thru it all was amazing to him.

As Sarah drove into the driveway, Becky took Sam up to the car to meet her.

Loading both of them up with packages, she said, "This must be your Sam!"

Becky replied, "Yep!"

Then Sam joined in by saying, "And you are without a doubt, the wonderful Sarah, Becky has told me so much about!"

After Sarah had settled into her soft easy chair and Becky fixing her favorite tea, she decided she would like to take them all out for dinner so they could relax and enjoy a good meal they would not have to prepare.

During dinner, Sarah asked Sam where he was staying. He told her he had not checked into a hotel yet, but that was actually his next question, as to where the closest one was. She said there was no need to check into a hotel, if he did not mind sleeping on the couch.

Sam replied, "As tired as I am, I could sleep anywhere."

Sarah told Becky she could bunk with her and they should all get a good nights rest.

At six a.m. Sarah woke everyone with breakfast on the table. She said they would have a lot to do today and with her parents arriving or all ready there, they would want some time, too. Just before leaving the house, the phone rang and it was William. Becky answered and he told her they would arrive later than expected. He said they would be at her graduation and meet her afterwards. Becky informed him that Sam had flown in for her graduation and her plans were to fly back with him the next day to be with Dusty.

He asked, "We won't have much time to visit, but could we take everyone out to eat after the ceremony?"

Becky thought that would be a great idea and told him where to meet her following dismissal. Then tenderly she said, "Dad!" "I love you!"

He told her how proud he was and that he could not wait to see her. Then added, "Becky, I love you too."

Commencement began right on schedule. After all the graduates were in place on the platform, the administration introduced the faculty, followed by the awards and honor certificates. Out of the first three awards, Becky received highest achievement for over all test scores. Others received awards based on their four-year academic achievements. The housemothers gave their speeches immediately following the diplomas. And when it came time for Miss. Woodward, Becky could not resist by starting a hip hip hurrah. Blushing fully as she took the podium, she spoke on how proud she was with all her girls. And she became completely chocked up when she said she would miss them all as they went on to college and began their journeys on their way thru life. She introduced the instructors and each gave a short speech as well. Taking the podium once again, Miss Woodward called Mrs. Miller to assist her.

Then she said, "At this time we would like to give, "No!" we are extremely honored to give the highest honor to the one student who far exceeded any student who ever attended the Boston Academy."

They looked at each other with smiles beaming and at the same time called out, Rebecca Stanley. Becky in shocked, made her way from the back row to stand at the podium. Both Miss. Woodward and Sarah hugged Becky.

Then, Miss. Woodward stated, "It is with great privilege of this academy to award you with a five thousand dollar scholarship to attend the University of your Choice. We are proud to have had the honor of being part of your life."

They turned over the microphone to Becky and she was speechless. She looked to the sky for words as tears flowed down her blushing cheeks, but found none to express her feelings at that moment.

Sarah quickly stepped up behind her and gently placed her hands on her shoulders, leaned forward with her face next to Becky's and said, "Thank you," for her.

The cheers from the crowd, along with her fellow students, gave Becky a very special feeling of the love from so many people. At that time, the ceremony ended with the usual caps flying thru the air in every direction. Then the dean dismissed the class, and the crowd edged around the platform to greet the new graduates.

It took William, Elizabeth, Sam and Becky quit a while to get to their meeting place through that crowd. Becky had grabbed onto Sarah before leaving the platform and wanted her parents to meet her. After the introduction, William invited everyone out to eat. They enjoyed a fantastic steak dinner, followed by a cake Elizabeth had brought for Becky. Sarah suggested they all come back to her house so they could visit more and be more relaxed. William accepted saying he would really like to talk with Sam. The look on Sam's face could have stopped a train! Becky busted out laughing and William joined right in.

At Sarah's, Elizabeth thanked her for going out of her way, making her daughters transition easier and most of all, being such a good friend. Sarah told her that she needed Becky probably even more than she needed her. That if it was not for Becky, she may have never been able to get on with her own life. She did not go on to explain the details, but Elizabeth somehow understood without any explanation.

Becky joined Sarah and her mother in the kitchen saying, "Dad wants coffee!" His way of politely saying, he wants Sam to himself."

William discussed his bad behavior to Sam and apologized for not taking the time to get to know him. He went on to say that mistrusting his daughters judgment could have been a tremendous loss if Becky was not the person she is. He said he could have lost her forever and it would have killed him in the end.

Adding, "Becky has always been able to see through other people. I don't know how she does, but it is a gift, I'm sure. I was too quick to judge and almost lost her. It won't ever happen again."

Sam agreed about Becky's gift, saying, "She can bring out the good when everyone else would walk away."

They went on to talk about Sam's family and his plans for the future. William listened intently, as Sam always included Becky when making decisions. He liked the idea of them joining forces and complimented him.

Becky had Elizabeth and Sarah peak around the corner with her at the same time, so to break the ice or any chill that might be in the air. William thought it was very funny, and then assured Becky that everything was just fine. He sat back in his chair, sipped his coffee and asked Becky what her summer plans were. Becky apologized for the short notice of her and Sam leaving the next day for San Diego. William and Elizabeth knew most of the wedding plans from Dusty, so they were not at all surprised. Sam had told William of his orders for boot camp.

And then Becky said, "Daddy", I'm staying at Dusty's mom's house while I'm there and..."

William interrupted stating, "I don't need you to explain all the little details Becky, you are very well capable of making good decisions on your own. And I trust you!"

She smiled, and asked, if it would be all right for her to come back when Sam left. She looked forward, into making up for their lost time together. William told her he would look forward to having his little girl at home again. Following the hugs and kisses, William shook Sam's hand and welcomed him into their family.

Sam, Becky and Sarah visited for a short time, and then the three were all ready to retire for the night. Sarah asked if she could drive them to the airport and expressed that she would really like to see them off, just in case it would be the last time she would ever see them.

Then she quickly apologized, saying, "I'm sorry, I didn't mean it that way."

Becky said, "I know!" And you're right, whether you say it or not. I'm going to miss you so much."

Giving Sarah a big hug and Sarah left the room. Becky handed Sam some pillows and bedding, then kissed him goodnight and followed Sarah.

Sarah's phone rang at five a.m.... It was William and he immediately apologized to her for calling so early, but he needed to speak to Becky.

She was already up in the kitchen drinking her coffee when the phone rang. Sarah handed her the phone and with a big grin on her face said, "Good morning daddy!"

He returned with, "How is my sweet pumpkin today? I wanted to catch you before you left for the airport. I have some money to give you and I'm sure you could use it."

She said, "That would be great dad!"

He told her what he was giving her was her graduation gift. Then asked, if they could stop by the hotel on their way to the airport. Becky asked Sarah, and she said the hotel is on the way, so there would be no problem. Becky repeated to William what Sarah had said.

Then Becky added, "Daddy, I am so happy we are back together as a family again. I love you and life is too short to spend it upset. Let's make a pack to never have an argument again."

William returned, "That's my girl, from now on we will keep the lines of communication open and I love you too."

Becky chuckled as she said, "I'll see you soon."

"I'll see you sooner." William replied, in a full laugh, as he hung up the phone.

Sam woke up to find both Becky and Sarah, coffee in hand, staring him awake.

He looked up, rubbed his face with both hands and said, "You two are quit a pair!" I'll have both of you on my case if I don't get moving."

Sarah laughed and said, "Breakfast will be ready in five."

Then Becky with a hug smile blew him a kiss and followed Sarah to the kitchen.

While they waited for him to join them, Sarah gave Becky a very nice brief case. She told her she did not wrap it because it was not anything special. She had used it when she first started teaching and thought she could use it for college. Becky opened it to find a phone book, pens, writing paper, stamps and a sealed letter.

She said, "Don't read the letter now. Wait until after all the festivities of the wedding are over and things calm down."

Becky told her about the gift she had received when she had to leave her friends behind in California, and thanked her as she explained how much she cherished gifts from the heart. She hugged Sarah and then reminded her she would be back in a few weeks. Then thanked her again, for not only the gift, but for everything she had done for her over the past months.

Stating, "I would have never accomplished near those grades, if it hadn't been for you. When I look back now, your life as well as mine came together in blessing form for me to find you and share your life too. I love you Sarah, you are a part of my family now and always."

Sarah added, "Always remember, love has no miles and I will be with you where ever you are and wherever you go."

Sam joined them at the table and for the next thirty minutes, they shared funny memories while devouring Sarah's famous banana pancakes.

After picking up Becky's luggage and saying goodbye to all the girls and Miss. Woodward, the next stop would be the hotel. Sarah had managed their time well, in order to give Becky a few extra moments with her parents. She felt that if she were in her shoes, she would have wanted all the time she could spare.

Sarah and Sam waited in the lobby. Becky told them she would be no longer than twenty minute and flew up the stairway to their room. Elizabeth answered the door when she knocked. Becky immediately walked into her mothers arms. She had not had that forever so longing closeness that a mother-daughter shared between them in a very long time. She whispered in her mother's ear for her to make special plans when she returns for just the two of them.

Elizabeth stepped a half a step back, then put her hands on Becky's shoulders and felt her hair and said, "It's been so long!"

William broke in and said, "We must keep this short or you will miss your flight!"

Then Becky replied, in an honoree type voice, "Yeap, Yeap!" I have twenty minutes and the clock in ticking."

They laughed a few minutes then settled down.

William handed her an envelope and said, "Come on girl, open it!"

She sat at the foot of the bed and opened it, then gasped for air! Inside was a check for five thousand dollars and cash totaling another thousand?

Becky said, "This is far too much!"

William told her, "I have money. If I cannot give it to my family, what good is it? You have made us so proud and you worked so hard, we want you to be able to have a great time on your trip."

Becky hugged her dad for the longest time.

Then Elizabeth said, "I want some too!"

She thanked them and said she would spend it wisely. As she left the room telling them how much she loved them both, she just said, "I'll see you soon."

With saying that, she headed for the lobby.

The rest of the way to the airport was quiet. Becky sat staring out at the scenery, not knowing how to say goodbye. Sarah finally broke the silence and told Becky she would not be going in with them.

Her words were, "I do not like goodbyes. So, I'm not going to say it."

Becky only came back with, "O.K...."

After she drove up to the sidewalk of the terminal, Sam unloaded the luggage and Becky hesitated to step out of the car. She closed her eyes, praying to God for Him to watch over her, then managing to hold back her tears, stepped out.

When she leaned down, one single tear had escaped her eye and with a forced smile said, "I'll see you soon."

Sarah smiled back with a warm loving and reassuring expression, then slowly drove away.

Becky turned to Sam, now in many tears, smiled and said, "The beach awaits us."

With that, they checked in their luggage and strolled hand in hand to the gate.

Chapter Three

As the plane landed in San Diego, Sam looked over at Becky saying, "I told Richard we would probably be late this evening getting to Dusty's. Would you accompany me this beautiful evening for a picnic on the beach?"

She smiled, then replied, "I would be delighted, Mr. Malloy!"

The weather was warm, with a soft cool breeze as they carried their luggage to Sam's van. Closing the back doors, he quickly ran to open Becky's and with a big smile said, "One stop at the market, and we're on our way."

Becky, just so happy to be back together, all she could do was smile. No words came to her worthy enough to express how she was feeling, so she just enjoyed the familiar sights and smells of home. At the market, they found ready-made sandwiches and fruit. Along with some bottled water and a few sodas. A display caught Sam's eye, of a romantic setting with flowers and wine goblets. He asked the clerk if he could purchase the glasses and she told him they were just plastic and he could have them, as they were going to change the display that day anyway. Then he asked her to hide them under the counter so Becky would not see them and thanked her with a tip. He had another special moment planned for this evening that would top everything this day could possibly bring. Wanting every moment perfect, he prayed for the words to be exactly what Becky wanted to hear.

When they arrived at the beach, Becky took off her shoes and socks, climbed out of the van and ran from the parking lot on to the beach. She could not wait to squeeze her toes into the warm sand as she had remembered doing months ago. Sam looked on, laughing as if she had never set foot on sand before, with a childish delight for such a simple experience. After a few moments, she grasped some sand in her hands, tossed it into the air, and then sat down rubbing it all over her feet. While Becky continued to amuse herself, Sam gathered up a blanket and the food, and then walked over to her.

With his arms full, he leaned down and asked, "Are you glad to be here or what?"

She looked up at him, slowly coming to a stand, and then jumped on him, knocking him down to the ground. They wrestled for a few minutes playfully, then jumped to their feet and picked up their things. Becky twirled, sang and hopped as they made their way towards the old favorite spot.

As the evening progressed and the cool breeze turned damp and cold, they wrapped up in the blanket, stalling their departure.

They sat quietly staring out into the surf and then Sam softly said, "Becky!" I do not want to wait until after boot camp to get married. I want us to start our life together now. I know it's not as if we would be able to throw a wedding together like Dusty's, but we could always do it again at another time. Then he asked, Am I making any sense or am I completely out of line here?"

Becky wrapped her arms around him and without any hesitation replied, "I want to be your wife now, too. I know mom and dad will be disappointed, but we could have another ceremony and I'm sure that would please them. Then she asked, but what about your parents?"

"I have the most understanding parents alive! He replied, then, they will be so happy for us and my mother will put together a family reception like nothing you have ever seen. There will be music and dancing, food stretched out across table after table, with flowers right from her flower beds to put any florist to shame."

Becky settled into his shoulder and just tried to imagine a picture of it in her mind of a place she had never been and the family she had never met.

The wind off the ocean was now too cold to stay any longer. It was after nine p.m. and they needed to check in at Dusty's house. On the walk back to the van, Sam asked her if she was going to share their plans with Dusty and Richard.

"I don't think we should say anything yet. Dusty has so much going on and all her thoughts should be on her wedding day. I don't want her to have to help plan ours too. Then she added, we can actually plan what we are going to do without her even knowing."

When they arrived at Dusty's, Richard had just beaten them there by a few minutes. They had been out for dinner and a movie.

Dusty screamed out, "Becky", when she saw Sam's van that had driven up behind them.

Sam yelled out, "Richard",

Becky yelled out, "Dusty".

Finally Richard yelled, "Enough already!"

With all of them laughing, Dusty's mother rushed outside to see what all this yelling was about. She saw Sam and Becky with Dusty clung on her side and walked over to greet them. She gave Becky a big hug and told her how good it was to see her home again. Then asked them to keep down the noise and went back into the house. Dusty hung on to Becky in fear that if she were to let go, she really would'nt be there. Richard suggested they go to there old café where they could talk for a while and catch up. But Becky was feeling the length of the day and asked if they could go tomorrow after a good nights sleep. So many plans going through her mind and all the busy days ahead, not mentioning the past few weeks, she needed to just stop and rest.

Sam told Dusty, "It's been a long hard day, with the flight and goodbyes for her. She could really use some sleep."

Then Richard said, "It would probably do us all some good and I'll buy dinner tomorrow night as a rain check."

"Sounds like a plan to me!" replied Sam.

Richard kissed Dusty goodnight, then hugged Becky saying, "Welcome home."

Sam shook Richards hand, patted Dusty on the back and took Becky by the hand to unload her luggage.

After carrying everything in the house, he kissed her and whispered, "Soon!" just as we said. I don't want to be away from you anymore."

As he walked out the door, he told her to call him in the morning when she knew what was going on.

Dusty had no idea what Becky's day had consisted of, but by the look of her eyes, she could see how tired she must be. She grabbed Becky's suitcases and suggested they settle in and get ready for bed.

Following behind her Becky said, "I'm sorry to be such a party pooper, I promise to perk up after a good nights rest."

Dusty said, "Becky, we have lots of time to get things done. There are only a few things left to do. Mom has taken over and she has been terrific."

Up in Dusty's room, she handed Becky a nightgown from her drawer, saying, "There's no need to unpack tonight. Let's hit the sack so we can start fresh and revived."

Becky had no argument on that and after she changed, she sunk into her pillow. Dusty looked over at her as she reached for the light switch and Becky was all ready out.

She said in a quiet voice, "Welcome home, my very best exhausted friend."

When Dusty woke the next morning, Becky was still fast asleep. She gathered her clothes and left, to let her wake on her own. There was nothing pressing, to wake her up early. Dusty and her mother visited over breakfast with the rest of the wedding details.

She told Dusty, "The only thing left for you and Becky to do is your final dress fittings. Everything else I will take care of unless you have any changes or need to add something."

Dusty thanked her mom for arranging everything so perfectly, and then said, "I could not have done what you have accomplished in such detail. And I owe you a multitude of hugs and kisses."

Then Alice explained to Dusty, "It was very easy!" Your wedding is the wedding I dreamed of having as a young girl. I should be thanking you. You are all grown up and it seems like yesterday, I held you in my arms for the first time. All this planning has taken me back in time even before you were born. I have walked thru my mind with every precious memory you have given me from your beginning. It has made me feel sad, happy and grateful to have such a wonderful daughter. I am very grateful also to be able to share this conversation. Then she asked, "Honey, your not ever going to be too far away, are you?"

Dusty answered her with, "Mom, I don't know where Richard will be stationed after boot camp, but where ever it may be, we will always be back to visit as often as we can. And anytime you need me, I'll be here."

She hugged her mother and then they both vowed not to talk about anything that would make them feel sad.

Becky came down just in time to have lunch, saying, "I guess I was tired. I've been getting up so early for so long, this was a real treat."

"I made another pot of coffee to prime you for this day." Dusty replied.

Becky asked, "Are we in for a busy one?"

"Oh!" have you and I ever not had a busy one? Asked Dusty, then added, if you are up to it, we will do our dress fittings and then have dinner with Richard and Sam. We will keep it light and relaxed. I think you could use some, no brainer days."

Sipping her coffee, Becky said, "The last few weeks, months, have been very heavy, in every way you could imagine. I feel like someone just took a hundred pounds off my shoulders and I don't know how to think or act."

"Actually Becky, I don't think I could have come through what you've been through, as well as you have. I admire your strength. You're a tough one!" she stated.

Becky stood up from her chair, took the last sip of her coffee and said, "I'm headed for the shower. I'll be twenty minutes tops and ready to go."

Dusty told her not to rush. Becky made a funny face, and then ran up the stairs, leaving Dusty in stitches.

Walking into the dress shop, Becky eyes lit up at the sight of all the beautiful dresses. At that moment, she felt she would never wear a wedding gown such as these. For their plans to wed, would be a simple service and yet no less meaningful, but somehow she still had a sadness in her heart. She began looking through the gowns, while Dusty had her fitting. As she flipped through the gowns lining the wall, one dress on a manikin kept catching her eye. She finally stopped and walked over to it. One of the clerks walked over and asked if she would like to try it on.

She hesitated for a moment, and then said, "This just might be perfect."

In the dressing room, she kept asking herself, why she was even thinking of this extravagant, unnecessary purchase. She just ignored those negative thoughts and put on the dress. It had a small cap sleeve, the neck line scalloped down to a vie, with small roses gathered at the front of the arm pit, as if to hold the dress together and ribbons sewn into the seams to give just a touch of the rose color throughout. She looked at herself in the mirror and knew it was her dress. Then she quickly took it off and hung it back on the hanger. Finding the courage to look at the price tag, she made the decision, that she would be married in this dress. No matter how simple her wedding would be, she was going to have a special day to remember.

The tag had no price listed, so she called the clerk back to the fitting room and asked, "What does a dress like this one cost?"

The clerk answered, "This dress is new to our shop and the price is three hundred dollars. "But!" the clerk added, Your friend bought her dress and all the attendances dresses here, so I can sell this to you for half price."

Becky held up the dress once again, pressed it to her body, gazed into the mirror and said, "I'll take it."

Then ask the clerk, not to say anything to her friend. She hugged the dress and hung it on the wall in the fitting room, then went to see Dusty in her dress. Her gown was beautiful too. She had chosen a traditional design of long lace sleeves, with the lace covering the whole gown over a satin base.

Becky, admiring how beautiful she looked, said, "It's perfect!" You look like a model from a bridal magazine or even a china doll, perfectly placed in an exclusive department store window."

"That's a very nice statement to make me feel really beautiful," replied Dusty.

Then she asked the clerk if Becky could have her fitting and she said that would be fine.

When the clerk came back with the maid of honor dress, Dusty said, "It's a perfect dress for you Becky!"

It was soft lavender in satin, in a simple cut, full length and sleeveless.

"Dusty", Becky stated, "It gorgeous!"

Then Dusty asked the clerk, to bring Becky back with her dress on, so they could stand together in front of the large wall mirror.

As they stood together, Dusty asked Becky, "Have you ever seen anything as cool as this?"

Becky in ah replied, "Only in the movies!"

The clerk asked if they would like a picture and Dusty requested an extra one for Becky. They went back to their dressing rooms to change and Becky put on her own wedding gown once again. Even though she had not made any plans with Sam as of yet, she just had to have Dusty's opinion of this fabulous dress. She would swear her to secrecy, never to tell him anything about this dress until a much later date. Back in front of the mirror, the clerk came over with a beautiful headdress of white and rose flowers.

She adjusted it from behind saying, "a lot of brides are wearing this type of head dress instead of vials."

The colors went together, as if they were a set. Becky whispered she would take it too and called Dusty over to the mirror. Her mouth had dropped open at the first glance and stayed frozen there until she spoke.

With her hand on the sides of her face, she said, "Becky!" That gown and the flowers are, "Breath taking!" Then she asked, are you just trying on, or is there something you haven't told me?"

With a big sigh, Becky answered, "It's for real!" Sam doesn't know it yet. He has asked me to marry him, and I accepted. "Dusty!" You have to keep this a secret! We are getting married secretly very soon and when I saw this dress, I decided that no matter how simple our ceremony is, this is the dress I am going to be wearing."

Dusty was so surprised, she couldn't think of a thing to say. Her loss for words of any kind, were over come by questions and the warmest feelings of joy she had at that moment. Becky, looking at Dusty's encumbered state, suggested it was time for a heart to heart pow-wow.

Saying, "I think its time for a nice cup of coffee and some good ol fresh air."

Dusty hugged her in silence, and then asked, "How about this coffee in the park?"

"That's a great idea, we can collect our thoughts and I might be able to answer a few of all those questions that are over taken your mind," replied Becky.

Becky had not told Sam of the money her father had given her. He knew she was getting money, but had no idea just how much. She paid for her purchase and asked the clerk if she could hold her dress at the shop for about a week. She assured Becky that would not be a problem and they headed out the door.

With coffee to go and Dusty rushing to the park, her questions flowed like running water.

Becky had to intervene by giving a big time out with her hands and saying, "Woe girl!" "Slow down," one question at a time. I should have bought you decaf."

Sitting down at a picnic table, Becky spilled the beans of their plans they had made the night before. She once again told her, she could never let on that she knew. Dusty promised to keep everything secret just between them.

Then she asked, "When?", "Where?"

Becky replied, "I have no idea! We haven't made plans beyond, as soon as possible."

Taking in a few deep breaths of the cool breeze, Dusty then said, "I would really like to be there when you do get married. Please let us be a part of that special, one and only wonderful beginning of your new life."

"Dusty, I'm sorry; I didn't want to put all this on you, and cause all this confusion with your wedding. Everything in my life has happened so fast, and I guess that is just the way my life is supposed to be. I just don't know."

Taking Becky's hand, she softly said, "You're not messing up my wedding! This is what friendship is all about. We have been together all our lives, and shared everything, which shows just how much we love the other. "So", you are not messing up my wedding. It would have been crushed me, if you had left me out, and you know that because of the relationship we have shared. Then she asked, do you remember, not really that long ago when we dreamed about getting married and raising our families, and what you used to say? That plain old Becky would become an old maid! What do you want to say now?"

Becky laughed and recalled those days, then replied, "You grew up at the normal pace, I, on the other hand, had to grow up all at one time."

Dusty agreed saying, "You know you are extremely correct with that statement. Can you just imagine? soon, very soon we will both be married and starting whole new lives."

Dusty glanced at her watch, then jumped to her feet and hurriedly said, "Its five o clock, Richard and Sam will be starting to get worried."

Becky said as she came to her feet, "I doubt that, they know when we are together, we always manage to take all the time we want."

When they arrived back at the house, Dusty's mother had left them a note.

It said, "Richard had called and he and Sam are running late. They had their fittings done and had a few errands to take care of. They will be here at the house by six or six thirty to go to dinner."

Becky said, "Good, I have time for a relaxing soak in the tub." Dusty told her to go ahead, that she had a few things to do in her room.

By six thirty, both girls were dressed and ready to go, but by seven, they were still waiting and starting to worry a bit. At eight, they pulled in the drive.

"Where have you been, Richard?" asked Dusty sharply.

"Honey," Richard replied, "All good things take time and time it took."

Sam walked over to Becky and gave her a kiss and hug. She whispered in his ear, "I've missed you today."

"Me too." he whispered back.

Dusty was still a little hot for not knowing where they had been so long, blurted out, "Richard!", You make me so mad when you worry me, but because your so darn cute, I'll let it go this one time."

He smiled and gave her a quick mischievous grin, then said, I'm starving, let's go eat."

During dinner, Becky asked what had kept them so long. Richard and Sam looked at each other, paused,

Then Sam said, "We had guy stuff to do."

Keeping his eyes on Richard and both having sneaky smiles on their faces.

"Richard!" Dusty asked again sharply, "What sort of guy stuff did you do today?"

Trying not to laugh, he kept his eyes on Sam and answered, "We did our tux fittings, had lunch, and "Oh yeah", some shopping, and, you know, guy stuff."

"Evidently, this stuff was something we would not have approved of." stated Dusty.

"Oh no!" he said, stuff you would approve of, but, we can't tell you, yet!"

Then after dinner, they went back to Dusty's house and visited a while with her parents. When they retired for the evening, the four of them played cards at the kitchen table until two a.m., giving all the plans and upcoming events a rest. Before leaving for Richards, Sam asked if he could have Becky later in the morning. Richard said that would be good for him as he had some shopping to do with Dusty.

Then Becky asked, "What time this morning do you have in mind. Will it be eight, nine, or ten thirty?"

They all thought that was funny and laughed until they reached the car, then he said, "I promise, it will be eightish!"

Becky was a little suspicious as to what Sam and Richard had been up too. She knew in her heart, that whatever it was, it would turn out to be terrific in the end, and she didn't feel the need to ask him.

Eight a.m. sharp, Richard in his car, Sam in his van, pulled into the driveway. Sitting on the front porch steps Becky and Dusty gave them the impression they had been waiting a long time. Dusty's mother pocked her head out the front door and asked if they would be in for dinner. Richard answered and said they would probably be very late getting back and he would bring pizza so she would not need to cook for them.

Becky waived to Dusty and Richard, as she climbed in the van. Both girls not knowing anything as to what the boys had in store for this beautiful day, they had decided to take it all in stride and have a good time.

Sam leaned over, kissed Becky, then said, "Good morning my love."

She smiled and asked, "What do you have planned for us today?"

"Breakfast first!" he answered.

Rolling her eyes and smiling she said, "You read my stomach, I am famished!" "Oh!" I have a confession to make. I did, or let me start again. I bought something yesterday. I don't usually spend money extravagantly, but this I could not resist."

"What are you talking about?" asked Sam.

"Well, I was lost in the moment, a selfish moment. And, and I probably, "no!" I should have discussed it with you first." Becky stuttered.

He wondered what she could have bought that she would be so concerned he might be upset by, then asked her again, "Becky!", What are you talking about? I won't be upset with you; you know you can have anything you want."

"I know," she answered, then, but it was far too expensive."

Trying to contemplate what she was trying to tell him, he said, "Let's talk about this over breakfast."

Richard, pulling into the parking lot of the mall, had Dusty very confused.

They had finished all their shopping the week before, so she asked, "Richard?" What are we shopping for today?"

He replied, "Honeymoon stuff!"

"What sort of, "honeymoon stuff?" she asked.

He laughed so hard. What he would have given at that moment to have a picture of the expression on her face was priceless.

He just had to say it again, "You know "Honeymoon stuff."

Sam took Becky to their special little café and she requested they sit at their table. After placing their orders, he told her, he needed to tell her his whereabouts of the day before.

He said, "Before you tell me what you bought, let me explain what I've been doing."

She listened quietly.

Then he started, "Yesterday, I had a lot of time to think. First, I went to the courthouse. I found out it takes five working days to get our marriage license. Then I found a little chapel. I want to take you there today to see what you think." Stopping for a moment, then, "Becky", do you think I am getting out of line? And added; I do not want you to feel that I am making all the arrangements and pushing you too fast. Tell me, what you are thinking."

Smiling at him, and then reaching for his hand and replied, "I would really like to see this little chapel. No, you are not going too fast! We don't have that much time to put all this together and it sounds like you have done a great job so far."

"Oh", he sighed with relief and said; that is a big load off my mind! I was so excited, yet so worried that it would upset you and you mean so much to me, for me to just take over and exclude your opinion, I have felt miserable. Now that I have told you what I've been up to, tell me about your extravagant purchase."

"O.k.," but first I must make another confession. I broke a promise. Dusty knows about us getting married."

Sam broke out laughing and said, "I did too, I told Richard."

They were so relieved, to have that off their minds, they thoroughly enjoyed their meal.

When the waiter came to take their plates away, Sam ordered another two cups of coffee to go. Finishing off the cup she had, she went back to their conversation.

Saying, "Dusty and I went for our dress fittings and I found a wedding gown. I told myself it did not matter how simple our ceremony would be, that, that day is going to be a once in my lifetime experience. I said to myself, this is the dress; I will wear to married Sam. And, I just had to see what Dusty's expression would be when she saw me wearing it."

"Well, what did she say?" Sam asked.

"She liked it." Becky replied.

Then he asked, "How extravagant was this dress?"

"It was half price because Dusty had bought all her wedding parties dresses there, so, mine came to one hundred and fifty dollars," shrugging her shoulders as she confessed.

"Wow!" that must be some dress!" he added.

After that, they both agreed to get their plans set together so they would not have different things going on at the same time.

Their first stop was to start the license procedures and check out the chapel. They planned to get married the morning of Dusty's wedding. Richard and Dusty could stand up for them and they would have plenty of time to get back for their wedding without anyone wondering where they were. Becky was feeling guilty about keeping all these wonderful plans of their marriage from her parents. It would be a strain on them to have to rush out there and then fly back again. She knew they would understand, with her plan to have either a reception or another ceremony, but it still weighted heavy on her mind. Keeping their plans secret was extremely important. She knew they would be devastated to hear it from someone else and they had restored one major mishap, and another would be even more traumatic. The only way to handle this was face to face and very gently.

On their way to the chapel, after they had finished their paperwork, Sam told Becky, they could find another place if it did not suit her. When they arrived, Becky was astounded! It was, even more than she could have imagined. They walked in, hand in hand, and welcomed by an older woman. She was the sweetest person Becky had ever met. Insisting they call her by her first name, Beth. She went over how the service was preformed, and then added some suggestions.

Stopping to say, "But don't let me interfere. This is your wedding and you should tell me to butt out."

Becky could not help but giggle when she said that and replied, "Beth, this is so perfect and more than I dreamed. All your suggestions are wonderful, but there will only be four of us attending. So the simplest version would be the best."

"Oh," four can be even sweeter than hundreds" Beth stated, then, well, in that case, maybe I could come too."

Becky took her hands, shook them softly and said, "I wouldn't have it any other way."

Beth checked the calendar to make sure the chapel was not booked at the time Sam had requested, and had them take a seat while she fetched the Reverend. When she returned, she introduced a very small man as, Reverend Sean O'Brien.

He shook Sam's hand with a firm hold, then turned and said to Becky as he took her hand, "It's a pleasure to meet you both. I hear you would like to be married in my chapel! Let's have a seat and talk for awhile."

He went over the service once again and then told them they could say their own vows, or he could read from his book, whatever they preferred. Both Sam and Becky wanted him to do the honors and he agreed.

Beth wrote them in on the calendar saying out load as she wrote, "June tenth."

Reverend O'Brien peered over her shoulder, and then added, "According to Bethie, nine a.m. Is this correct?" he asked.

Sam affirmed the information and everything was set. They sat and visited for a while, then headed back to Dusty's house.

Richard had left an envelope with Dusty's mother.

Alice met them at the door and handed it to Sam saying, "Richard asked me to give this to you as soon as you arrived. They have been gone all day and didn't say when they'd be back."

After he thanked her, he said they were going to dinner and would call later. They climbed back into the van and Sam opened and read the note.

It said, "Meet us at the little café. Come hungry!"

He handed Becky the note after reading it aloud and shrugged his shoulders.

When they entered the café, Richard, Dusty and the members of Sam's band surprised them and throughout the room, streamers hung meticulously to a wedding bell just above their table. Once the initial surprise settled a bit they explained they had rented the café for the evening and told them, they thought they should have a reception of some sort for this special occasion. Starting out with dinner, the small group gave toasts for a wonderful life and many happy years together. Then Dusty went into the kitchen. The lights went out, except for the candles on the table and she rolled in a cart with a wedding cake. Sam and Becky stood giving them toasts of thanks and making their evening one to remember for a lifetime. They cut the cake in the normal traditional fashion, fed each other the first piece, and then served the party.

The rest of the evening was filled with pictures and dancing, and Becky was so happy, she cried from time to time, but always with a smile. Sam invited the band members to the wedding and drew a map to the chapel on a napkin.

Richard asked Sam if he would sing some of the songs they had written together and he said, "Only if you join the band. It is a rule! If you write it, you sing it."

Richard replied, "I'll give it a good try!"

As Sam and Becky thanked them again, Dusty added, "We will be celebrating more than anyone will know at our reception and it will be the best memory that friends could ever share."

Becky and Dusty exchanged a high five and laughing once again, and they headed for home.

With all the plans set and fittings done ahead of schedule, Becky asked Sam if it would be all right with him if she and Dusty spent a few days together. She told him it would probably be a long while before they would see each other again and was glad they could finally relax and maybe just kick back.

Then he said, "I have some things to get and I need to wrap up everything in the apartment, so you have a great time, but call me when you can."

She promised to call at least twice a day and then they said goodnight.

The next two days, Dusty and Becky brought each other up on everything they had done over the past five months. They enjoyed spending time with Dusty's parents and helping out around the house. Alice was beginning to show little signs of stress in her actions, so they jumped right in with the cooking for all the out of state relatives soon to be arriving.

June ninth came so fast. It was rehearsal day followed by a dinner for the wedding party. The dinner was held at the hotel were the reception would be, and Dusty took Becky off to show her the wedding suite for her honeymoon. Everyone else was busy visiting as the two girls disappeared down the hall. Dusty had told her days before about booking the room and Becky had planned to arrange for her and Sam also, as a wedding gift. With all the distractions, it completely skipped her mind. Dusty stopped at the front desk for her key and the clerk handed her two. Becky instantly knew what Dusty had up her sleeve! Such a wonderful friend, Becky thought, as she was feeling a little ashamed for forgetting about this gift.

She handed Becky the other key in the elevator, saying, "This is from Sam. I had nothing to do with this. He wanted to surprise you, but I thought you might like to do a bit of surprising of your own." Then she added, "Tonight, after everyone leaves for the house, you and I will do some extra decorating in your room. I had this idea for my room, so I just doubled everything."

Becky asked, "What things do you have?"

"Richard and I did some shopping, remember? I knew about your plans from Richard, obviously, and we thought it would be a nice gift, if we could make your first night together just as special as ours." replied Dusty.

Becky opened the door to find the whole room filled with flowers and candles.

Then Dusty simply said, "You see!" Just little personal touches, add so much, for such a perfect beginning. And there is still much to do."

Returning to the party, Sam asked Becky where she had been. His face was beaming to hear what she would come up with, with the entire crowd gathered round. Becky's face flushed!

Dusty looked over at Richard, winked, and then answered for Becky. "We took a little walk for girl talk."

He knew Dusty had taken her to the room, but no one told him anything about Dusty's decorating plans. She had told Becky that he would really be surprised.

Becky, having the upper hand now said, "You just never know what two girls can do together in a short span of time."

She and Dusty busted out laughing and Sam decided to let her have this moment on him, knowing in his heart, whatever she was up to, would turn out to be pretty special.

One of Dusty's chores the day of rehearsal was to pick up all the gowns and take them to the church. Becky had helped her very early that morning and they managed to keep Dusty's mother from inspecting the church dressing room. Dusty had left Becky's bridesmaids dress underneath Becky's wedding gown in the trunk. She was close enough in size to be able to wear Becky's bridesmaid dress for Becky's wedding and planned to spring it on Becky at the chapel. They still had to decide where they would dress.

Becky told Dusty about the woman at the chapel saying, "If anyone can help us with this dilemma, its Beth. Dusty, she is the sweetest woman you will ever meet. She has a way about her that beats anyone. You can't help but love her."

Towards the end of the evening, Richard finally got up the nerve to sing his song. With a heavy case of stage freight, Sam stood up with him and together they sang that beautiful song directly at Dusty. The words of his story were exactly how their lives had come together. Each verse was a chapter of the years they had spent together and would always cherish, with the ending praising God for his blessings.

When everyone started to leave, Richard and Sam said goodnight to the girls and then helped the band load their equipment. Alice told Dusty not to keep the girls up too late; stating they all needed their rest for tomorrow. Walking to the elevator, Dusty told all the girls she would meet them in their room after she changed her clothes.

Turning to Becky, she said, "Mom wants us to get plenty of rest, she must be exhausted. There is no way I will be able to sleep after hearing that song from Richard. It just plays over and over in my mind."

Becky agreed with her as she stepped inside the wedding party's room.

Dusty planned just for the girls to meet in their room after everyone else had gone home. She had snacks and games to last well into the wee hours of the morning.

Apparently, all the dancing and festivities had worn out everyone. They tried playing different games, but it just did not turn into a party atmosphere. Dusty suggested that they all try to get some sleep and there were no refusals to that suggestion. Becky slipped out with Dusty and they quietly completed all the decorating on both rooms. Dusty called the front desk before Becky went back to the other girl's room to get some sleep and asked the clerk for a very early wake up call. Then she asked Becky how she might be able to wake her without disturbing the others.

Becky assured her she would not need to be called, stating, "I won't be able to sleep a wink!" there is so much excitement in my heart; my thoughts will keep me on overdrive until dawn. I'll be here at your door even before your call comes thru."

Becky was exactly right; she knocked on Dusty's door just as the phone rang. When Dusty opened the door, she was all ready dress to leave. She had to call her mother and give an explanation, as to where she was going, and then they were clear to leave. Alice asked Dusty, if there was anything, she could think left to do. Dusty told her she had done such a thorough job, there was no way they had missed a thing.

Taking the initiative at the most opportune moment, she told her mom, "Becky and I are going out for a private breakfast, we will be back here by noon, and mom, relax, everything will work out great."

Alice made her promise to be back at that time and told her to have a nice time. Grabbing coffee and rolls to go, they headed for the chapel. They were to meet Richard and Sam there by eight fifteen a.m.... Then after the ceremony, they would change again, go to breakfast and meet at the hotel as if they had not seen each other all night.

Arriving fifteen minutes early, Beth was ready and greeted them at the chapel door.

Dressed in her Sunday attire, she took a glance at the girls and asked, "Are you getting married in jeans?"

"Whoops!" said Dusty, as she ran back for the car.

Becky just stood smiling.

Beth then said, "You don't need to explain anything to me."

Becky giggled, then, asked if there was a place, they could use to change into their dresses.

"Absolutely!" she replied, then, Come along and I will show you. I hope I can be of some assistance. The best part of setting up the chapel for a wedding is to get to be included. I feel like all the couples are my family and that it's my purpose in this wonderful life I've been blessed with."

Becky knew how she felt and had her working zippers, tying bows and when they were dressed, she had Beth place on her headpiece, as she completed the results. She could see in Beth's expression, just how fulfilled her heart was and she was happy just to have the opportunity to make someone else feel loved and needed. Standing side-by-side, Becky and Dusty astounded her.

She said, with watery eyes, "You both look radiant!"

Dusty asked her if she would take their picture and after she did, she volunteered to snap some more for the entire ceremony. Knowing how well she had made all the arrangements, they were thrilled for her to do the honor of taking over the camera. Having them wait in the back room, she explained how she would go place Sam and Richard, and then she would take their picture and return for them. Standing in front of the chapel, all the boys waited until Beth called them in. Sam paced back and forth, while Richard would give teasing remarks about his nervousness.

He pointed his finger at Richard saying, "Your next buddy!" and when the other boys laughed, he added, with his finger, "Your day will come and I hope you will remember this moment and laugh at yourselves for me."

They all laughed in agreement and Sam shook off his tension as Beth opened the door and called them inside. She adjusted their collars and straightened their lapels, just to impress a kiss on their cheeks. She then asked if they were ready.

Sam answered, "I could never be more ready then I feel at this very moment." She lined them in their places and Reverend O'Brien took his. Awing over them, she took a few shots and then went back to get the girls.

Beth, back in the girls holding area gave her final instructions of cues to start their slow precise walks and then headed for her piano to play the wedding march. Sam was smiling with a calm warm feeling that came over him as Dusty walked up the isle. Her dress was beautiful and everything was perfect. Taking his eyes from Dusty to Becky's appearance at the back of the room, his face changed to an awesomely astounded look. Never before had he seen anyone so beautiful, so perfect and he realized at that moment, just how enormously God had blessed him. He praised the Lord for her and promised he would always hold her near to his heart forever. They joined hands and the ceremony began. When Reverend O'Brien finished their vows, he added a special blessing of his own for them, knowing in his heart, it was obvious, that this marriage, was indeed, brought together by the highest power.

After everyone had congratulated Mr. and Mrs. Sam Malloy and pictures were completed, Becky and Dusty flew to the back room to change. Beth accompanied them to give some assistance. She also wanted to understand why they were in such a rush and thought the girls might let her in on what was going on. While slipping into her jeans, Becky explained the whole situation in just a matter of minutes. Their time was getting to short for idle chitchat and she wanted to have a nice breakfast with her new husband. Beth listened intensely, without interrupting, just nodding her head, yes, as if she was in complete agreement, even though she was a bit confused. When Becky finished, Beth's thoughts were not to mettle and she changed the subject asking for copies of some of the pictures for her scrapbook. Saying goodbye, Dusty promised to send her, her photos as soon as she got them back. Becky hugged her and gave her a look with a loving smile.

Richard and Sam arrived at the café, where they were to meet and ordered the girls meals to save time. Only a few minutes behind them, they whisked into the café just dancing, with Becky singing the song, "Singing in the rain", which had everybody in the café giggling. When they sat down, Becky gave Sam a long kiss.

Richard said, "Becky, it isn't raining!"

She replied, "No", and then sang out, "But I'm happy again, I'm happy again with or without any rain."

It was just after noon when they finished eating. Dusty glanced at the clock on the wall and just about had a fit!

She jumped out of her seat, grabbed Becky up out of hers saying, "I promised to be back by noon!" We have to leave now!"

Becky leaned down to swipe Sam's lips as Dusty pulled her away without saying goodbye to Richard.

Rushing to the car, she kept repeating, "My mom is going to be furious, I promised."

Screeching tires through the parking lot, Becky started in, "Calm down!" We will be there in a few minutes and she won't be angry. Its better we get there, than have an accident and not get there at all."

Dusty came to her senses and slowed down, but still exceeded the speed limit to make up some time.

Finally back safely at the hotel, Becky had Dusty take a deep breath and said, "We need to act carefree and happy."

Dusty settled herself while walking into the lobby and told Becky, "We'd better find mom and start helping her set up the tables first."

Entering the reception room, Alice waived them over to her. She said, "You're late, but that's o.k. now. "We have a problem!" I went to the church to check the dresses and shoes. Everything was in order except Becky's gown."

Dusty quickly replied, "I must have left it in the trunk of my car. I'll go check to make sure."

Becky almost laughed at the serious face Dusty had put on, but pinched herself in order to keep a straight face. When Dusty returned, she brought it in draped over her arm, wrapped in its plastic cover. Alice snatched it up and said she would put it in her car to make sure it is not lost again.

Becky wrapped her arms around Alice and said, "You are so good at this!" Everything is done, ready to go and now you can relax for a while and then spiffy up for the big moment. We have so much extra time and I think you could use a nice cup of tea with your daughter."

Alice thought that was a wonderful idea and took both girls by the hand to the dinning room. Within a short time, she began to let go and gather her thoughts. She had gone over the arrangements so many times, that she had caused confusion and panic in her own mind. Dusty and Becky talked to her, as if they had not a care in the world, projecting over them an array of quiet, gentle peace. For those well-needed minutes, Alice came to realize she had been in a battle of her own doing needlessly. She thanked the girls for being so perceptive of her, when all this was about Dusty's day.

"How you can be so calm, is beyond me." said Alice, and then asked Dusty, "Where does this come from?"

Dusty replied, "You have done the most wonderful job putting everything together. I had no doubt in my mind, that this day would glide along just as smooth as glass. "And!" I also had my best friend by my side these last few days, which really made all the difference."

Becky added, "We have been a pair for so many years, that one can't possible do anything without the other."

While they were sitting in the dinning room, the caterers came in and gave the details as to when they would set out the dinner.

With nothing left to do there, Alice said, "Well, I think I'll head back to the house and get ready. I will meet you at the Church no later than four. You need to be there at that time to dress and start with the photographer. Please, don't be even a few minutes late!"

"Becky and I are going to my room to freshen up and throw some curls in our hair. And after we play around with some make-up, we will be on our way. This promise I will keep." Dusty replied.

Grasping the arms of her chair, after Alice had left, Dusty looked at Becky and said, "Next stop, up stairs!"

In the elevator Becky asked, "Where is all this energy coming from?"

Dusty grinned, and said, "I'm not sure!" All I am thinking about is, if my wedding is half as wonderful as yours, its going to be fantastic! And you know? I don't feel the least bit tired."

They stopped in at Becky's room, just so she could see it all fixed up again.

Dusty said, "But, before we leave, I have one more thing just for you."

She went to the dresser and motioned for Becky to open it. As she pulled the drawer open, there was something wrapped in gently folded tissue paper.

Dusty said, "Open it!"

Becky pulled back the tissue paper to find a beautiful nightgown with a matching robe. Dusty lifted it out and held it up to Becky in front of the mirror.

Becky asked, "Where did you find such a gorgeous set?"

"You haven't had much time to shop for yourself, and probably wouldn't have anyway. When mom and I were out shopping I saw this and went back to that quaint little shop by the name of, "Just for her", replied Dusty.

Becky thanked her and said, "Dusty! You've done so much and you just keep adding more. This is the prettiest gown I've ever seen, full length and as pink as it can be."

"Mine is similar, but I choose a cream color with small roses, added Dusty, then, lets hang it up in the bathroom to take out the wrinkles and I'll show you mine when we get to my room."

Becky hugged her tight saying, "You're the best sister, I could have ever had."

Becky had purchased a greeting card that expressed her exact feeling on their friendship, along with some money tucked inside; she decided it was the perfect time to give it to Dusty. As she rummaged through her things in an oversized tote, back in Dusty's room, she had her sit down for just one second.

Finally finding it at the bottom, she handed it to her and said, "This is my gift to you."

Dusty opened it not paying any attention to the cash, only reading the words with tears streaming down her cheeks. She hugged Becky without saying anything, and held on.

Becky said, "Hay!" check out the rest!"

"Wow!" went Dusty, then, "Becky! This is too much!" "You can't do this!" "I can't accept this!"

Becky laughed saying, "You have no choice, I want you to have it and besides, it's a gift and you can't give it back."

Overwhelmed, her knees buckled and she fell down on the bed. Becky sat beside her and explained how she could afford to do this, telling her about what her father had given her for graduation.

"And like my dad said, what good is all my money, if I can't give it to my family!" Then she added, and if you don't dry those tears, young lady, your eyes will be so puffed up when they take pictures and you won't like a one of them. Now let's fix your make-up and curl our hair."

By three thirty, they were ready to leave for the Church. Alice met them at the door and took them out around the building to the dressing room. It had completely skipped their minds as to where they were going and Alice figured Dusty was a bit nervous at this point. As they dressed, one of the bridesmaids brought Dusty a lacy blue garter.

Becky looked on and said, "Something old, something new, something borrowed and something Blue! Now we have blue and I have something new!"

She handed Dusty a small box, wrapped in silver paper, tied with thin white ribbons and a small white rose for the bow. She didn't want to open such a pretty box and hesitated for a moment.

Becky said, "Dusty! Open the box. You can save the rose!"

Very gently, she untied the ribbon, saving every piece to keep forever. As she lifted the lid and folded back the tissue paper, her eyes lit, her mouth dropped open and she reached ever so carefully to lift out, it was a beautiful pearl drop necklace.

Dusty whispered, "It so beautiful!", "Oh Becky!", "It's so beautiful!"

Becky lifted it from her hand and fastened it around her neck.

One of the other bridesmaids said, "I have something you can borrow!"

She handed Dusty a cameo that her mother and grandmother had worn when they married. None of them could think of anything old. Becky suggested the cameo could be both, something borrowed and something old. They all laughed and agreed that would be acceptable.

Alice peaked in the door to see if everyone was dressed.

Becky walked over to the door, reached for her hand and said, "Come see your beautiful daughter."

Dusty turned to face them and Alice, with a hankie to her nose, started to cry.

Becky motioned to the other girls to come outside and softly said as they walked out, "Let's give them a few minutes alone together."

The photographers were calling for the wedding party to line up for a few shots. Richard, Sam and three other attendants took their places. Dusty's father came to get her and Becky escorted him to the dressing room. As the wedding march began, the bridesmaids started slowly down the isle. Becky knocked on the dressing room door, and then took her place in line. As she walked towards the altar, her eyes fixed on Sam's, and all the memories of the morning ceremony flashed through her mind. It was extremely difficult at that moment for her to hold back her tears, but somehow she managed and took take her place.

Arm in arm, Alice, Dusty and her father, Chris, walked up the isle all together. Chris put Dusty's hand into Richards and the ceremony began. Her wedding was just as beautiful as Becky's was, filled with all the memories that best of friends could ever have. After the newlyweds and wedding party had greeted the guest, they departed out of the Church, and the photographers once again took control. Dusty had asked them for additional shots for Becky and they took as many as they could.

The reception began with a dinner buffet of roast beef, turkey and ham, and all the side dishes in an array to please any taste, set between the dance floor and the cake table. Toast after toast went out to Richard and Dusty by friends and family members. The band set up shortly after and Sam started the first dance for Richard and Dusty, with their special song Richard had sung for her at the wedding rehearsal dinner. Becky sat dreamy eyed as she watched Sam sing, and the way he sang that song, she knew it was just for them, but also directed straight to her heart. He had the band play just music for a dance or two, to enable him to break away for a dance with Becky and one with Dusty. Then the rest of the evening, Sam took song requests, which kept him on stage.

At eight, Richard and Dusty cut the cake. People were already starting to leave as the evening was winding down. The photographers finished up their pictures and by ten, the only ones left were Dusty's family. Chris and Alice packed up the gifts and leftover cake, while Richard and Sam helped the band load their equipment. Dusty was ready to take off her dress shoes and took Becky to an isolated table were they could relax and talk. Within a half hour, after Chris and Alice kissed their daughter and welcome their new son-in-law to the family, they left for home. Richard and Sam joined their wives with the last of the punch Richard had poured into four glasses. Delivering them as if he were a waiter and announcing it to be champaign for the newlyweds.

Dusty gave a toast by stating, "May we always stay best friends forever!"

Becky followed with, "Let this day be just one of many more precious memories we have make together!"

Richard and Sam tapped everyone's glass as they stood and held their hands out to their wives.

When Becky woke the next morning, cuddled in Sam's arm, she felt a peaceful completeness. She laid quietly watching him sleep, feeling his heartbeat until he woke. They talked for a while of how happy they were and took their time showering and sipping their coffee. The room was booked for the day and neither wanted to leave. Sam ordered room service for lunch and they set up a picnic on the floor.

Richard and Dusty passed by their room as they left the hotel for Dusty's house. They had to see off the family that had flown in and Alice had planned a gift opening dinner for them.

After seeing the, "Do not disturb", sign on their door, Dusty told Richard they would make some kind of excuse for them not being there.

Just before check out time, Sam told Becky there was something he needed to tell her.

There bags packed and set by the door, he said, "My orders came in to report to the recruiting station on the fifteenth. We don't have as much time as we originally planned. I would like to keep our room until I leave and hold you in my arms just as long as I possibly can."

Becky, holding back her emotions said, "I would like that too. It's going to be so hard to say goodbye again. I will do my best to stay strong, but this time."

Then, before she could finish he added, "Six weeks, "Becky!", and then you can come wherever I'm stationed and we will find a place of our own."

He put his arms around her and she began to cry.

Lifting her chin to look in her eyes, he said, "Think of all the things you need to do, breaking the news to your parents, Sarah, and spending as much time as you can with them before you leave again. It will make those six weeks fly by."

With a soggy face, Becky said, "For us, I can do anything! I'll be cheerful, thinking of our place and picturing in my mind how we will fix it up just for us, if we can go five months, we can surely do six weeks."

With that, they stood up, wiped her tears and headed for the lobby.

At Dusty's, when Sam and Becky arrived, they were still opening their gifts. Alice fixed them a plate of food, while they watched Richard and Dusty's delight with each package. When they finished, Richard announced his orders to the crowd. They were the same as Sam's and Becky looked at Dusty, to give her some strength, as he spoke. Later that evening, after everyone had left and Dusty and Becky had helped do all the dishes, Dusty asked her mom and dad to join them in the living room. Becky told them she had an announcement of her own to make and Sam stood by her side as she broke their news.

Alice quickly responded with, "Both my girls married on the same day! What a day this will be to remember."

Becky went on to explain to them that she wanted to tell her parents when she returned to Boston. They agreed that would be best to give them the news in person. Chris shook Sam's hand and gave Becky a big hug, with Alice right behind hugging everyone. Sam informed them they would be staying at the hotel until he left and Dusty and Becky would be making their plans afterwards.

Chris said, "This night deserves a special toast!"

He went to the kitchen and came back with six glasses of champagne.

As they tapped glasses together he said, "May all your years together be as glorious as ours has been. Full of love and blessed with good children with many happy memories to see you through your senior years!" They sat and talked about their wedding and some of the short-term plans they had made before leaving to go back to the hotel.

Just minutes after getting back to their room, a knock came at the door. Sam opened the door and there stood Richard and Dusty.

Dusty said, "We have our room, too."

Richard wrapped his arm around Dusty's neck, seeming to drag her off and said, "See ya later!"

Sam and Becky watched in laughter as he continued to pretend to drag her down the hall.

The next few days had vanished into mid air. Before they new it, they were at the station trying to get enough kisses and hugs in to last as long as possible.

As they started loading up on the bus, Sam told Becky, "Remember, stay busy, have fun, try to keep your mind busy making plans. I will write just as soon as I can and you start a letter today. I love you, "Becky". As he stepped on the bus, he turned back and said, "I'll see you soon."

She threw him a kiss and kept a smile on her face until the bus was well out of sight.

Dusty took Becky by the hand and went back to the car.

She suggested to Becky, "Let's go back to the house. Dad is gone for the day and mom would like to be with us right now. She knows how we feel; she's gone through pretty much the same thing with dad."

Alice turned out to be a real comfort. She told them funny stories like how they were married, and the short time they had together before he had to leave. Trying to keep up their spirits, she added things in just to make them laugh.

Becky stayed with Dusty another week, helping her pack and getting ready to move wherever Richard would be stationed. They both talking about how they could, most likely move to the same place. Then silently thinking about how they would have a great time if they were in the same place.

The day before her flight home, she called Sarah and told her of her arrival.

Asking if she could pick her up at the airport, Sarah replied, "You betsha", I have missed you so much and I cannot wait to see you. I have spent quit some time with your mother. We have been unpacking and your father has been busy setting up a small business. He is so happy here; you will be amazed at what we have been doing!"

Becky was not her usual talkative self, and Sarah knew she was in need for some cheering up. She went on asking Becky questions about the wedding and Becky would give her short direct answers, but not the way she normally would have. Sarah figured she would talk when she came home and did not push her. Becky gave her the flight information and cut the conversation short.

Dusty was more optimistic than Becky. As quiet as Becky had become, with Dusty going on and on, talking and planning, no one even noticed how sad Becky really was. She managed to hide her feelings from everyone. In the back of her mind, she knew Sarah knew, and she was glad that she would be the one picking her up.

At the airport, Becky kept on her happy face and Dusty was so excited about their moving that she just kept chattering about what her imagination could picture for their future. Becky didn't want her to feel the sadness she felt and let her just go on jabbering.

When the announcement of her flight came, and as she walked towards the gate, leaving Dusty waiving, she looked back, and a feeling came over her, that she would never see Dusty again. She found her seat on the plane and began trying to convince herself that all this was just in her mind. She was upset over Sam leaving, her leaving Dusty, and it was her mind playing tricks with her thoughts. Taking a slow deep cleansing breath, she prayed. With her eyes closed and no one interrupting, she continued to pray and then meditate during the entire time she was in the air. By the time the flight attendant came over the intercom to fasten seatbelts, she had felt a peace come over her and some strength, to keep going through the rest of her day.

Chapter Four

Becky's flight arrived in Boston much earlier than scheduled. Even so, as she entered the airport terminal, the first face she saw was Sarah's, and a warm comfort came over her, as she grew closer. Sarah, with open arms and a welcoming smile, wrapped Becky up with all the love she could give at that moment, exactly when she needed it the most.

The drive back to Sarah's was an emotional one for Becky. She could not hold back her sadness of this separation. As her tears fell into her hands cupped to her face, Sarah reached over and put her hand on Becky's shoulder. She said nothing at all to stop her crying; it was Becky's turn to let it all out. By the time they reached the house, she had had a good cleansing downpour. After parking the car, Sarah asked if she would rather be with her parents. Becky composed herself and told Sarah she would like to stay with her a day or two. She had no problem with that request; in fact, Becky could move in with her and stay forever as far as she was concerned. To her, Becky was the sister, the daughter, the mother and most of all, the most precious friend she had had since Brian. No doubt, she would move Heaven and earth to be able to take all the pain that was so heavy in her heart.

With the car unloaded and Becky still in silence, Sarah fixed them a pitcher of ice tea and set it out on the patio. A warm breeze had filled the air with the sweet fragrances of the flowers in Sarah's beds that lined the fence around the back yard. She hoped the warmth and familiar surroundings might enable Becky to open up and discuss what was so painful and heavy on her heart.

After still sitting in her silence, Sarah asked, "Please talk to me? Then adding, I can't help you unless you fill me in on what's troubling you."

Finally, she took in a deep breath, looked into the sky and said, "Your right!" What am I doing? "But, it's so hard!"

Sarah took Becky's hand saying, "Tell me everything that's happened from the time you left here."

Gathering her thoughts for a moment, she started with the flight back to San Diego. Well into dusk she continued talking, describing every detail. And following Sarah to the kitchen as she fixed supper, Becky never stopped until the food was set on the table. Then after they had finished eating, she started right where she had left off before their meal. Sarah just let the dishes set; she did not want to miss any detail of Becky's life changing events. When she finally came to a halt, she had covered everything to saying goodbye to Sam at the recruiting station. Sarah, at this point had come to understand Becky's emotional state. But it was so late and Becky looking extremely exhausted, she suggested they get a few hours sleep and start putting all this into perspective in the morning. She walked her to the bedroom and sat her down at the side of the bed.

Becky looked up and said, "I'm so glad to be here with you, I don't know what I would do without you."

Sarah kissed her forehead and leaned her back to the pillow. Sarah sat down beside her and stayed until she had fallen to sleep.

Becky woke at nine, but not too eager to face her parents with her news. And she knew the longer she waited, the harder it would be for them to understand. Sarah notice by the look on Becky's face she felt better, but as far as rested, that would come later.

During breakfast, Sarah brought up some of the best times Becky had described the night before. After a while, her attitude lightened to became brighter. She realized it was easier to think of the good things and that would see her through the next few weeks. Keeping in thought Sam's words to fill her mind and his strength to fill her heart.

Sarah asked her if she would like to borrow the car and go see her parents.

She was a bit reluctant and said, "Actually? Then, I have a huge request to ask."

"Anything!" replied Sarah.

"Will you go with me?" she asked and, I know it sound a bit childish to need someone with me, but if I say something wrong, you could jump right in to rephrase my thoughts. And besides, you are family too."

Sarah contemplated that statement for a while then answered, "Well, I won't be saying much and I'm sure you will do just fine." Then she gave in saying, "You don't know your way to the house. I wouldn't want you to get lost and not be able to come find you." Becky finally laughed and Sarah did as well.

She called the house to make sure someone would be home and her mother answered the phone.

She said, "Mom, I'm home!" Elizabeth had no idea she would be back so soon. She thought she would be another week or so. With this unexpected delight, she was very grateful to hear her voice and anxious to have her back home. Elizabeth told her, that William was at home and working on the yard. Then she said he would be extremely surprised when she arrived, saying, "I'm not going to tell him your back. I want to see the look on his face when you walk in."

"Mom!" Becky jested, then, you are getting pretty ornery, I must be rubbing off on you or you have been suppressing a side we haven't seen." Then changing the tone in her voice she added, "I can't wait to see you! I've missed you so much."

"Me too, honey," replied Elizabeth.

As Sarah drove up the lane towards the house, she stopped a few houses away. Becky, with her mischievous grin told her she would sneak into the back yard to surprise them. She told Becky she would give her a two-minute start, and then she would pull on into the driveway. Becky managed to enter the side gate and reach the patio without noticed. She quickly sat down in the shade and waited for William to look back from his pruning to see her. Elizabeth saw her from the kitchen window and slipped out to join her prank. His attention so focused on the shrubs; Sarah had parked the car, came through the house and was sitting with Elizabeth and Becky without his acknowledgment. When he did turn and look towards the house, he thought at first his eyes were playing tricks on him. Standing to disbelief for a moment and rubbing his eyes, his face flushed then beamed with excitement. Mumbling something, he rushed over to Becky; they could not help but laugh.

He picked her up as if she were a rag doll, twirling her around saying, "My baby's home."

"Wow", Becky blurted out, then, I didn't know you were this strong! All this moving and yard work has put you in great shape."

Then he said, "It's so good to see you. When did you get in?"

Becky answered, "Yesterday afternoon."

"Is everything alright? We thought you would be another week or so," asked William.

Becky went on to explain, how Sam and Richards orders changed and she decided to come sooner than expected.

"Well", said William, then, let me clean up a little and I'll want to hear all about your trip."

While he freshened up, Elizabeth and Sarah took Becky on a tour of the house. Starting to feel more at ease, Becky was hungry for her mothers special home cooking.

She asked, "Mom", have you made anything for dinner yet?"

Elizabeth replied, "When you called this morning, I knew you would be ready for something good. I made your favorite casserole, the Mexican chicken dish! Asking, do you remember?"

She answered, "I can't remember when we had that last, it was always was my favorite."

Becky went on to say what a beautiful day it was and Sarah suggested they eat out on the patio. The flowers were in full bloom and just as sweetly fragranced as they could be. William told Becky the landscaping is what sold him on this house; every plant; flower and scrub in this yard most likely involved a professional gardener. Then he took her by the hand and they walked around the yard. Elizabeth, watching them from the kitchen window told Sarah, that for the first time in Williams's life, he had settled to love being at home. His work had taken up most of his life and he finally has found just how happy he can be with the simpler treasures.

Elizabeth's casserole made a big hit with everyone. Becky even thought it might be her best accomplishment since chocolate cake.

Elizabeth laughed and asked, "How did you know I made a chocolate cake too?" Becky told her the aroma was still in the house and she smelled it while they were taking their tour.

Sarah insisted on clearing the table and cleaning up, while Becky began to tell them about her trip. She moved quickly so she would be back at the table when Becky broke her news. Her words flowed perfectly as she led up to the part of her marriage to Sam.

Very slowly and choosing just the right timing she said, "Dad, mom, I am."

William interrupted with, "You are Mrs. Malloy!" We figured that by the ring on your finger. We cannot get angry with you. Your mother and I were married at sixteen. We can't throw stones. In fact, we had an idea this would happen, even though we would have loved to have been there with you."

Becky apologized and explained how fast everything had happened. She told them about the little chapel Sam had found as she handed them the pictures she had brought back with her. Elizabeth asked if she could take them to a photographer and make them some copies for her album. Becky told her she had planned to do that for them. As Sarah viewed them, she thought one in particular would make a nice wall pictured, framed in maybe a silver or gold frame. They loved her dress and Elizabeth asked if she had brought it back with her.

She quickly answered, "Of course. I would put it in a frame too if it would fit."

"I would really like to see you in it sometime," said Elizabeth.

Sarah knew of a great photographer in town and Becky could put her gown on for a single picture for their wall. William joined the conversation and suggested they have some sort of a reception when Sam finished boot camp.

Elizabeth said," That would be a wonderful way to show him how welcome he is in our family. You will need to make me a list of people to invite."

Sarah asked Becky how many people, off the top of her head, she could think of.

She thought for a few minutes and then said, "Really, it would just be us. I don't know the girls from school that well and I will probably never see them again.

"We will have a reception to remember!" said Elizabeth.

They went on and made plans for a nice elegant dinner and Sarah said she would order the cake. At that point, Sarah and Elizabeth went to the kitchen for desert and coffee.

William had Becky to himself for a few minutes and took advantage by asking, "How are you really doing? It has to be very hard on you to be separated so soon."

She moved her chair closer to his and put her hand in his, then laid down her head on his shoulder and said,

"You know me pretty well, don't you dad. Then she lifted her head and added, I broke down at Sarah's, but she let me get it all out and helped me realized how much love I have right here. We have much to catch up on and so many beautiful sights I want to show you. And just wait until you see how wonderful it is to see the seasons changing. You will like the winter, it gets very cold, but the peacefulness it brings is breath taking."

She apologized again for not calling or inviting them to her wedding. Looking back now, it would have been the icing on the cake, if her father had walked her down the isle.

The exact thought was also in his mind, which sparked an idea he presented to Becky by asking, "Well kiddo, and what do ya think? Want to do it again?"

Elizabeth and Sarah had just stepped out on the patio at that moment; Becky pushed back her chair and stood up with the biggest smile her face could project. She walked out to the middle of the yard, William following and they stopped. He leaned down to her shoulder, put his hand on her arm and pointed to a special group of flowers.

"What about putting up a trellis right there?" He asked.

"It's perfect!" She replied. She turned around to hug him and said, "This is going to be a dream come true, "Thank you, daddy!"

Sarah and Elizabeth stood watching, wondering what they were planning.

He took Becky back to the patio and told Elizabeth, "We're having a wedding!"

The look on her face, as William put it, was worth more than a million bucks and he hugged her with tears in both their eyes.

The rest of the evening, they discussed a number of ideas. And when they agreed Elizabeth would write it down. Becky stayed in the room they had fixed up just for her. They had no plans for the next few days as Elizabeth insisted that Becky, get some well-needed rest. She had admitted feeling extremely exhausted and thought her mother was right on her assumption.

Over the next few weeks, they had kept Becky's mind very occupied with the wedding plans. She assisted William while he built the trellis and did the painting of each piece prior to his assembling. Sarah made some calls and found out where Sam had rented the tuxedo he wore, and then ordered one as a gift. William helped Becky with her flower order, and added a list of plants for the yard. By the time Sam arrived, they would be ready for this ceremony, no matter how short a time he had.

Becky received a letter sent to Sarah's from Sam. She rushed it over to Becky, as she knew it would cheer her spirit and ease her mind. It had been five weeks since he had left and she was beginning to worry. When Sarah arrived, Elizabeth said she was so glad she had brought it right over. Becky was not feeling well and had spent most of the morning in bed. Sarah took it to her and found her as pale as the bleached white sheets. She asked if she could get her anything and Becky told her nothing was staying down. She suggested some tea and Becky said she would try.

"Enjoy your letter and I'll be back in a few minutes," said Sarah.

She held the letter to her chest, and then thanked God it had finally come. The writing was messy, as if he had a lot to say and no time to get everything down. It said,

My Dearest Becky,

Oh, How I love my sweet Becky! The vision of our wedding has kept me going. Everyone in my platoon has been so worn out with maneuvers training, target practice and marching, that whenever we go to write, most of us fall asleep. Today we have a break and our first sergeant assigned us to write home. I have missed you so much and I am counting down to the hour when I will see you again. I hope the news went well with your parents. My next letter will be to mine and they will be happy, I'm sure. Sarah must have been shocked too!

We have just one more week to go. Then there will be a ceremony. We will have thirty days before I report to wherever they send me. Richard has applied for mechanics and so have

I. But that could change at any given time. They look at each individual's abilities and make their decisions from that. Richard is taking the bus to San Diego and I will get a flight to Boston as soon as I leave the base. I will leave a message at Sarah's with my time of arrival. With thirty days off, I would like to get to know your parents better. Then I would like to take you to meet my family. But we will need time to get to where we will end up. And then, there's setting up our place too. Well, there is a lot to think about, so I will stop just for now. We never know how much time we will get and I had better write mom and let her know everything that has happened.

"I Love my Becky!"

"I'll see you soon"
All my Love, Sam

Sarah returned to Becky with sweetened tea and toast, as she had suggested would give her some strength. She sipped the tea slowly and nibbled at the toast for quit some time. Then told Sarah she was feeling a bit better. Over the next few days, she would have a good day, than some not so well. By the time Sam arrived, she was feeling better. She sized her illness up to being homesick for him and just plain old tired.

Elizabeth agreed and told Becky she should really start taking better care of herself saying, "The next time you get sick, it could be much worse and you could end up in the hospital."

William welcomed Sam into the family with a two handed shake and then a strong hug. Elizabeth was next, giving him a hug then a gentle kiss on his cheek. Sarah had Becky thinking he would arrive the following day, so he could surprise her by showing up unexpected. And that she was, when he walked out onto the patio where they were all taking in some sun. She laughed and cried at the same time, rushing to his arms.

Elizabeth planned a cookout for that night so they could all visit. William gave Sam his tour of the house, then to all the landscape of his yard. Becky told him how she and her dad had built the trellis together, one piece at a time. Then William asked Becky if he could ask Sam for an extremely special request.

She walked over to her dad and said, "He's all yours!" But don't hurt him too bad!"

Sam's eyes opened wide, with his eyebrows raised, his lips pressed in a funny grin, as he had no idea what they were up to next.

The first thing William told him was, "My request is not funny!" Elizabeth and I would like to see our daughter married. We would like to have a small ceremony right here."

"That explains the trellis!" replied Sam, then went on to say, I cannot think of a more perfect setting and after all, you and Becky did all this work, we can't let it go to waste! So a wedding there will be!"

Back at the table, they informed him of all the plans they had made over the past few weeks. But as long as Becky was happy and it made her parents happy too, it was the least he could do. After going over all they had planned, a date was set for the coming weekend. Elizabeth and Sarah cleared the table, giving William the hint to give Sam and Becky some time alone. William acted as if his day had worn him out and excused himself to hit the sack. Becky still feeling weak thought a good night's sleep sounded wonderful. Sam picked up his duffle bag in the hallway as Becky drug him up the stairs. Elizabeth and Sarah sat down to the last of the coffee and afterwards Sarah went home.

Becky had so many questions to ask, but felt they had both better get some sleep.

As they lay in bed, she could not help but ask, "Sam, where are we going?"

"Have you ever been to Texas?" He asked.

She answered, "No", but it will be an adventure."

He smiled, took her in his arms and drifted off to sleep.

The next morning, Sam was up at six. He joined William in the kitchen for coffee and they discussed his orders. He told William he had to report to Fort Hood Texas by August thirtieth. Richard was to report to the base in San Diego and he said Becky would not be too thrilled with that news. We won't get any further information until I report in. William asked if he had planned to see his parents before they moved. Sam told him he would really like them to meet Becky and show her the farm.

"That is a lot to do in thirty days. Said William, and then, I hope Becky is up to the trip."

Sam looked at him with a concerned expression and asked, "What do you mean? Is there something I don't know?"

William told him about her being so sick after she had come home, then added, "Elizabeth and Becky thought it might have been that she was just homesick for you. But I'm not so sure."

Sam assured William, he would have her seen by a doctor if anything came of it and that she would have a good checkup when they got to the base. William felt more at ease when Sam said that and he knew he would take good care of her.

Later that morning, Sam questioned Becky about how she was feeling. He told her what William had said to him earlier and how worried they were concerning the extreme weakness she had suffered. Becky reassured him saying she was feeling much better and would be just fine to do all the traveling and visiting, they were both looking forward too.

Although he was not convinced with her attempt to reassure him, he said, "While we are here, I want you to rest. If you are not feeling well, tell me! We can put off the farm for our next trip when I get a few weeks off again."

By the time the weekend rolled around, the weather was gorgeous. All the flowers around the beautiful landscape were in full bloom. Perfectly setting the stage for a wedding fit to please a queen. Elizabeth set the dining room table with her fine china and Sarah decorated the buffet with flower arrangements, and then set the cake in the midst of the entire colorful array. While Becky rested, Sam helped William finely manicure the yard. When they had finished, William pulled out paper ribbon to stream around the patio for his grand finally. By noon, everything was finished. Now it was time to freshen up and dress before the minister arrived.

Sarah had scheduled a photographer and he arrived shortly after the minister. While they were waiting for Becky, Sam held out his arm to Elizabeth and escorted her up the imaginary isle. Next, Sarah walked slowly and took her place. As Becky stepped out on the patio where William was waiting, Sam noticed a mystical radiance about her. He thought back for a moment of their wedding in the chapel. She was indescribably beautiful then, but now, even more so. William paused to kiss her and tell her how beautiful she looked before walking towards the minister. This ceremony was just as wonderful as their first. Although Reverend O'Brian and

Beth were not there, Becky felt them in her heart. Another day to cherish was Becky's innermost thought. Then after their vows and the traditional kiss, they lined up for pictures. Before the photographer left, Becky asked how soon he would have them done. He told her the proofs would be ready in three days and once they made their choices it would take another three days and he would deliver them. Becky told Elizabeth and Sarah that she would like to fix up a very special album for Sam's family and it would be nice to have it with them when they arrived on their visit.

Elizabeth's dinner was delicious! From her prime rib to the homemade dinner rolls. The cake Sarah ordered was as perfect as it could be; Italian crème with a satin icing and just a few scattered little roses around the edges.

After devouring large pieces of that delicious masterpiece, William stood at the head of the table and everyone thought he was about to give a toast to the newlyweds, instead he gave a blessing through prayer;

"Oh", Dear Heavenly Father, I come to you in thanksgiving this day, for all the blessings you have graciously and lovingly brought into our lives. May we continue to strive in our lives to do your will for without you we are helpless! I ask for your blessings today upon our family, we gather at this table in celebration of a marriage brought together by your mighty hand. Let them live for you with honor all the days of their lives. Bless them with good and obedient children that will carry on for your namesake! We thank you Lord, for what you did to save us. Please guide us to continue to walk in your path through our lives and keep all evil from us. In Jesus name, Amen."

The room echoed with quiet Amen's, then a few moments of silence. William had captured in his prayer all anyone could have ever said. There was not one eye without tears in the room. The overwhelming love felt by all at that very moment, would be the most precious memory of their lives.

Sarah stood next, thanking William first, for taking her into their wonderful family, and then she went on with, "We never know where life will take us, but wherever that may be our love for one another will continue to flourish. For Sam and Becky, their lives will move to Texas, William and Elizabeth here to explore Boston, and for me, my next adventure takes me to England. I would like to announce that I have taken a position at Oxford University. A few weeks ago, I met a professor from Oxford. We have been dating and I made the decision to go and pursue this relationship. I am keeping my house here for the time being, to see how this special person may fill my life. This move is the biggest step I have ever made and I would have never considered it, if it weren't for Becky. She helped me to live again and let go of the pain. I do not know, how I could ever repay her, but I do know that God sent her to me. William, when you said, we have been graciously blessed, you were not ever aware of just how many blessings we have received. So the only thing I can say is, thank you so much for all the love you have given, I will always love you all."

Becky got up from her chair, circled around the table and hugged Sarah. Then she stepped back, but kept one arm around her and said, "You deserve all the love your heart can hold. I pray this new person in your life will come to find how precious your love can be."

Everyone gathered around her giving big hugs towards her happiness.

Elizabeth brought in a roll cart mounded with gifts, while they were all still visiting with Sarah. She asked that they come into the living room and gather round. She put Sam and Becky in two dining room chairs just behind the cart and William, Sarah and Elizabeth took their places on the sofa to watch them open them. They opened everything from a toaster to bedding sheets and towels. Sarah handed Sam a small box after they finished with the mounded cart. Inside the box were four keys.

With puzzling looks on their faces, Sarah explained, "One key is to my home, where you are welcome anytime. Another key is to this house, where you had better visit as often as possible. The other two keys you will have to go out front to figure out."

Still, the baffled looks projected on Sam and Becky, William led them out to the front yard. There in the driveway sat a shiny brand new ford van. William said they knew Sam liked vans and with all their stuff to take, they needed allot of space.

"This way", he said, you can drive to Missouri and go on to Texas from there very comfortably."

They were dumfounded and overwhelmed! Never in Sam's wildest imagination would he have thought they would give such an expensive gift.

Hugs and more hugs circled the family once again, until William said, "Climb up in there!"

As he climbed into the driver's seat, there was an envelope taped to the steering wheel. When he opened it, the note just said, "Traveling expenses!" along with a check for two thousand dollars.

"What terrific people these are and how blessed we are by their lives," Sam thought to himself. All he could force out of his emotion was, Thank you all, so very much!"

The day could not have turned out more perfect. William, Elizabeth and Sarah just went on and on, as they picked up the dishes to clear the dining room table. Sam and Becky went to change and Becky just had to call Dusty. She had not called her since she arrived and all this good news would blow her away, thought Becky as she raced to the phone. There was no answer at Richards place so she called Alice. When she answered, she told Becky they had gone on their honeymoon.

Then Alice said, "He took her to Alaska on one of those tour ships and they are due back sometime next week."

So Becky filled her in on what all had transpired, just in case she would be unable to talk to Dusty before they left for Missouri. Alice was so happy for Becky and told her that Dusty will be delighted to hear her news. Becky gave her addresses for her parent's home and Sarah's. Before she hung up, she thanked her again for all she had done for her and asked her to tell Dusty that she would be in touch as soon as she could, but not to worry if it might be a while with their trip to Missouri and Texas over the next couple of weeks.

After she finished her call, she joined everyone in the kitchen.

She just could not thank them enough for all they had done and William finally told her, "Honey!" We know how much this day has meant to you. Your happiness and love is all the thanks we will ever need. "So!" Let's just relax and enjoy each others company."

The next day Sam took out a calendar and sat Becky down to plan their trip according to the time they had left. He did not want to rush into just any place when they arrived in Texas. Then after several hours and Williams help, they managed to finish a complete schedule. They would leave for Missouri, Monday the eighth. That would put them near the farm on July thirteenth, if all went well. They would have three days there to visit, before heading for Texas, giving them just over a week to settle into a place on or near the base.

The rest of the day Sam spent packing the van to enable them to get an early start the next morning. Becky rested while she visited with her mother and Sarah. William helped Sam organize the van, leaving a full rear seat open for Becky to lie down and sleep along the way. Then they huddled at the kitchen table to work out their map strategy. William bonded so close to him, that he felt he had acquired the son he had always dream of having. Letting them go know, he knew, was going to be the hardest goodbye he had ever experienced in his entire life. He would have to be strong for everyone else, but inside, that deep burning loneliness would cripple him for the lack of words he would need to give others comfort.

As they reminisced over their cherished memories and exchanged their thoughts over the future, each one of them knew how painful the morning goodbye would be. Sarah had given Becky the address and phone numbers where she could be reach at any time and they avoided the wonderful conversation they could have had if it were not so painful. Shortly after they had finished dinner, Sarah abruptly had to leave. Unable to say goodbye, she just got up and left. Elizabeth moved over by Becky as she began to cry, knowing it would be her turn soon. William did not want this evening to be full of sorrow and asked Sam if he would bring in his guitar and play for them. Sam thought that was a great idea and he knew why William had made the request.

He played and sang songs of only cheerful melodies. With lyrics that were funny and uplifting. Becky's thoughts were on Sarah the entire evening, even though she kept it from showing on her face. She wondered if she was able to find some comfort being all alone at home.

And she tried to keep from visualizing the image of her sitting in the living room, curled up in a chair by the window just starring out into space. She prayed that her newfound friend would show up at her door and become the comfort she could not be. Then her mind moved forward to picture her parents, standing in the driveway holding on to one another with their tears as they drove away. At that moment, Sam felt inside that Becky was beginning to get down even more so than before and brought her attention back to the music by asking her to sing with him. She forced herself at first, but once she was into the song, she started to feel much better. Then she reminded herself that leaving was a new beginning, not an end to any of her family or friends.

Breakfast consisted of a cup of coffee and a slice of toast as they headed for the van. Without saying, they all knew it would make things worse if they were to start any conversations at this point. Becky held back her emotions just as hard as she could, and then after they hugged each other and said their goodbyes, Elizabeth broke down. William took her in his arms and Becky quickly climbed into the van. Sam patted her shoulder and shook Williams hand, then followed Becky's lead and drove away. Taking Sam's hand, Becky starred out the window and just let the tears run.

By evening, Becky had become ill once again. Sam watched for a motel as they drove through town after town. When he would come up on one, there would be a no vacancy light on and he would have to drive further. Finally, he found a roadside rest area and pulled in for a while. They walked around for some fresh air, thinking that would help Becky's nausea, Sam drank coffee while Becky tried to sip on a soda. She told him she would be all right, that it was just an upset stomach from saying goodbye. He asked her if she could sleep and be comfortable on the back seat until he could find a place to stop, and with her stomach now settled, she told him that sounded like a good idea and assured him she would be very comfortable curled up in her blanket and pillows. Then she asked him if he needed to sleep for a while before going on. The caffeine from all the coffee had him wired.

His answer to her question was, "I am as awake as I can be with the thought of seeing my family, and I am ready to be there. I can drive straight through without a care in the world about resting with the excitement building in my mind." He told her he had called his mother the night before and told her when they would arrive. Then, climbing into the van and tucking her in the back seat, he said, "If you need me to stop at any time, just let me know." She smiled; he kissed her and wrestled to his seat.

When she woke, it was dark and she asked how long she had slept. To her it felt like just a few minutes, but actually, it had been hours.

He told her, "Just an hour or two."

Rubbing her eyes and stretching a bit, she asked, "Do you need to stop and rest?

His answer was, "If you don't need to stop, "Baby", I'm good to go."

Sinking back into her pillow, she whispered just loud enough for him to hear, "I'm fine, goodnight."

Stopping for breakfast the next morning, Becky woke to become furious with him! He had driven over twenty hours without any rest or food.

When she asked how far they had yet to go, he answered, "About twenty minutes."

"You're kidding?" asked Becky.

"No." He replied, then, "You've slept the whole trip and just as soon as we get to Texas, you're seeing a doctor. Something is not right! Becky. And if I can make an appointment with the doctor in town, you're going!"

She agreed saying, "If it will ease your mind, I'll go. But I'm sure, I am just fine."

It was a real fight to keep down her breakfast, but she did not want him to know, so she ate just as much as she could.

Pulling up to the house, Becky smiled and said, "What a great place!" It's beautiful here."

"I'd forgotten just how beautiful and peaceful it was growing up," replied Sam.

She watched as his brothers and sisters, mother and father poured out the door to greet them. Sam told them very little of the events and wanted to see their faces when he gave them their news. He introduced Becky and in the same breath, announced she was his new bride. They joyfully extended her a country welcome into the family and then Sam's mother whisked her into the house. The rest of the afternoon, stories filled with tall tales of childhood memories exchanged, one after another. It was so much fun and very hilarious at times, that time just flew by. Becky had never been around a large family and they made her feel at home the minute Sam introduced her. Sam's mother, Anna, announced supper was ready and everyone scattered for his or her chairs. Sam explained to Becky, that here on the farm, lunch they call dinner and dinner is supper.

The home cooking filled the ten-foot long table. Becky tried to be selective, but with all the different varieties, she put small amounts of each on her plate. Then hoped she would be able to eat it all. With all the chatter about the table, no one notice she had hardly touched her food. Her nausea had become so unsteady; she excused herself from the table and went outside for some fresh air. Sam followed directly behind her knowing she was not feeling well again. His concern now had become stronger than ever. He knew it was more than a case of homesickness or the fact that leaving her family had anything to do with it. When they were alone outside, he asked her to explain exactly what she was feeling. Standing by his side, she turned her head to talk to him, and then fainted into his arms. He hollered out for his mom and everyone came running. By the time Anna reached them, Becky had come to and wanting to get up. Sam at this point was now frantic! Anna took charge, helping Becky to her feet and back into the house. She walked her to her room, had her lie down on the bed and asked her to tell her what she was feeling when she fainted. Becky explained how hectic her schedule had been over the past months and she felt it was just her body telling her to slow down and relax. After she had explained her transfer to Boston, the problems with her exams, graduation, Dusty's wedding as well as her own, then flying back to Boston and renewing their vows there, it had all just caught up with her. Anna still puzzled, felt her forehead to see if she might have a fever. Other than being so pale, she could not find anything and thought Becky may have hit the needle to the thread.

She said, "I'll talk to my son and calm him down, but, if you have any more symptoms or if you feel this way again, I will call the doctor myself."

Becky told her that maybe she should be check, just to make sure there was not something going on. Anna told her she would call the doctor right away then and left the room.

Sam and his brothers were waiting outside for their mother's word on Becky. She stopped and called the doctor at his home and he told Anna he would be there within the hour. Then she went outside and told everyone what Becky thought this might be concerning her schedule over the past few months.

Sam agreed, then went on to say, "Mom", she has had a rough time, but she's tough and this is not like her at all."

Anna took his hand and told him the doctor would be there soon. She knew deep in her heart this was not due to all the commotion, but she also had a feeling that Becky could very well be pregnant. Feeling it was not her place to diagnosis, she kept still and the doctor would confirm it, if that were the case.

When he arrived and went in with Anna to see Becky, Sam spent the entire time just pacing from one side of the house to the other. His father and brothers looked on, but said nothing. After about an hour, which felt like the whole day to Sam, Anna called him into the house and took him back to Becky's room. The doctor was sitting on the side of the bed and Becky, propped up with several pillows, had a huge smile on her face. His first thought that came to his mind was, "she was right and now she's going to let me have it for being so worried." She reached out for his hand and had him sit beside her on the other side of the bed.

Then she simply said, "We're not sick!" We are going to have a baby!"

The shear relief on his face suddenly turned to overwhelming joy! He leaned over and kissed her, then asked the doctor what she should and should not be doing. The doctor explained to Sam that her nausea was completely normal, but the fainting may be a sign of her blood sugar dropping. He wrote down some instructions as to how often she should try to eat and specifically what she should and should not consume. Then he said she should rest during their traveling, stopping every hour and to walk for ten minutes, just to keep her circulation flowing. He gave her a bottle of vitamins to try, but if they upset her stomach, to just eat right until the nausea subsided in a few weeks. Before he left, he also told them to see a physician as soon as they could find one on the base.

With two days to rest before heading for Texas, Sam asked his mother if they could wait until their next visit for the whole family to get together.

When Becky heard him say that, she put her hands on her hips saying, "I'm not sick!" I want to meet everyone; this is the time to celebrate! They have not seen you for so long."

"I know, "Becky", he said, then asked, "Are you sure you're up to all the people we're talking about?"

"Absolutely!" she answered.

Anna told them they would not have to do a thing. That Jennie and Virginia would be in charge of all the cooking, the boys would be in charge of setting up the tables and other than the music, there was nothing else to do except be there.

Sam just shook his head with that incredible deep dimple grin and threw his arms in the air saying, "Let's do it!"

While everyone prepared for the family get together, Sam took Becky for a walk around the farm. He pointed out the fields they planted and told her how they change the crop every year from one field to another, pointing out all the different types of machinery and what each one did as they walked.

Looking out over the pond, Becky said, "What a wonderful place for children to grow. Then, whatever made you want to leave?"

His answer was, "When I first left, it was to see different parts of the country with the band. I really needed to see what the city life was like. We only read about it in books and newspapers. And now that I'm back, I think it would be great someday to have a place for our kids to grow up."

He asked her how many children she would like to have.

She thought for a minute, with her hands on her tummy and answered, "At least three or four." Then she asked him the same question.

He knelt down on the ground and picking a wild flower answering, "As many as the good Lord will give us."

By that evening, all the tables were set up and the cooking completed, that Anna could possibly do the day before. After a mildly spiced supper of chicken and dumplings was devoured, Anna took Becky out on the front porch to talk while they sat rocking in the worn out chairs that were every evening the place to complete the day.

Becky woke early the next morning to find the kitchen full of confusing commotion. Making her way to the kitchen, introductions of aunts, uncles and cousins swarmed her path. She did not stand a chance to remember all their names. Wanting to help them in their preparations, but had no idea where to begin. Anna nuzzled her way through the crowded kitchen with a tray of milk and toast for Becky. She took her once again to the porch, this time to have a little peace while she ate. As Becky started kibbling, she remembered the album they had put together for her and excused herself for a moment. It was the perfect time for Anna to glance through it before she would have it pulled away and passed through the family. Sam was still sound asleep and she knew he had to be exhausted after drive all that way without resting, so she quietly took the album from her suitcase and slipped back out without waking him. She handed it to Anna and apologized for not giving it to her sooner. Then as she finished her milk, she explained all the events of the album. Anna's eyes were watery as she flipped each page after Becky gave the details. She would say every once in a while how beautiful the scenery was, then the dresses and just be in a trance as if she were right there standing by their side. When they had finished, Anna told Becky they would be going to Church in about thirty minutes and afterwards the whole family would arrive for their big picnic. Becky said she would wake Sam and be dressed in no time. Anna did not expect them to go, but was thankful that they were.

Coming back from town and driving down the lane towards the farm, Becky could not believe the amount of cars and trucks headed in the same direction.

So she asked, "Are all these cars family?"

Sam laughed and answered, "Yes, Dear!" Adding, each car has at least four people inside."

"Its going to be an exciting day!" replied Becky with an enthusiastic smile.

And it was! The food they had all prepared covered four makeshift seemingly endless tables. There were children running in every direction, with couples together laughing and the sound of the music was unlike any she had ever heard. Anna had Sam introduce her from the stage his father had put together. Otherwise, she would have never been able to meet everyone. They ate, danced and played their instruments throughout the entire day. Then, as quickly as they came, by six they had all gone home. The mess was gone, the stage put away and no evidence of a party ever being there. Becky ate often and light just as the doctor had instructed, which had her feeling much less fuzzy. Her lightheadedness was gone and she had had a fantastic day. Winding down from this event would take some time for her. Everyone else was ready to hit the sack by seven, so Sam sat with Becky on the porch and they just rocked until she felt she could get to sleep.

The days there flew by so fast and before they realized it, it was time to move on. Anna handed Becky a package before they left. She opened it to find the most beautiful wedding ring quilt she had ever seen. Her mother had one and Dusty's mother did also, but neither of them could even compare to the detailed handwork of this one. Her eyes filled with an overpowering flood of water, as all she could say was how beautiful it was and how thankful and blessed she was to receive such a gift. Becky hugged her tight and promised to always, take gentle care with it. For Anna it was just a hand made item that she made for all her kids when they married. To Becky, it was irreplaceable and far too precious even to use. Sam was pushing now to hit the road, Becky hugged Anna one more time, then Sam's father and they loaded themselves in the van.

He drove allot slower than before, making sure to stop often to stretch their legs and grab a bit to eat. Becky felt better than she had in weeks. Just knowing she was pregnant with a baby already loved by so many, was enough to help her feel good. Sam hadn't said too much, but she knew he had so much on his mind with finding a place and settling in before he had to report for duty.

Pulling into town, they checked into the nearest motel Sam could find closest to the base. It was very late and his plans for the next day were to find a doctor and make Becky the soonest appointment possible. He was excited and wanted very much to show her just how much, but until he knew for a fact that she was fine and the baby was fine, he wasn't about to show any emotion. If there might be something wrong, he would not want to add any more worries on her. He recalled one of his brothers wives loosing a baby they were both ecstatic over and it almost cost them their marriage. The pain they endured was more than he had ever witnessed and would not want that for anyone.

After a good nights rest and a nice breakfast, Sam drove to the base hospital to inquire about how to see the doctors. The hospital referred them to a clinic on base, where no appointments were required. It was sign in and take a seat. Sam, bound and determined for their baby's examination that day, they waited. After a two hour wait, they took her to a room. She saw the doctor, he did his exam finding her about ten weeks pregnant, then sent her off to the lab for blood work. The nurse told her everything with both her and the baby checked out fine and handed her a form to get prenatal vitamins down the hall. She also gave Becky specific orders of, no heavy lifting, and then come back in for another visit with the doctor in four weeks. Even though Becky was doing fine and she was starting to get her energy back, Sam felt an uneasiness he could not shake off. He said nothing to her and planned to ride it out, but he would keep a close eye on her for any indication of what it might be haunting him. That night was a sleepless one for him. He laid holding Becky as she slept and his eyes were wide open with questions flooding his mind of the, what ifs he could possibly handle. So much so, he was shortly out of bed and on his knees in prayer.

With three days of looking at apartments and house rentals, they made their decision on a house. The town was just a few miles from the base and seemed quiet and peaceful. A small cottage type home with two bedrooms and all the appliances furnished. It was within their budget and they could move in right away. Next was the utilities and that was simple to take care of in a small town. Becky had noticed a used furniture store near the motel where they were staying. They found a nearly new bed, a decent sofa and a kitchen table with three odd chairs. The owner said he could deliver everything when he could find someone to help him load the truck. Sam offered his help and the owner closed the store and they loaded up. Becky told Sam she would do some grocery shopping while he unloaded the furniture. He told her not to get too much, going into detail about her instructions on no lifting.

She laughed and said, "O.K., daddy!"

He pointed his finger at her and she made him a funny face, then said, "I know what the nurse said about lifting and I won't do anything to hurt this baby. I am fully capable to decide dos and don't. And, I will try not to get too bossy or short tempered with you. So please! Just have patience with my raging hormones."

He kissed her and apologized for telling her what to do, then asked her to pick him up some razor blades and shaving crème.

By the time they had unpacked and put everything away, they still had four days to sit back and enjoy their new surroundings. With the telephone installed, it was time to call her parents.

Elizabeth answered when Becky called, and was so happy just to hear her voice.

Becky asked, "How are you doing, mom?"

"I'm doing just fine honey," replied Elizabeth, then, I want to say I am sorry for making it so hard on you when you left. Will you forgive me?"

"There's nothing to forgive," answered Becky softly and then, we both had the same feelings, it's always hard to say goodbye and that's just the way life is."

"So tell me all about your trip," asked Elizabeth.

Jumping right in, she told her all about her new family, how friendly everyone was to her, how they work together and play music at their family picnics.

Then, "The food!" said Becky; there were tables of all sorts of homemade everything. The scenery was so beautiful and peaceful. And before we left, Anna gave us a quilt she had made by hand. Mom, it is unlike anything I have ever seen! The detail of her stitching and the pattern, like yours is the wedding ring. She is a wonderful person and her family is just like her." Then she went on to tell her about the house they had found to rent in a small town just a few miles from the base.

Elizabeth asked, "Do you have everything you need to set up your housekeeping and furniture?"

She answered, "We have more than enough to get started. All the gifts you, dad and Sarah gave us filled the cabinets. We found a used furniture store not too far away, where we bought a sofa, bed, and a kitchen table with three chairs. Everything is unpacked and we're all set up."

"How are you feeling?" asked Alice.

"Much better than before, in fact, a lot better than before!" answered Becky. She knew it was now time to give her the news about the baby. She asked if her dad was home and Elizabeth told her he was outside tending to his flowers. Then Becky asked her to call him to the phone because she had something very important to tell them both. When he came in and took the phone, Becky said, "Dad", before you ask me any questions I want you and mom to share the receiver so you can both hear me at one time."

He said, "We're listening."

"Well!" she started, then, I don't have the flu and it wasn't that I was homesick. "You're going to be grandparents!" Silence came over the wires as Becky repeatedly called out to them, "Mom!", "Dad!"

Sam sat watching Becky's expressions as she filled them in on all that the doctor and nurse had told her. Both their attentions grew when Becky asked them their thoughts on the subject.

Elizabeth feeling so surprised said, "It's hard to describe! On one hand, my baby is going to have a baby.

On the other hand, I am going to be a grandma! This is going to take some time to soak in. But, I'm very happy and becoming a grandmother is another dream come true."

William was so dumbfounded; he didn't know what to say.

So, Elizabeth answered for him and said, "Grandpa is so happy, he's crying."

"Me too, dad." relayed Becky. After giving them her new address and phone number, she asked her mom to make sure Sarah gets this information before she leaves for England.

Elizabeth paused, and then told Becky that Sarah was already gone and would write just as soon as she could.

"Wow!" that was fast!" stated Becky.

Before she ended the conversation, William took the phone again and gave her instructions to get plenty of rest and eat enough for two.

Becky's next call was to Dusty. She dialed Alice's number to get a current one for Dusty and Dusty answered their phone.

Becky asked, "Are you still living at home?"

She laughed and asked Becky, "How are you? Where are you?"

"Which do you want first, how or where?" responded Becky.

"Where!" Dusty replied.

"Texas, she quickly answered, and then, just a few miles from Fort Hood."

Then Dusty asked, "How are you?"

Jokingly her response came, "Lets see! In a nut shell I can say, happy, healthy, married and pregnant!"

"Oh my goodness!" replied Dusty.

Teasingly Becky said, "Is that all you can say, Oh my goodness?"

Laughing and crying at the same time Dusty answered, "Yah!"

"So, tell me what's been happening with you and Richard." Becky asked.

"Well", we went on the most fantastic cruise to Alaska. Now we are packing to move to Germany," Dusty replied.

Becky knew she was excited, but still asked, "Its not what we had planned on, is it?"

With a long deep heartfelt sigh, Dusty answered, "No, asking Becky in the same breath, "Is Sam being sent anywhere?"

Becky told her he didn't have to report to the base until the twenty-fourth and he didn't get any other information on anything.

Then she asked her, "Why did Richard get called in early?"

Dusty replied, "After we came back from our trip, he went to the base and ran into his platoon sergeant. He asked him if he would like to choose between Germany and Cambodia. The platoon sergeant told him, if he chooses he may have to leave sooner and if they chose, he might have to leave me here. So, Richard chose Germany. It is somewhat confusing to me, but I think that's how Richard explained it to me. I'm so nervous about going to another country and not knowing anyone, it's a wonder I'm sane at all."

Becky knew how she felt, leaving her home and going to a place not knowing anyone, so she tried to lift her spirit by telling her she was going on a new journey, saying; "when I had to take that first one, it turned out to be a blessing in disguise. Then, all things work out to be better than we think in the end. Continuing her positive reinforcement, she added, "No matter what! You keep your chin up! We will be back together in no time. Besides, you do have Richard on your journey and I'm sure there will be tons of sights to see. Make it fun and interesting; send me post cards and pictures."

Dusty smiled with a new optimistic outlook as she asked for her address and phone number, then said she would send hers just as soon as they had one. She promised Becky she would stay in touch.

Becky immediately told Sam what Dusty had said about Richards orders. She thought, maybe he would be lucky enough to get the same kind of orders.

Sam simply said, "Different base, Becky. There is no way I will be able to find out anything until I report in. I have a feeling I am here for more intense training. Before we finished boot camp, I received a transfer into expert rifleman. Richard was so much better at mechanics and I did better at target practice, which separated us into different squads. Not to change the subject, sweetheart, but we still have a few things to do at the bank. Because of hearing how Richard is being sent overseas, we need to set up our bank incase I get shipped out."

At this point Becky was feeling uneasy and a little frightened.

He took her in his arms and said, "We knew this could happen and it may not happen, but I think we need to be prepared. I put in for medical school and eventually that will change a lot of my traveling. Let's take life one day at a time and keep our thoughts on trusting our Lord. He will get us through anything that comes our way."

Sam took Becky to the bank that next morning. They opened an account and between the new account associate and himself, they taught Becky how to use and balance the checkbook. Remembering the envelop containing her graduation money still inside, she pulled it out from the bottom of her purse. She handed him the cash she had left and her check for five thousand dollars. Together they decided to put the cash in the checking and the check in a savings account to use towards a home of their own someday.

The day came for Sam to report to duty and Becky made plans to explore the shops on the square in their little town. Just a few houses from the square, walking would be her means to see everything. Standing on the sidewalk in front of their house, she looked down one way and then the other. To her left, three houses down was a huge Church with another building attached. Across the street from the Church was a park. Then looking to her right, she saw all the shops, the bank and the market around the square. In the center of the square was a fair size building, which was city hall. Setting her walk, she decided to begin around the square and maybe end up in the park. Everyone she passed by, gave friendly greetings with warm smiles. There was one road in to town; it circled around the square then right back out. She walked down passed the bank, then the market and stopped in the flower shop to see all the pretty arrangements. They had a gift section and a wall full of greeting cards. The clerk inquired if she was just visiting or a new resident in town and Becky introduced herself telling her she and her husband had rented a house down the road. She gave Becky a handful of carnations and welcomed her to stop by anytime to visit. Becky smelled the flowers then thanked her as she continued her walk. Missing her morning coffee as she came upon a small café, she thought a milkshake really sounded good. Sitting alone in a booth, a woman approached her and introduced herself as Merriam Holdman.

She joyfully volunteered, "I believe we are neighbors. I live two houses down from you, right next to the Church."

Becky asked if she would like to join her and she sat down. After Becky introduced herself, she told her they had just moved from Boston. Visiting for just a short time, Merriam apologized saying she could not stay, but asked Becky to visit her anytime and she would tell her everything she knew about their town. Becky thanked her for the invitation and said she would be by soon.

Back on the street, she passed by business offices, the barbershop, a beauty salon and the variety store. Passing her own house, she continued towards the park. In the center of all the beautiful shade trees with flowers planted around each one, was a large gazebo. She stopped and rested in the shade, taking in the cool breeze and listening to the Church bells ringing from across the street. They gave her such a soothing sense of peace, she decided to go in and say a prayer. Before she crossed the street, she noticed the sign in front of the building attached to the Church. It was an orphanage run by the Catholic Church. As she walked into the Church, she sat on the closest pew from the doors and knelt to pray. She looked above the altar at the tall stain glass windows that glowed with color rays of the still quiet, and it took Becky's breath. One of the Nuns joined her, sitting beside her quietly and projecting a warm smile of approval. After Becky sat back on the pew, they began to talk. With her hands folded on her lap and sweet smile on her face, she told Becky her name is, Sister Ruth.

"But everyone calls me, Sister Ruthie." She said in a humorous tone.

Becky in returned said, "My name is Becky Malloy. My husband and I just moved here from Boston and he is stationed at Fort Hood."

"It's nice to meet you." She stated, and then asked, "Will you be coming to Sunday service?"

Becky told the Sister she was not Catholic, but wanted to attend. Saying she didn't think the Lord would mind if her intention is to be in his house to worship him.

The Sister shook her hand and told her to come by any time, she giggled and said, "I'm always here."

Becky laughed quietly as the sister slipped away, through a door on the side of the Church. Then Becky headed back for the house to rest.

When Sam came home, he found Becky fast asleep. He quietly showered and changed into his jeans and waited for her out on the porch. She woke feeling rested and refreshed from all the pleasantness of her day. Noticing Sam was home; she fixed him a tall glass of ice tea and sat with him on a swing hung by chains from the roof of the porch. They talked about how each of their days had gone and then Sam followed Becky in to help her cook dinner. After she cleaned up the dishes, she asked him if he had any new orders. He told her that he and fifteen other men in this unit would join with other units for a specialized training course that would last about eight weeks. He wasn't sure why, but he said he would find out soon enough.

Attending Church on Sunday morning they met most of the people who lived in town. Becky received all kinds of invitations to luncheons and tea parties. Delightfully, Merriam always escorted Becky to each event. In between times, she spent her days helping the Nuns take care of the children.

There was a special area just for the infants and Becky grew quite attached to them.

"These tiny babies left abandoned on our doorstep, Sister Ruthie told her, "The horrible part of all this is, no one ever adopts them. And in the near future, we will no longer be able to keep them. They will be sent away to other places, maybe not so loving!"

"What a terrible way to grow up, said Becky, then, will they take the smallest children as well?"

"We're not sure of that either, unfortunately." She replied.

Then Becky said, "I will pray for them."

Sister Ruthie smiled and said, "As we all do."

Becky met Sam on the base for her second checkup with the obstetrician, referred to them by the clinic family practitioner. His name was Dr.Phillips and he told them the baby was growing at a normal rate and that she should be seventeen weeks along, giving her a due date of March seventeenth. He told her everything she was doing was fine and to stay active. The nurse walked them out and said to come back in another four weeks.

Sam was almost finished with the training course and still had not received any new orders. The other men in the units thought maybe they were training for a just in case squad, to be placed on stand by and not even receive orders to be shipped out. But Sam did not feel that was the case. Something was telling him to get prepared. Although he tried to hide his concern from Becky, she knew there was something weighing heavy on his mind.

She kept her parents up to date on her pregnancy and Sam called his mom almost every week. His entire family was extremely excited and wrote to Becky all the time. Yet there was still no word from Sarah. The information she had left with them was either incorrect or she had moved. Merriam's son was the school principle and with his help, they sent a letter of inquiry. After weeks of waiting, the return letter from the Deans secretary said, there was no instructor on campus by that name. Elizabeth tried on her end by contacting Miss. Woodward, but still nothing more, except that Sarah had sold her home. Becky became very upset with that news. Sam reminded her that she needed to concentrate on the baby, getting all worked up over something that might not be a bad situation at all, would only weaken her. She knew he was right and said she would be patient. Receiving a letter from Dusty, with pictures of the apartment they were living in, was just what Becky needed to ease her mind that not everyone was lost. She wrote they were doing well and she spends a lot of her time shopping with the other wives in her building. Along with her address and phone number, she asked Becky to write soon.

On November tenth, Sam came home from the base with a very worried look on his face. He sat Becky down at the kitchen table, telling her he had received his orders. Her face grew pale, as she knew they were not what she wanted to hear. Her heart sunk as he told her he was going to Cambodia.

Then he said, "It's a special mission that we can't discuss with anyone. My orders are to get our personal affairs taken care of within the next two weeks."

"Sam!" Becky cried, then, "You're scarring me!" "What if...?"

Sam quickly put his fingers to her lips saying, "Everything will be fine, I will come home. No matter what happens I'll be back." Then she melted into his arms.

Later that evening, they discussed her returning to Boston. But she felt an overpowering urge to stay for the babies at the orphanage. Sam insisted it would be in hers and the baby's best interest to be with family while he was gone. Reinforcing his concern, he told her it would ease his mind to enable him to concentrate on his duties. She gave into his insistence knowing her family had to be first priority and Sam didn't need the extra burden on his mind.

He worked on the packing and arranged a moving company to load everything, including the van, which would be stored as well. That way Becky could fly to Boston and have the care and support without all the hassle. In between those two weeks, he had to be on base for briefing. When he went to the base, Becky spent most of her time helping Sister Ruthie and the other Nuns. Every chance she could she would go to the Church and pray for guidance, the safety of her husband and all the other men in his squad. Mother Marie prayed along side Becky each time she came. They all knew how frightened she was and felt her sorrow. But with faith and all theirs prayers, they knew if its God will, he would come back to her.

The day before he left, Becky went to see Dr. Phillips. Both mother and baby were doing fine and the baby was right on schedule. Sam asked him if it would be safe for her to fly. He told them as long as it was within the next two weeks, after that he would have to say no. Becky signed releases forms to take her medical records and Dr Phillips told them both to take care. Sam scheduled her flight, but the earliest flight available was on the first of December. He had no choice but to take it, leaving Becky there alone for another week. She assured him that Merriam and all the Nuns would take good care of her.

The moving company was to arrive the same day Sam left. Becky had a small travel bag to carry and saved room to keep some pictures close. Merriam came over to see how things were going and asked if she could help in any way. Sam told her there was a big favor he needed to ask.

"Anything!" she said.

He tried to explain Becky's flight schedule and when he would be leaving, then could not find the right words to ask.

Becky saw that he was having a hard time getting out what he wanted to ask, so she jumped in for him asking, "What Sam is trying to ask is, he would like to know if you would look after me and put me on the plane?"

"Is that all?" Merriam asked. Then she told him he could rest assured, she would be thrilled to have Becky as her guest and the airport was no problem either.

Then adding, "You go do what the army needs and I'll take care of Becky's needs. It has been so long since I have had a guest come stay with me. My big old house longs for sounds of people having good times. And she will more than brighten up that dingy old place."

Sam thanked her for being such a loving friend and Becky looked forward to her company.

"Now I had better go and prepare something special. You kids come over when things are finished here tomorrow." Merriam finished, as she continued out the door mumbling to herself.

To get Becky away from the house and starring at the packed boxes, he took her for a walk. She asked if they could pray together and they went inside the Church. Father Mathew met them just inside the large double doors. He took them to the front of the Church, where he gave them a personal blessing. They thanked him and he excused himself to check in on the children. He really wanted them to spend some time alone with their own prayers together.

As they were walking back to the house, Sam asked her if they could eat out and then have a quiet night. Becky said that sounded nice and suggested the café down the street. After dinner, they walked the short distance to their little cottage and sat down on the old swing.

Rocking slowly she said, "We're going to miss the festival everyone has been telling me about."

"There will be lots of festivals for you, me and?" He started to say, then stopped for a moment and asked, "What are we going to name our baby?"

"If she's a girl, what would you like her name to be?" asked Becky.

"I would name her after you." He answered.

"And a boy?" she continued.

"Maybe, Joseph or James." answering out of the blue, then he said, I'm going to let you be in charge of the names and that way I will be surprised when I see him or her for the very first time.

He had only started the conversation to get her thinking of something cheerful. He, himself had far too many concerns to even carry on basic conversation. It was very late when they went in to go to bed. He held her all night, rubbing her tummy and taking in the aroma of her sweet perfume in remembrance to last until his return. Becky knew this mission was going to be far more dangerous than he let on. Yet still she stayed strong, knowing their love would see them through, giving them the faith to endure.

Their sleepless night became dawn like a flash. Sam had asked one of his friends to pick him up at the house on his way to the base. He didn't want Becky to go through a long drawn out goodbye. She made him a pot of coffee while he dressed and finished packing his duffle bag. He made her promise, always to believe he would come home, as he waited for his ride. She told him she would keep that promise, forcing back the ocean of tears waiting behind her eyes. As the car pulled in the drive, he embraced her and told her he would keep her heart to his with their love rushing through his veins.

Walking out the door, he looked back at her and said, "I love you Becky and if I'm not back before little Frankie comes, let him know he has a father that loves him."

She forced a smile, but the tears had taken their toll and she went back in the house as he rode away.

The movers arrived at the exact time Sam had scheduled them. Becky had finished what was out in the kitchen and the bedding. With what little possessions they had, it was not long before they finished. She gave them the keys to the van and they were pulling out for Boston to put their things in storage. Sam had told her he was storing their things, but until the movers told her the storage facilities address was in Boston, it left her feeling cold, stunned and hollow. Her concerns grew even dimmer than before.

Merriam came over as soon as she saw the movers leave to help Becky clean. When they were finished, they took her bags over to the house. Becky told Merriam she needed to stay busy and it would do her some good to play with the babies for just a little while. She told Becky to go on and that she would hold dinner, and then reminded her not to over do, as she walked towards the Church. Her first stop was her pew and Mother Marie was there when she walked in. They silently prayed together over an hour, then sat back and watched the stain glass windows loose their glow as the sun disappeared into the evening.

She returned to Merriam's about eight p.m.... Although the dinner Merriam had prepared was delicious, Becky had to force down her food with her lacking appetite. Once they finished, Merriam showed her to her room and told her to get some rest. She cleaned up the dishes, looked in on Becky and found her sleeping peacefully. Over breakfast, Becky told Merriam how she was not looking forward to leaving, and wanted desperately to relinquish the promise she gave to Sam that she would be with her family.

Then she said, "But these babies, you, and the Nuns are my family too now. And what will become of them?" she asked.

Merriam softly told her, "It's all in Gods hands and you know He has a plan coming to be as we speak. We do not know what it will be yet, only that it will be in the best interest of each one. For know we must keep our faith and fill our hearts with hope."

Merriam and Mother Marie worked very hard to keep Becky's spirits strong. During those last five days before she left, they had her helping with their Christmas preparations and shopping for the older children. Becky found wrapping the gifts with Sister Ruthie extremely hilarious! She would always somehow get herself tangled in the ribbon and the tape in the dispenser would fall back, taking her forever to pick it back to get a good hold again. The funny part about the whole thing was she wasn't fooling around; she always had problems when it came to wrapping and Mother Marie always had her involved that she might get better at it. Her patience are incredible, Merriam would tell Becky through her laughter. And so, together they wrapped and decorated each gift with lots of ribbons and bows.

Saying goodbye to everyone and looking over the nursery was almost too much for Becky to bear. Her thoughts were; she would never see them again or if they would be loved and treated kindly. She had to stop and not let herself go on dwelling with such sorrow, her baby too, at stake, would need her devotion as well. Pulling herself together as she left the nursery, she touched each Nuns hand as she left the building. Mother Marie and Sister Ruthie followed her outside and stood looking on as Merriam drove off.

On the short drive to the airport, Merriam told Becky she was welcome anytime.

Becky thanked her and said, "I may hold you to that. I really don't think I am going to be able to stay away very long. There is something pulling me back and I haven't even left yet."

"Always remember, my home is your home, always." Merriam ended as she leaned over to Becky giving her a kiss goodbye.

And the last thing Becky said was, "I'll see you soon!"

Chapter Five

Both William and Elizabeth were waiting when Becky walked from the plane into the airport terminal. Elizabeth took one glance at her daughters face and knew how emotionally drain she was. Only having one carry on bag they quickly headed for home.

After a few days of rest and some familiar home cooking, she began to come back to life. She received a letter from Sam after being home just over a week.

He wrote,

My Dearest Becky,

So far, we have not had too much to do. At this moment, we are still aboard a naval ship in waiting. I hope all went well with the movers. You will not be able to write to me for a while, until we get to where we are going. I will keep writing as often as I can.

Remember when I said to you, "Little Frankie?" You can name our baby, it does not have to be that name. I just said that in fun. It is a part of my name, so I guess that is why I said it.

I miss our place. We were just starting to feel like we were home. Someday we will have even a better place, with trees and flowers to pick for a vase every day. We will have a dog and many kids to play in the yard too. When you can write, tell me how you would picture our place in your mind.

While I have been on ship, I have had the opportunity to work with the physician. It has made me even more determined to pursue my career. I have observed surgeries, set fractured bones and not once did I get queasy. As soon as I get back, I will push to start college.

I miss you so much. Maybe this will be a short mission. Some of the men seem to think this trip has become a total loss and they will bring us back. Every time I listen to them talk, my hopes get higher to be back with you.

Well Honey, I have got to go for now. Remember always, I carry you well into my heart and you need to take good care of yourself for me. I am not there so you must take charge. Be strong, Becky! We will be together soon.

All My Love, Sam

Any news from him helped her regain her strength to hold tight. When he mentioned there mission could be canceled she really started raising her hopes. She even thought he could be home before the baby arrives. William told her not to count on it, that it would be a great let down if she did. Taking his advice, she put those thoughts in Gods hands.

During breakfast one morning, Elizabeth asked Becky if she would like to pick out the Christmas tree.

"That sounds like fun!" Becky answered.

Then Elizabeth went on to say, "I'll make the cookies we all like so much and we can decorate them later."

William brought out one of his old jackets for Becky to wear; her coats would not reach to fasten over her stomach now.

There was no snow in the near forecast, but the temperatures were extremely cold. William and Becky searched from one end of the tree lot to the other. They had made a plan to find the most spectacular tree that would fit in the house. By the time they got home, Elizabeth had cleared a place in the living room where they would be able to see the tree from the dinning room and kitchen. William trimmed the bottom before placing it in the stand and had to cut more than eight inches in order for it to fit in the house. As tradition in their family, he put on the lights and Elizabeth and Becky placed the ornaments. After placing the star at the top, they took time for prayer. Their prayers included all those in need, the sick, the elderly, the widows and all the orphans. Adding some especially for those who might be alone or lost.

By Christmas Eve, a foot of snow had fallen. William cleared the driveway early so they could go to Church. The service was magnificent! The choir sang beautifully and the atmosphere was enlightening with everyone having only a candle to light the hall. In the morning, they opened their gifts and saved Sam's for when he came home. Elizabeth had prepared the turkey feast with all the extra trimmings she could possibly think of.

When they finished, Becky said, "We ate this great meal, like little piglets!"

Agreeing in laughter they all helped with the dishes to work off the discomfort of the three little pigs.

About seven p.m., the phone rang and it was Sam. He was calling ship to shore and only had just a few minutes for his turn. As Becky took the phone, she felt she had received a special gift from God. He had to talk fast, so she listened quietly. He said his unit would be on board the ship at least another two weeks and he had been training as a medic while they waited. He wished them all a Merry Christmas, told Becky he loved her and the baby and missed them both so much.

Then he had to go, saying, "I'll see you soon, my love."

She had manage to tell him she loved and missed him in between words and sentences, but what mattered most was just to hear his sweet voice.

January tenth, Becky finally had an appointment with a doctor referred by the base staff. Everything was good with the baby, but Becky needed to gain some weight. The baby's weight was right on schedule with the due date, but she was far too thin to be seven months pregnant. Elizabeth assured the doctor she would have her eating more.

During the next month, they prepared and did shopping for the baby. Becky was getting her walking exercises in the mall and Elizabeth was cooking up a storm. When it was time for her to see the doctor again, she had gained seven pounds and he was pleased. Everything was ready and they were starting to get excited. Becky spent a lot of time in the rocking chair her father had bought for the baby's room. Many times her mind would take her back to their cottage porch and she would dream of Sam sitting by her side and placing his hand on her stomach to feel the baby kick. By keeping her dreams of warm and loving thoughts, she kept her tears from falling.

Another letter came from Sam. This time he told her they were getting off the ship in just a few days. He could not say where they were or where they were going. The letter was very short and he apologized for not having enough time for more. With the training, he explained and briefings, they were only getting two to three hours of sleep. He asked her not to worry and take care, that he loved her and as always, would see her soon.

This letter worried her. Even though he tried not to let his concern show, she knew that whatever his mission was, was about to begin. She gave the letter to her dad when she finished and went to her room. Elizabeth followed her and as she began to cry, Elizabeth did her best to console her. But Becky was scared, now more than ever before.

After a while, she composed herself, taking in deep cleansing breaths to calm her nerves and then Elizabeth suggested a nice cup of herbal tea. Becky thought for a moment and with somewhat of a smile, told her mother she would meet her in the kitchen in just a few minutes. Walking down the hall towards the kitchen, her water broke. She stopped, placed her hands on each side of her tummy, looked down and called out for help. Both William and Elizabeth ran from the kitchen to her side.

All she could say was, "It's not time!" "Something is wrong!" "It's not time!"

Helping her into dry clothes Elizabeth tried to tell her that many babies come early and reminding her that the doctor had said the baby was doing just fine. William grabbed the pre-packed case they had ready in the coat closet and rushed out to start the car. Before they reached the hospital, her pains had begun, coming every two minutes. Within one hour of reaching the hospital, she had delivered a five pound, eight ounce baby boy. What a beautiful sight it was, when William and Elizabeth walked into her room to see her holding her precious bundle of joy.

As they reached the bedside, she looked up and said, "I'd like you to meet, Franklin William Malloy!" She passed him in his snug little bundle to Elizabeth and said, "This is your grandma and grandpa, Frankie!"

Elizabeth kissed him on the forehead and unwrapped him just enough to put her finger in his tiny little hand. William looked on closely, wanted to hold him when he grew a bit bigger.

After Becky came home from the hospital, she called Dr. Phillips at Fort Hood Texas. Asking him if there was any way he could get the news of the birth of her son to her husband. He told her he would do everything he could on his end to try to reach him, but he had to apologize for the Army's sake if it weren't possible. Then she called Merriam with her news and asked about the babies at the orphanage. Merriam was delighted to hear that her baby boy was born in good health. She reassured Becky by saying the babies were doing well and all was fine at the orphanage. Merriam asked about Sam, and Becky told her everything she knew, which wasn't much. Then she asked Merriam to tell everyone hello for her and to give each one of her babies a kiss. She promised Becky she would, and then told her she missed her very much. Becky said the same and prayed to see her again when Sam came home.

Months went by without any news. Becky kept busy with Frankie, but longed to get a letter or even a quick phone call to ease her mind.

William would try to keep her spirits up by telling her that, "No news is good news."

It would help for a while until she would start to feel the panic creeping back once again.

Elizabeth and William made a suggestion to her about taking Frankie to Missouri and visiting Sam's family. Explaining to her that the pictures were nice, but they would thoroughly enjoy being able to hold their grandson. She liked the idea and called Anna. William arranged their flight and within a few days, Becky and Frankie were on their way to the farm.

While she was there, she helped can tomatoes, green beans and corn. She was not much help when it came to dressing chickens, but she had no problems feeding or gathering the eggs. Anna would rock Frankie to sleep while she talked about how good Sam was as a baby.

She'd say, "He never cried much and she checked in on him a lot to see if he was breathing. He was the happiest baby out of the nine and throughout his childhood the most content." Then went on to inform Becky that Frankie was the spitting image of his father.

After three weeks on the farm, Becky decided to fly to Texas. She had that pulling feeling again and she knew Merriam would be happy to see them.

"Delighted!" was the word Merriam used when Becky called. Anna asked her to come back as soon as she could and Becky told her that she would and Lord willing Sam would be with them.

Anna told her she would pray for them and Becky said, "As I do several times through out each and every one of my days."

She could not wait for that flight to end. Frankie seemed to enjoy traveling and all the passengers seated close to them would make him laugh by making funny faces to pass the time. Even though Frankie had become the center of attention and all was well, she felt a strange and uncontrollable nervousness engulfing her. As she entered the terminal, there to meet her was Merriam and Sister Ruthie. Minutes seemed like hours to Becky with this overwhelmingly uncomfortable state that she just could not shake off. She wanted to rush them from their ooze and ahs, which was not in her character ever. Keeping the forced smile and pleasant greetings coming through her lips she kept her patience intact. Finally, in the car on their way, she felt the tension releasing slightly. She asked all about the babies and Sister Ruthie went on and on about how they had grown and all of them doing extremely well, and then asking Becky if she remembered this or that, one then another. Becky joined right in returning things they were doing when she had left naming each one by name. They spent the rest of the afternoon in the nursery and they had dinner with the Nuns. Becky felt like she was finally home. There was such a sense of peace she found there and a fulfillment that was indescribable. Her feeling of nervousness had lightened by the end of the day, but in the back of her thoughts, lingered warning signals of something coming that would devastate her world and absolutely nothing she did could ease her mind.

Sister Ruthie had taken an extra crib over to Merriam's for Frankie; and Becky spent her days as before helping in the nursery. She knew she would need to go back to Boston soon to keep the promise she had made to Sam before he left. Her parent's home was comforting and they always had lots of fun, but here she felt so alive and the happiest, making it very difficult to leave once again. But she had a couple of weeks that she could put that time out of her thoughts and enjoy all the time she could have with the babies she had grown so much to be a large part of her life. Her routine was back as it was when she left, each morning stopping in the Church to pray along side Mother Marie and each evening before she went back to the house.

Early one morning, before Becky had left the house, William called. His voice came through with that stern strong tone he used when something was terribly wrong. She quickly braced herself and listened closely. He told her that two men in uniforms had come with a letter.

She immediately asked, "What are you telling me dad?"

There was no way to say it but straight out, so he did, "Sam is missing in action."

Becky sunk to her knees; she was thinking he was going to tell her he was dead. Merriam stood close to Becky with her hands gently on her shoulders. He went on to tell her they would be coming to her with all the information they had at this time. Becky was numb, William called and called to her, and then Merriam took the phone. She introduced herself then asked what had happened. William explained what he had told Becky. He asked her if they should come and she told them she would call back after Becky had absorbed what he had said. Giving him reassurance, she told him Becky would have someone with her at every moment. He gave his appreciation by thanking her and said he would wait for her call. Becky slowly coming to a stand, walked over to the crib where Frankie was sleeping and leaned down to gently picked him up. Taking him and holding his small little body close to her heart, she sat in the rocker quietly sobbing while he slept.

It took two days before the men in uniform knocked on Merriam's door. Becky was now a bit more prepared, listened as they told her what her father had said on the phone. Then adding that they had found three men and Sam had bandaged their wounds.

After they gave her that information, Sam's words flooded her mind, "I promise I will come home." Those words were all she could think of and she vowed to herself to be strong and hold on to that promise no matter how long it took.

Each week thereafter, she would call the United States Defense Department to see if they had any news. Never giving up, she would call just to receive the same answer as before; "We're sorry Mrs. Malloy, there is no word this week."

During a prayer session one morning on her way to the orphanage, she reflected on the promise she had made to Sam before he left. Her visit here was becoming her home. She knew she needed to return to her parents and the longer she stayed the harder it would be to leave. And before she got up to go help with the babies, she asked Mother Marie if she would have some time to help her sort out some problems going through her mind. Without saying a word, Mother Marie stood up and took Becky by the hand to her office where they could talk freely without interruption.

Becky told her of the promise she had made and explained how much being here helped. Mother Marie asked her different questions concerning her family and brought to her attention Frankie's need to know his family.

With her palms face up, and both equally matched, Mother Marie said, "Your decision is clear, you either keep your promise, or you don't. Adding, When I have a decision to make I weigh it out and bring it to the point of the answer being yes or no. It helps simplify all the possible rights against the wrongs in every situation. And as far as you staying, I would love to tell you to stay. You have made a great contribution here, but your husband is the head of the household and whether he is here or not, remains the same."

Becky knew she had to leave, but just did not know how and with Mother Maries input, her mind had cleared. She thanked her for her guidance and told her, her wisdom was truly from the Lord.

After dinner that evening, she called Elizabeth and told her she would be coming home on the next available flight. Both her parents were excited to hear her plans. William took his turn on the phone asking Becky if she wound like him to make her reservations.

Becky told him, "Thank you, dad, but I need to learn how to take care of these things on my own. Its high time I showed some responsibility for both myself and Frankie."

As proud as any father could be, he said, "You have grown up to be an outstanding person, Becky. I am so proud to be your father."

Then before they ended their conversation, he had lifted her spirits with some holiday plans that Frankie would thoroughly enjoy. Which included a train set that went all around the Christmas tree. Becky felt a little guilty now after hearing the excitement in his voice and scolded herself for being so selfish.

She managed with ease to schedule their flight, bound and determined to think of others more than she had in the past. A new Becky was blooming and the time for innocents and dependence was gone. Giving herself no time to indulge in the self-pity of her loneness when she had so many right there and showing their love, she scheduled out her days on a calendar and gave herself little time to dwell on anything.

With a smile on her face and not one tear from her eyes, she said goodbye once again and flew to Boston. When she arrived, the first of November, her calendar reminded her to call the Defense Department giving them the address and phone number where she could be reached. There was no updated information and their answer to her was the same as weeks before.

William was first to notice the cold change in her attitude. Just by watching little things, she would do in the ways she had never been so articulate. As far as the way she treated people, she seemed to stretch out of her way and give no thought to her own feelings. Concerned about how overboard she had become, he intervened by having long discussions during the evenings after Frankie had been laid down the night. It was not long before he came to realize she was so full of guilt over not keeping her promise to Sam that she was punishing herself to the point of a breakdown. At the rate she was moving, it would take its toll very soon. Knowing her as well as he did, he used their discussion time and brought up fictitious people to bring about his point. At times, he would ask her advice on how to help these people. Then after a while, it dawned on her, there were no others and without mentioning it, she began to soften and ease up on herself. Later, while they were in a prayer session together, thanked the Lord aloud for working so gracefully through her father to help her let go of her guilt.

They celebrated Thanksgiving by donating their time and enjoying a meal with the Salvation Army's homeless shelter. William and Frankie visited with people while Elizabeth and Becky helped cook and serve the feast. It was Becky's idea to help others at a time when they all needed the comfort. Staying as busy as she could was the best thing she could do to keep her mind occupied.

The day before Christmas Eve, Sarah showed up at their door. She had just flew in from England and wanted to surprise Elizabeth and William. William was extremely surprised and very happy she had come. Elizabeth and Becky had left him to baby sit while they finished the last of their shopping. Frankie was down for a nap when she arrived and William took advantage of that time to fill her in on not only Becky's baby, but also the sad news of Sam missing in action. She was devastated and apologized repeatedly for not staying in communications with them. He told her she was here now and that he hoped she could stay a while. When Frankie woke up the real fun began! He was soaked through his clothes, very fussy and hungry. After his continuous crying through his bath William gave him, Sarah had his lunch ready and waiting. As she fed him, her eyes filled with tears thinking about the anguish Becky must be going through. This little bundle of joy that resembled his father in so many ways had to be what kept her going. He brought back a smile on her face when he played with the food in his mouth and laughed at his grandpas funny jesters. By the time Elizabeth and Becky came home, Sarah had washed his bedding and together William and Sarah had every toy out with Frankie sitting in the middle of all of them. He was laughing and playing, crawling back and forth to William then Sarah. Becky and Elizabeth had to wade through all the toys to greet Sarah. And before long they all sat playing with Frankie.

After they had finished dinner and Frankie was down for the night, Sarah told them that she was back to stay. Things had not worked out between her and the man she had met. His ways were set and when she would try to compromise, he would become so angry that she feared him. She said she could not live that way and came home.

Becky said, "Love doesn't threaten or give someone the feeling of fear. If two people love each other you both have to give."

William agreed and added, "We are all happy to have you here. There is plenty of room here and we'd like you to stay."

Sarah thanked them and said, "I have no idea what I'd do without you. I feel so foolish for even thinking he was the right man for me. I guess I wanted love so much in my life, I couldn't see this coming."

Becky and Elizabeth hugged her at the same time and then Becky told her not to be so hard on herself, that it was better to find out what kind of person he was before she married him. There was much more that Sarah had not revealed and they knew that eventually she would open up and tell them everything that had happened.

Christmas Eve Becky made her call to the Defense Department and nothing had changed. Dusty and Richard were not home and Alice, when Becky called her said they had taken a trip for the holidays. Alice wished her a Merry Christmas and told her how sorry she was to hear about Sam. Dusty had explained everything to her and she said they were in her prayers. Becky asked Alice to have Dusty call when she got back home and gave her holiday greetings. Merriam was delighted when Becky called to wish her a Merry Christmas. She was just about to leave the house when the phone rang. Her son had decided he would have the holidays at his home and she expected him to pick her up at any time. They visited while she waited and discussed everyone at the orphanage. All was well and everyone missed her. Becky said she might come again in the spring.

Merriam told her, "I can't wait! It has been so lonely in this big old house and she often pictured Frankie crawling across the floor."

She asked Becky if she had heard any news on Sam and Becky told her everything was still the same. Her son arrived and she told Becky she would call her back as soon as she returned.

Their Christmas began with a nice breakfast followed by a morning Church service. Once again, they had volunteered to help feed the needy and Sarah was eager to help. Towards the evening, while they opened their gifts Becky remembered last Christmas when Sam had called from the ship. It was all she could do to hold back her tears, but with Frankie pulling and tugging at packages, her attention focused on him.

Williams's gift to Elizabeth came in a large box.

When he gave it to her to open he said, "This is something from the past. You put these things away many years ago and lost the interest. I thought you might like to start over and, go ahead open the box."

There were all sorts of painting supplies, a camera and he had added a map of different sights in the area for them to see. Back when she was in her late twenties, she used to take photographs of scenery and covered bridges, and then paint them on canvas. She was ecstatic! How he knew she wanted to try again was beyond her. He had managed to give her the gift of encouragement, which meant more than anything he could have possibly purchased. His gift to Becky was a sewing machine. Although she had never done any sewing, he thought she might like to tackle something new. She was very happy to receive it and planned to give it her best shot. Elizabeth and Becky handed Sarah an album they had put together to send her with pictures they had collected from the time she left. They had no idea where to mail it and that worked out for the best. Becky gave her father gifts of yard tools and a few books he had mentioned he would like.

Elizabeth bought him a new winter coat so he would get rid of the oversized dingy one he had bought the year before. Frankie made out like a bandit! He had toys to please any toddler and he didn't know what to play with first. In all it had been a good day. After Becky tucked Frankie in for the night, she gave everyone a kiss and a hug, and then retired to her room. She sat on the side of her bed well into the night waiting for some miracle that the phone would ring and she could hear his voice after all this time. When it did not come, she slipped into bed and sobbed quietly to sleep.

After the New Year, Sarah took her position back with the Boston academy and found another house. William and Elizabeth had started taking day trips for her photographs and Becky had become restless for the orphanage. Therefore, she decided it was time for her and Frankie to take a trip. She wanted to visit the farm and Sam's family, but with winter in full force decided to start their trip in Texas and then stop in Missouri for a few weeks in the spring.

When she called Merriam to ask if they could come, Merriam said, "I had been thinking it was about time for you. We knew it would not be long before you would have to return. It sounds bad, but all the Nuns including Mother Marie have been placing bets on the month you would be back. It looks like Mother Marie has won the prize."

"What is the prize?" asked Becky.

"There is no prize, dear; just having you here for a while is prize enough for all," Answered Merriam.

Becky said she would call her back after she made her reservations and thanked her again for being such a good friend.

Becky asked her father if he would help her with her schedule so that this time she would not overextend her stay at any given place. Together they came up with three weeks at each place and back home in just a month and a half. She then made her reservations and called the Defense Department with this schedule so they could reach her at any time. Within two weeks, Becky and Frankie were on their way to Texas.

Frankie's sweet disposition through the entire flight was a blessing for Becky. Her mind swelled with memories of the six babies she would soon be able to hold in her arms once again. She wondered how they had changed over the past few months and if they would remember how much she loved them. Frankie was saying a few words and calling her mamma now and the others even more so advanced in their vocabulary, she thought about Ruthie having her hands full and even more confusion with them all walking. The hours they were in the air passed with ease. It seemed like they had just took off when she heard the captain announce they would be landing and for all passengers to return to their seats. Her heartbeat increased with the anticipation of being where she knew she belonged.

Sister Ruthie was there to pick her up this time. Upon Becky's arrival, she told her Merriam had to take care of some business and was unable to leave town. Frankie remembered Sister Ruthie and reach for her with his arms extended so far, Becky could hardly hold onto him. She took him and twirled him around and he laughed with the biggest open smile his little mouth could project. All the way to the car, Sister Ruthie and Frankie chattered some kind of foreign language as if they knew what they were actually saying, which kept Becky in stitches to tears. By the time they reached Merriam's house, she had him calling her, "Ruffie".

She told Becky that all the babies call her that name and then said; evidently it's easy for them to say."

When she pulled into the driveway, Mother Marie was standing out in front of the Church waiting their arrival.

Becky told Sister Ruthie they could get the bags out later stating, "I just have to go see my babies!"

Leaving Frankie with Sister Ruth, Becky ran to Mother Marie, and then hugging her as if she had been gone for years. Becky started in with question after question regarding everyone and Mother Marie just stood with a smile shaking her head until Sister Ruth caught up with them.

She looked at Frankie and said, "My goodness!" What a big boy you are." His face in the full dimpled smile just like his fathers and his arms stretching for her, she said, "You just come over here to Mamma Marie!"

Becky was at a point of bursting and they went through the Church to the nursery keeping up with Becky's snappy pace. Merriam came in just after feeding the children and stayed to help get them ready for bed. Then she and Becky took Frankie home. After he was down for the night, they stayed up well into the night catching up on the past few months.

After a week Becky made her call to the Defense Department and as always, they had nothing new to tell her. It had been just over a year and she could not understand why they could not tell her something, but she remembered his words and went on with her day. Sarah called and said she had a new student that reminded her of Becky and she just had to call to hear her voice. Becky told her she would be back in five weeks according to her schedule and they would be able to spend a lot of time together then.

Becky started a journal back in Boston and wrote every little change and funny thing Frankie had done from the beginning of his life. She took an afternoon with Merriam to do some shopping and thought she might pick up six more journals for her little ones at the orphanage. It was a free day for her and Frankie had stayed with Sister Ruthie so she could enjoy the shops. As the day progressed, Becky had an unusual feeling of deep despair come over her. She told Merriam; unexpectedly she needed to go home. Finished with her shopping she told Becky they could leave right away. Driving home, she tried to explain the feeling that had come over so hard on her, but why or what it was baffled both of them. Her first thought was Frankie, had he fallen or become ill or, something to do with Sam, her mind wondered on endlessly. She ran to the Church when Merriam pulled into the drive, only to find Frankie peacefully sleeping along side one of the other babies. While Frankie finished out his nap, Mother Marie took Becky to her office to find out what was happening. Becky explained how this feeling could have knocked her over it was so strong and hit her suddenly out of nowhere. She told her that every time something is about to happen, a feeling hits her, but this one had been the hardest ever. She knew something was coming and this time it would be the worst. Mother Marie suggested they go into the Church and pray. Becky was right up out of her seat ready and waiting. They spent the next two hours on their knees and Becky pleaded for God to watch over everyone. When they had finished she checked in on Frankie and he was up and ready to go home.

Mother Marie softly spoke these words as Becky left, "It's all in Gods hands and He will be with you whatever this may be. If you need us our lights are on all night."

Later that evening, Becky called her parents home and got no answer. She tried Sarah's and she was not home either.

Merriam, trying her best to comfort said, "Maybe its nothing, dear, today was the first day you had to yourself in a long time and you might have felt guilty. Only time will tell and lets keep our spirits up that it just a simple quirk."

Becky was not feeling any different and bottled it inside, in order not to upset anyone further. They had had a long tiring day and both decided to go to bed early.

At ten p.m., the phone rang. Merriam pick it up and Becky flew to her side. It was Sarah and she needed to speak to Becky.

Her voice was very unsteady and she immediately said, "Becky", there's been an accident!"

Becky calmly asked, "Sarah just say it."

"It's your parents Becky. She said, and then, they have been in an accident. You need to come as soon as possible. I am here at the hospital and I will pick you up at the airport. I don't know the numbers here, so I'll call you back in just a little while so you can give me your flight information."

Becky started to ask one question after another.

Sarah stopped her saying, "Please don't ask me anything until you get here."

Becky's mind went blank to what she had just said and calmly told her she would call the airlines as soon as they hung up.

Sarah replied, "That would be best," and hung up the line.

Becky quickly called the airport and booked the first flight out that next morning. Waiting for Sarah to call back, Becky frantically told Merriam what Sarah had said while she threw clothes for her and Frankie into a suitcase.

"Becky?" Merriam asked gently, then, would you let me take care of Frankie?"

Not knowing how bad they had been hurt in the accident, she thought it would be the best thing for him.

"Are you sure, Merriam?" She asked.

Merriam replied, "He's no trouble at all and we will have a great time."

Becky hugged her and said, "I've told you this before, but, you are one of the most precious friends I've ever had."

"Were not just friends anymore, dear, we are family now," stated Merriam.

Sarah was there when Becky arrived, meeting her with an embrace much different than she had ever felt before. Outside the terminal, she started telling Becky the desponding details of the accident.

She said, "They had taken a day trip sight seeing, then, your mother wanted to take a picture of a covered bridge to paint during these winter months. They were coming up to the bridge and the police say your father did not see the other car coming. He did not wait and hit head on. The man in the other car will be all right. "But your mother!" Sarah stopped and paused to regain her strength, and then, your mom didn't make it through surgery."

Becky numb to any emotion asked, "And dad?"

Sarah softly taking Becky's hand into hers said, "He's not going to make it, Becky."

Sarah drove straight to the hospital and Becky followed her right into the intensive care unit. She rushed to his side, grasped his hand and called out to him to let him know she was there. The nurse came over and told her that he had been in and out of consciousness and calling her name.

She sat down by his side, rubbing his hand she said, "Daddy, hold on, we can get through this, I need you and Frankie needs you." Then she laid her head down to kiss his hand and cried.

Late that night he woke for a moment, long enough to call for Elizabeth, and then he was out again. The next two days Becky only left his side to freshen up. Sarah brought in food and Becky forced down only what she could.

On the third day, he woke to recognize Becky. He smiled then began to cry, blaming himself for the accident. She tried to comfort him, but there was no use. He knew Elizabeth was gone.

Then he told Becky, "I want you to go to the house. In my briefcase on the top shelf in the hall closet, is everything you will need." Using all the rest of the strength within him, he drew a short breath and whispered, "Becky", and he was gone.

She stood from her chair and laid across his chest. After a long while, she rose up and looking at his face, she cupped her hands to each side, and then kissed him. She asked if she could sit with him, a while longer and the nurse drew the curtain and left them alone.

Sarah gave her quit a while and went back in placing her hands on Becky's shoulders and said, "Its time to go."

Back at the house, she found the briefcase William had told her she would need. Sarah had already made the decision on Elizabeth's casket and started the arrangements with the funeral home. Becky placed the case down on the kitchen table, and then sat down. Sarah took her hand and told her it was late and they could put this on hold until morning. She suggested they try to sleep for a few hours, and then Becky got up, walked over to the patio door, and starred out.

As tears dripped off the sides of her face, she said, "What wonderful times we had together, and now, everything is gone."

Sarah now in tears went to Becky and stood by her side.

Once Becky was asleep, Sarah went back to the kitchen and read Williams' instructions, he had written up with his attorney months before. She made a list of things they would need to do and William's attorneys name and phone number. All Becky had to do was contact him and he was to take care of the majority of arrangements.

When Becky woke, Sarah fixed her coffee while she read the list. When she finished reading, she took Sarah, coffee in hand and went out on the patio.

Somehow, she said, "This crisp cold air adds a bit of peace to all of this."

Not one footprint lingered in the eight inches of snow that covered the back yard. The plants dormant in waiting to revive at the first spark of spring and she pictured them together, standing at the trellis, she and her father had so carefully put together. In her mind, the shrubs and flowers swayed in a slow gentle breeze. She pictured their faces happy and still, with no cares in the world. She smiled at Sarah without bringing her thoughts to her attention and she knew Sarah had a similar picture in her mind as well.

Becky's first phone call was to check in with Merriam to see how Frankie was doing without her there. She was able to give Merriam all the tragic details of the accidents and keep herself composed. Merriam told her Frankie was doing just fine and that was exactly what she needed to hear. Not knowing when she would be back, she told Merriam to call her at any time and she would be there as fast as she could.

Merriam said, "You take all the time you need. Frankie and I will be right here or with the other babies at all times."

Becky did not know how to thank her enough for all that she had done and stuttered, as she began to cry again, "I thank God for my family of friends, I would be lost." Then she stopped, as she could say no more.

Sarah took over the phone, and talked to Merriam for a few minutes longer and then told her they would call back after the funeral.

William's attorney immediately took over everything after Becky called his office. He told her he would personally go to the funeral home and handle all the requests William and Elizabeth had made.

"After the funeral is over, he said, then, a day or so, whenever you are ready, we will go over their will and the estate."

Becky thanked him and said she would call soon.

A few days late with her call to check on Sam, she just could not bring herself to make it. She couldn't handle their unsuspecting sarcasm they projected in their own subtle way and asked God to forgive her for feeling this way, but it was the truth. Sarah never mentioned calling and knew she could only handle what was before her at this moment in time. She had been unable to reach Alice or Dusty on the numerous times she tried and figured she would tell them later when things began to settle down.

After finalizing the funeral arrangements, the attorney called Becky and asked if she could come to the office. They set a time for that afternoon and Sarah drove her over. He explained all the arrangements he had made of the graveside service they had requested and the minister she knew from her wedding ceremony to conduct the service. It was to be the following morning at a cemetery not far from the house. He went over what he would need for the insurance company and asked if she would mind if he took care of that also. She had no problem with him handling the details and told him so as she thanked him for all he had done. After he finished he made them an appointment to meet back in his office two days following the funeral to go over the will.

On their way back to the house, Becky asked Sarah if they could stop at a Church, they had attended during the holidays. Inside, Becky took the pew in the back row and knelt down to pray. Sarah along side knelt and said her prayers and then sat back and waited for Becky. When she sat back after quit a while she became a little light headed. Sarah asked if she would like to go out to eat before returning to the house and Becky thought that would most likely be a wise decision.

The service was beautiful. William and Elizabeth had written prayers and left Becky letters, just in the event something might happen. Each one in their own words gave thanks to God for their lives. They took turns mentioning funny memories Becky had forgotten over the years and left her a special message that they would always be watching over her and her family until the day they would meet again. As the minister read on, she felt exuberantly touched by their words, and she knew in those moments, their intent gave her the most wonderful gift of hope. The messages they gave and the words they spoke she would carry with her all the days of her life.

When she spoke, she told them how very much she loved them and in her heart, she would know she would never be alone no matter what she had to face.

Her last words to them, "I'll see you soon."

The day after the funeral, the investigating officer came to give Becky his warm regards. He told her the man in the other car was doing well. He also informed her that neither driver was at fault. There were no signs posted on either side of the bridge. The highway department had taken them down to replace them. She thanked him for bringing that information to her and he gave her a copy of the report before he left.

When he was gone, Becky said, "I hope dad heard that it wasn't his fault."

Sarah replied, "I'm sure he did."

The meeting with the attorney did not take very long. They had left everything to her and she was quit shocked to hear how much money they had in the bank and the insurance policies. He asked if she wanted to keep the house. She told him she would be going back to Texas as soon as she finished with everything here. Then he said she could sign a power of attorney over to him and he would take care of the sale of her fathers business and the house. Then he would transfer the funds when everything was final. She quickly agreed to his offer and she signed the paperwork. Before leaving his office, she told him she would arrange an estate sale as soon as possible and than she would be ready to turn the keys over to the realtor.

Going through the house, they packed one room at a time. Becky kept all her mothers dishes and fine linens she had collected over the years, packing them separately to figure out later just how she would get them to Texas. Then she remembered all her household items are in storage right here in Boston.

Sarah came up with a great idea, "Why don't we have one sale of things in your storage you would exchange for your parents things? We could have them moved over here, go through and keep what you want, then sell the rest."

She thought for a minute and said, "There really isn't that much in there except, the van. How am I going to get all of this to Texas? Adding, I can't drive across country, Sam would have a coronary if he found out!"

Sarah reminded her that she would probably have more stuff to go back than they sent to storage here. Going on to ask, "How did you get it here?"

"Sam took care of all that, she answered, and then, I have no idea who the company was that moved it."

Sarah laughed and told Becky not to worry that she would find out and arrange everything that needed to be done. Becky feeling like an extremely confused idiot laughed right back.

Together they made a plan to move all Becky's things from storage there and repack everything going back to Texas for the movers to load before the sale. Within a week, Sarah had found the movers, had her possessions delivered, and between the two of them, they had repacked everything. Along with the help of the moving company, the sale would take place on the upcoming weekend. Becky was more than ready to be back with Frankie, but leaving Sarah behind was not going to be easy. At one time during their conversations, Becky asked her to move back with her. Sarah told her she would definitely give it some consideration but would have to finish out her contract with the academy.

With every item marked and all Becky's things on there way to Texas, they spent a few days in deep girl talk. Sarah told her that the reason why she could not reach her in England was; her teaching transcripts were still in her maiden name. The man that she had fallen in love with had given her fictitious addresses and phone numbers. She found out very quickly once she moved into her apartment that he wanted to control and use her. He had no intentions of a meaningful relationship. She broke off the relationship and finished out her contract with the University. Becky took her turn telling her about how she felt when her father called with the news about Sam being missing in action. Then, over the past year, she went on to say how all her friends had helped her cope. Becky asked if she really would consider moving to Texas.

Whispering, Sarah told her she had and then said, "I'm moving! I cannot stay here without you! Now there is no one here and you were the one that brought me out of that lonely state. I definitely do not want to go back to that life. But I will have to finish this school year and put the house up for sale."

Becky was so excited and said, "You just plan on living with me."

Then she jumped up and ran to the phone. She called Merriam and asked her if she still was interested in selling her house. Merriam said it had been off the market for some time, but if she were interested, she would sell it to her as long as she could stay for a while.

Becky said, "Stay forever!" I just need a place where everyone will be comfortable and by the way, Sarah will be moving this summer."

Merriam heard the lifted spirit within Becky voice and was very thankful.

Becky asked about Frankie, she put him on the phone, and he said, "Mamma come home?"

She had worked with him just in case she called when he was not sleeping.

She told Frankie, "Mamma will see you soon, and she loves you very much." Merriam said his eyes were beaming and then asked when she thought she might be arriving. Becky told her the sale was this weekend and it would only be a few days after that. Merriam told her to let her know the flight schedule and they would be there to pick her up.

It was difficult for Becky to sell the clothing and all the little things her parents found to treasure. At times, she would have to leave and go out back to compose herself to face the crowd again. By the end of the day, everything left; they packed up and gave it to a local charity. They had cleaned the house before the sale and after going over the floors one last time, she turned over the keys to the realtor.

Monday morning she met with the attorney and then booked her flight for the following day. Driving from his office back to Sarah's she told her she would like to pick up some flowers and say goodbye to her mom and dad one last time.

At the cemetery, Becky sat in the snow in between the two graves. She talked as if they were right there with her carrying on a conversation. Then when she couldn't speak anymore, she just sat calmly looking into space.

Chapter Six

Sister Ruthie was anxiously waiting Becky's arrival at the airport. She loved her as a sister and she was always thrilled when she would get to be the one picking her up. Merriam stayed home with Frankie on the count of rain. It was pouring down and the forecast warned of severe thunderstorms throughout the day. While she waited for her flight to arrive, she prayed for all the people traveling on this day.

By the time they had reached Merriam's house, the storm had worsened. The radio station warnings were for winds at eighty miles an hour and tornado watches in all the counties. Sister Ruthie told Becky they would have to leave the luggage in the car and get into the house as fast as she could. Becky fought her way to the house. She was soaked by the time she got there, and Merriam was waiting with a towel, after she got inside. Taking her to the basement, she told Becky of the dangers. A new updated warning was issued for three tornados spotted just a few miles west of there area and heading straight for them. Merriam had taken Frankie's playpen down earlier and covered him with pillows until she returned. Becky found him fast asleep, more precious then he had ever seemed before. How blessed she was to have him especially in this particular time of her life. She knew God had a plan for her, and Frankie was the gift that would encourage her to be strong.

As the house shook and the rumbling outside grew stronger, Becky picked up Frankie along with several heavy blankets that cushioned underneath him and huddled with Merriam behind an old mattress. It sounded like a train was speeded right into the house. They could hear glass shattering and things slamming into the walls. It seemed like it would never end and then suddenly there was silence. Becky wanted to go upstairs to look out, but Merriam told her they would need to wait until they receive the alls clear siren. Listening to the radio with news of the storm moving off to the east of them, the siren sounded the o.k., which was load enough for the entire town to hear. Walking slowly upstairs they carefully entered into the kitchen. Broken glass was everywhere. There were people in the streets calling to take account on everyone and assisting the injured.

The hardest hit was the little cottage just a few houses down where Sam and Becky had lived when they first moved to town. It had been vacant since they lived there, and now demolished. No one was seriously hurt that day, just dozens of cuts, bruises and a few broken bones. Merriam took Becky and Frankie to the Church.

Everyone in town was to meet there during any crisis. While Merriam assisted Mother Marie, Becky took Frankie with her to help with all the children.

Sister Ruthie along with Becky's help settled the babies into their cribs for the night. Then they went in to help the other Nuns with the older children. In the Church, the mayor held a meeting to see how many families were without places to stay. Fortunately, only a few had to be taken in for the night. Others brought in blankets, dry clothing and food. The pews became makeshift beds and Father Matthew held a short service in thanks for all the lives spared.

Early the next morning, the towns people gathered for breakfast and organized the clean up and repairs. Becky was amazed how everyone joined in to help their neighbor's piece back their lives without a thought of themselves. She had never been through anything like this before and was grateful for the opportunity to experience the love that lived in this small community. While Sister Ruthie and Becky tended to the babies, Sister Ruthie told her about other storms over the past years and how each time a crisis would come; every person large and small would be there to help.

Then she said, "If only the whole world could be this way without tragedies, what a wonderful world it would be."

Merriam's house was one of the hardest hit.

Becky still asking to purchase her home said, "This is the perfect opportunity to do some remodeling."

Besides the broken glass and the wet carpeting, they found slivers of both wood and glass throughout all the walls and doors. Becky called a remodeling contractor and the three of them worked out a plan to give the entire house a completely new look. He put in orders for all new appliances, they replaced the existing bathroom, adding on another and even had a play yard built with swings and slides for Frankie and all his friends.

By the time the house was finished it was like new. He had brought in men from surrounding towns to complete the job as quickly as possible. Within two and a half weeks, it was finished. At that time, Merriam and Becky had also completed the paper work on the purchase of the house. Merriam's son Steven had begged her to move in with him since the death of his wife. He was the school principle and with three children of his own, had become stretched to his limits. In addition, with Becky taking the house and helping at the orphanage she finally felt her need to be with them. She would have her hands full with two boys in high school and his problem, fifteen-year-old daughter all in one house. Becky had met him briefly when they were trying to reach Sarah in England and Merriam had filled her in on everything else.

Becky had again arranged for the movers to bring her things from storage the day after she helped with Merriam's move.

This time she thought to herself, "Let's just pray we don't have to do this anymore!"

This reminded her of her weekly call, only to receive the same answer as usual.

Steven's house was larger than Merriam's. It had seven bedrooms, three bathrooms and even a large music room where they played together in a band. Becky asked him if he new anyone who gave private music lessons. She told him ever since the time she saw Frankie dancing; she thought she might learn to play the piano. Before she left that day, he handed her a piece of paper with the name, Bessie Wallingford neatly printed on it. He told her she is the wife of the schools music instructor and that she takes on a few new students every year. Merriam told Becky that Bessie is one of the most talented pianists she has ever heard and all her students play extremely well. Then went on to say that her way of teaching is fast and you will play not only by reading the notes, but, you will be able to play by ear as well. Becky thanked them and called her that next day.

Not knowing anything about pianos, Becky went to Bessie's house for her first lesson. She arranged her time, so Frankie would be napping along with the other babies when she went for each lesson. Well into that lesson, Bessie told her she would need to practice everyday. Not having a piano, she inquired to Bessie about finding a nice used one for the house. Bessie said she would be glad to help her find one and that her husband, Stone would arrange the delivery.

Two weeks later both Stone and Bessie showed up at Becky's house to see that the piano and do some fine-tuning. Bessie introduced Stone to her and she introduced Frankie to them. Frankie was feeling his oats that day and showed them how he danced when Bessie played an enticing tune. Stone leaned down to Frankie and asked to see his hands. Frankie thought he was playing and put his hands in Stone's, to dance along. When Bessie stopped, Frankie stopped and Stone came to his stand. He looked over at Becky and told her she had a little musician on her hands.

Then he went on to say, "He has rhythm. When I held his hands, I felt the exact beat and movements of the music. He should learn to play an instrument starting now. As you learn the piano, have him sit with you to watch and listen. You will be amazed how much he will remember."

Becky told them his father plays the guitar, writes his own songs and sings.

All the time she was saying this, Stone was shaking his head, "Yes!"

Each day after her lessons, she returned to the orphanage to help with dinner and baths. Always, on their way home, she would take Frankie through the Church to her pew and stop to pray. Once home for the evening she would prop him up on a pillow beside her at the piano. Starting with one finger, she would show him the key, as she pressed down to make the sound. She repeated all the keys each night for months. He would sit in full attention quietly listening and without any fuss. Then his routine was off to bed to read and talk about his daddy. After putting, him down for the night Becky would do her household chores and practice her lessons while she waited on the laundry.

Bessie was extremely pleased with Becky's progress and told her she could now manage on her own. At this point, Frankie showed Bessie how he could press down each key correctly, as Becky called them out. She felt, after observing, he was ready for professional instructions. Becky asked her if she would take him on as her student and Bessie said it might be even better if Stone were to work with him. She knew a male figure would be a good experience and told Becky she would discuss this with Stone and get back to her.

Sarah had finally sold her home and had completed her contract with the academy. It had been two years since she had seen Becky and was extremely anxious to move. Becky had prepared a few rooms in the house to let her bring in her own furniture and to give her some privacy. With so many empty large rooms left, she had plenty of space to take on five more boarders. She was also thinking ahead for maybe a sewing room, a playroom for Frankie and another two guest rooms.

With school out for the summer, Stone called Becky to let her know he would be looking forward to work with his new student. Frankie now over three years old and well behaved, would be a delight for any teacher.

He told her, Frankie would have lessons twice a day, everyday at the same times, stating, "It is very important to have short lessons, but very often to begin. We don't want him getting board and loosing interest."

Becky thought that was fine and they made him a schedule.

She often thought how nice it would be for all the children at the orphanage to have the same advantages as other children, they did not participate in the after school activities such as sports or band and it just did not seem fair. This had to make them feel left out, and how that might affect them in the future, weighed heavy on her mind. She could picture their happy faces with instruments in hand or them running with other kids on a ball field and she knew that it was going to be up to her and her friends to make this happen.

Merriam visited often after she moved in with her son, her grandchildren were old enough to fend for themselves, which left her with plenty of time for herself. With Steven's twin boys starting college in the fall and his daughter always off somewhere, she spent her days visiting all her friends around town. Becky shared all her thoughts with her and she became just as enthusiastic as Becky did, when they discussed ideas concerning the children.

One Sunday afternoon Merriam invited Becky and Sarah to dinner. Mother Marie insisted that she should go and start getting out more often, explaining, they had plenty of help and it would do them good to be with their friends. So Becky, Sarah and Frankie spent the evening with Merriam. Steven had taken the kids on vacation so Becky thought dinner would be just the four of them.

When they arrived, Merriam introduced them to Arlin Hamilton, she informed them saying, "He is one of the judges for our county and a very dear friend of mine. I have told him all about you, and Sarah and of coarse, little Frankie. And I thought it would be nice for you all too finally meet."

During the evening, through dinner and long after, Arlin had asked Becky numerous questions. Becky not thinking anything of it answered all of them openly and honestly without hesitation. There was nothing in her life she needed to hide and found him to be very pleasant to talk too. He had no motive behind his questions, just found her exceedingly well adjusted for what she had been through at such a young age. After Merriam's delicious cheesecake, Becky said they should get started for home so Frankie could get to bed. Sarah remained very quiet; her last experience with the opposite sex had turned her from becoming too acquainted with anyone. She told Becky she found him to be a nice person and left it at that.

Well into the summer, Sarah thought it was time she started looking for a job.

Merriam sharing this conversation over morning coffee and said, "Steven had been interviewing prospective teachers and had not made any decisions as of yet." Directing the conversation to Sarah, she added, "It's not college."

Sarah quickly replied, "I'm open just to be able to teach again."

Merriam called his office and by the time she returned to the table, Sarah had an interview that afternoon. Becky had her hands full with Frankie's music lesson and Merriam volunteered to drive Sarah.

By evening, Sarah had a job and Becky came home with some astonishing news of her own. Both Merriam and Sarah could hardly wait for her to tell them.

With arms folded across her chest, she announced, "I'm not going to tell you! I'm going to show you!"

Frankie walked over to the piano, climbed up on the bench and just started playing. They were all thoroughly thrilled over the progress he had made. Becky had no idea until she had picked him up today and they let her see for herself. She also had asked Stone and Bessie if they would give the orphanage children lessons, stating she would cover all the costs of everything. Stone told her he would work with them on occasion and Bessie said she would start with the little ones and go from there, telling Becky not to expect any miracles that each child is different and music may not interest some.

When Becky went to bed that night, her mind took her back to all her special moments when Sam played his guitar and sang. Thinking how proud he would be, to be able to hear and play with Frankie. She prayed once again as she did day and night over the past, soon to be four years, then drifted off to sleep as she heard him singing in her head.

By the end of October, Bessie had all six children playing instruments. Stone had some of the older children now playing in the school band, whom had found interest in music. Nathan was almost five and very tall for his age. Bessie picked him to play a base guitar. She allowed the children in a large room filled with all sorts' instruments, and as she watched them, she made her decisions. Sarah Jane stuck with the piano, progressing more rapidly than the rest. Michael went directly to the drums and Bessie thought they could just cure his fidgets or at least put them to good use. Joseph was very quiet and so timid around the equipment Bessie chose the fiddle for him. Kayla, very closely attached to Joseph, wanted to do everything he did and she was doing well on the fiddle as well. Last, but hardly the least was Christopher who had an extraordinary desire to express himself.

Bessie said, "He is now picking his strings and working on led guitar."

She also told Becky that Frankie's true interest was the electric guitar. She only had one and Christopher and Frankie shared so well that she was thinking about getting another, but the way they work together, had brought her such pleasure, she put off the purchase for the time being.

With Sarah teaching and tutoring after school, Becky did not see her much. The holidays had been fun with all the children and they settling back to their routines. Becky worked on reading with all the children in-between running back and forth for their music lessons and was completely exhausted by the time she went to bed each night. But she never complained and would not have it any other way either. Her own schedule she attached to the refrigerator, and it started with her weekly call too when she did laundry.

Mother Marie received a very disturbing letter! The Church officials were in the process to begin the transfer of the children to other facilities suited for the opportunity of adoption. It said they would begin with the older children and move on to the younger. This transfer would begin two months from her receiving this notice. She spent the rest of that day and all night praying and asking for a miracle. Each day over the next month, she prayed along side Becky as usual, focusing her prayers on the children. The other Nuns had no idea of what was coming and she felt it was time to give them this information to prepare. When she gave them the news, she asked them to keep it to themselves for the time being. Sister Ruthie asked questions of why they needed to go and where, but Mother Marie would say nothing and told them all to take their concerns to God in prayer.

One of Sarah's students she tutored after school was Steven's youngest daughter. She was a senior in high school and barely making passing grades. She had been a stubborn child all her life and when her mother passed away, Steven lost control. Although Merriam spent a lot of time with her, Sally still would skip school and hardly ever complete her homework. Sarah had taken her under her wing and asked Steven to let her take a little more control over her life, by asking him if she could move her in with her and Becky for the rest of the school year. She promised to keep a close watch on every move she made and he agreed.

Sarah said, "Maybe a different atmosphere and further away from bad influencing groups might just be what she needs. Stating, Sally could spend some time along side Becky."

Steven knew all about Becky from his mother, so he felt he could trust the environment she would be entering.

"Who knows? He replied, then, you may have the perfect plan to bring Sally to a right way of thinking. Sarah, thank you for being the kind of person Sally needs so desperately in her life. No one else has been able to reach her and maybe in time she will confide her feeling to you. But please, let me know how she is doing and if I can be of any help."

Sarah told him she would take good care of her and would update him often.

Sally was reluctant at first, but with so much anger in her heart, she was ready to go anywhere. Becky welcomed her, as Sarah knew she would and Frankie took her by the hand to show her all his stuff in the toy room. She fell in love with Frankie at first sight. Sarah told Becky they may be only a small part of Sally's rehabilitation and Frankie could turn out to be a boy wonder!

During the evenings when Frankie would have Sally down on the floor playing, Sarah and Becky would have open discussions. Directly using their most personal memories, with explanations of how they overcame problems, were the topics of their talks. Even though it was hard to talk about the accident, Becky felt if she could help someone else through her pain she would be willing to hurt for a little while. To keep herself from becoming too emotional she would jump to another time when she met Sam and shared some of their beautiful memories. After a few days, Sally would ask questions and listening even more attentively. Soon, Becky felt it was time to see if Sally would like to share some of her feeling and started asking little insignificant inquiries so not to pry.

Within weeks, Sally was doing most of the talking and Becky was on the floor with Frankie. She even cried at times when she opened up about loosing of her mother. Every time, Frankie would go sit beside her and hold her hand. Her grades were improving and Sarah had her doing extra credit work in all her classes to enable her to graduate with her class. Steven would come often to visit and take them all out to dinner. She had become a completely new Sally, full of life and ready to plan her future. He encouraged her by telling her how proud he was to have such a wonderful daughter. Her conversations were lively and contagious and she told her father she wanted to either go to college or enroll into a trade school right after graduation. Not knowing at this point, what her best interest might be, she asked Sarah on several different occasions about what she might consider. Sarah did not want to overstep her bounds, so she made up a questionnaire with different likes and dislikes. When she had Sally answer the questions, they discussed a variety of careers she might pursue.

She had grown to love Sarah and on one evening during dinner with Steven, Sally told him with Sarah present, they should start dating each other. Now Steven and Sarah had been sharing their lunch hours together in the teachers lounge and had both been attracted to the other, but neither ever considered dating. It had been a long road for Steven having the kids to manage after his wife passed away and Sarah, with her past experience, wasn't eager to even try at love again, but yet in the back of their minds it seemed they had already connected a friendship that could develop into something more. Both of them dropped the conversation and went on to Sally's future agenda.

Steven asked Sarah what she thought Sally's interests might be. She told him about the questionnaire she had given her.

Then she said, "She loves children, so I'm thinking maybe a teacher or even going into nursing and working with children in pediatrics. However, she must decide this on her own. What I might think maybe completely the opposite of what she wants."

Surprising the both of them, Sally declared, "There is a two year program for LPN and then two more years to become an RN."

"When did you check this out?" asked Sarah.

"Well!" she answered; I went with some friends from school to a college about two hours from here. They were picking up some brochures and I talked to one of the counselors."

"Honey, Steven replied, if you want to go to that college, I'd take you there and arrange everything."

"I really think this is what I want to do, dad." Said Sally, and then, but I would like Sarah to come with us and help me get set up."

Sarah had no problem with that request and they made plans for a day trip the following week.

Later that evening Sarah brought up to Sally the discussion they had had earlier concerning her and Steven dating. She explained to Sally that her father might not be interested in her that way.

Then, Sally apologized saying, "Sarah, I'm so sorry for putting you on the spot like that! I know it's not my place to fix up you or dad. But you do have to admit, that you like him!"

"Yes, Sally I do like him, but that's something we have to work on and I may not even be the right person for him." She said.

Then Sally admitted she was right and ended to conversation by saying, "If it's meant to be, it will be."

Summer at hand, Sally had managed with Sarah's help to pass her classes and graduate. She chose to start her nursing career that summer and moved into the dorm. Steven's boys came home for the summer and would return to college in August. The three of them planned a fishing trip and Sally was happy to be in school. Staying in a cabin and fishing did not seem to sound like too much fun for her. Sarah promised Sally she would come and visit her and Sally was to call her with any problems.

Becky noticed for some time how quiet Mother Marie and all the Nuns had become. Every time she would ask if there was something wrong, they would evade her questions and change the subject. She had an uneasy feeling and no one could help her make heads or tails of it. Frankie had been sick with a cold that was not getting better. She thought maybe his sickness was this uneasy feeling and took him to the base clinic. After sitting for an hour, the nurse called them in. She took Frankie's weight and temperature then left the room. While the doctor examined Frankie, Becky told him how he had had this cold for more than just a few weeks.

His tonsils were seriously inflamed and he told Becky, "Due to the fact of this being so severe, he wanted to hospitalize him immediately.

Then he added, "When the infection is cleared, we need to take out his tonsils. I'm positive he will be just fine."

Becky asked if she could stay with him and he told her, "I will have the nurse get Frankie settled and she was welcome to stay."

After ten days of antibiotics, he was well enough for surgery. Merriam and Sarah stayed with Becky as she waited and paced the floor until the doctor returned. When the doctor appeared, she could see on his face, by his smile, that Frankie was just fine. He told her he did well and he would be in recovery for the next several hours and then she would be able to see him. She thanked him and then went to the hospital chapel to thank God. When she came back, Merriam and Sarah insisted she get some fresh air and food into her stomach. Becky nodded and followed along.

Just before they left the building, Dr. Phillips passed by and remembered Becky as his patient. He asked if everything was all right and she told him about Frankie's surgery. Then he asked about Sam and she informed him there was still no news.

"It's been how long since he was reported missing?" he asked.

Sadly, Becky answered, "Almost four and a half years."

Taking her hand in his, and pausing for thought, said before he left, "Don't give up hope. They could call you at any time saying they have found him. I have seen cases that took even longer."

"Thank you!" She said.

Looking back as he made his way down the hall added, "I'm here any time if you need me, just have them page me and we can talk."

When they were able to see Frankie, he was awake and very fussy. His little throat was sore and his tears just ran. After crying through the shot for pain, it was not too long before he was sitting up and enjoying a popsicle. His recovery was fast and he looked better than he had in months. His first day home Becky gave him a gift.

When he opened it and his eye danced with excitement. "My own guitar!" he shouted and then, "Momma!"

"My very own guitar!"

She asked Stone to pick it out for her; he had it tuned, and ready to play when Frankie opened the package. Instead of sitting in a chair to play, he just plopped on the floor. It was an electric guitar and Stone had the wires ready, but Frankie was playing it as soon as lifted it from the box.

After that day, any moment away from school lessons and his Bible study, he was playing his new instrument. Becky would bring the other children from the orphanage to play out in the back yard and he would have them all back in the house taking turns playing his guitar and Sarah Jane on the piano. So, Becky called Stone and asked him to purchase instruments the children played, to have for them at her home. Sarah came up with the idea to fix up one of the largest spare rooms as a music room and in a short time, that room became the most widely used room in the entire house.

With Frankie on the mend and Becky's routine back in full swing, she thought maybe a summer vacation to the farm would be a good idea. She mentioned this to Mother Marie during their morning prayer, but before they could talk about it, one of the Nuns called her away and before she left she asked Becky to join her for tea in the garden when the children napped.

Becky's morning began with the children's Bible lesson followed by going back and forth to their music lessons. In between, she read with them and worked on their reading and math. By the time they were down for their nap, she was more than ready for her break with Mother Marie.

The Church officials had temporarily postponed the transfer of the children, but today Mother Marie had made the decision to inform Becky of what was coming. It seems according to the States Child Welfare, that transferring the children to other facilities would give them a higher opportunity for adoption. At this time, the Church was no longer in control. The whole situation perplexed Mother Marie. Even though the children might have a better chance at adoption, it did not make sense to her to put them in foster care to achieve this goal, still knowing, she could absolutely do anything, she stayed in prayer.

Becky met her in the kitchen and they took a tray of tea and cookies out on the patio. For a while, they sat admiring the perfectly manicured landscape and the peacefulness of the warm breeze. Peace for Mother Marie did not last as she stood from her chair and began to pace.

Becky initiated their discussion by saying, "I've seen for some time that you and all the Nuns have a heavy burden that you can't discuss. Then she asked, is there anything I can do to help?"

Her pacing ceased and she sat back down in her chair, then reached for Becky's hand and said, "I have unfortunate news. I received information over two months ago and this information had to remain within the Church. Now it is in the hands of the State and I feel you need to know so you can prepare yourself for the inevitable."

Becky felt heaviness upon her shoulders and head as she listened to Mother Marie tell her of the transferring of the children. Her heart sunk lower with each horrifying word.

Her mind went wild thinking, "The children, her children!" Picturing, strange people pulling the children apart as they clung to one another frightened out of their wits and looking back at her with tearful questions of how could she let these people do this to them. This was more than Becky could handle! She pleaded with Mother Marie that there had to be some way of preventing this from happen.

All Mother Marie could say was, "It's out of our hands."

The rest of the afternoon Becky hardly spoke. On her usual passing through the Church, on her way home, she had even more prayers for God. Mother Marie, kneeling as well and Frankie waited quietly by her side.

When they walked out the door, Mother Marie said, "God will find them all a good place and everything will be alright, Becky."

With a reluctant smile on her face, she turned and took Frankie home.

Mother Marie had told Merriam about the children earlier that day so she would understand Becky's mood when she came home. Knowing how hard Becky would take the news, she did all the chores listed on the refrigerator so they could spend some time talking that evening.

Sarah and Sally were at the house when they walked in. Sally was busy packing her clothes and Sarah was telling Merriam all about the dorm where Sally would be living. They were as bubbly as teenagers were! Sally would run out to ask Sarah her advice on what to take and Sarah would be just as enthusiastic right back. In a matter of about twenty minutes, they were heading out the door to hit the road for Sally's college. Sarah told Becky she would not be back until sometime late the next day. Becky smiled and told them to drive safely as they pulled out the drive.

Becky just sat in her rocker and starred into space. She had no clue as of what to do next. Merriam played with Frankie a while and then had him dress for bed. When he came back from his room, he crawled into Becky's lap and she rocked him to sleep. Merriam carried him upstairs to his bed and knew it was time to discuss the children.

She sat down near Becky's rocker and said, "Mother Marie told me about the children today."

Becky stopping the rocking asked, "Why are they doing this? Don't they have any compassion in their hearts at all? These kids are loved and where they might be sent, it could." She stopped!

Her heart was pounding with fear and anguishing pain for her kids. They had become her life and with Sam in his situation, they were her fortress. Merriam grew even more concerned as she witnessed Becky face go limp and turn pale. When she brought up the postponement, she tried to convince her all this worry might be in vain. Yet Becky did not feel that this was simply going to fade away, they would be back and she needed to make a plan to stop all of it. Merriam told her she would help in any way she could and said she would call Arlin in the morning for his advice also. Becky thought he might have some insight and thanked her for offering to help.

That next morning, Arlin arrived at the door bright and early. Merriam had called him after Becky had gone to bed: she had spent the night and planned to stay for part of the summer. He sat down at the breakfast table with both of them, gathering all the information they had. The next item on his agenda was to pay Mother Marie a visit and see if she would share the letters, she had received. Father Mathew had been gone for several days, but Arlin said he would catch him when he returned. He told Becky that possibly they are shuffling this paperwork around trying to figure out what to do.

Becky replied, "If only they would let me deal those cards!" Then she apologized for her outburst.

He snickered when she apologized and said, "I know exactly what you mean, I've spent years in the court room and so many times I've held my tongue, so there's no need to apologize to me."

When he left the house he told them to hang tight, that it might take him a few days to cover this paper trail and Becky, wrapped in Merriam's arms said thank you once again.

With all the confusion over the children, Becky decided to invite Sam's family to come for a visit. There was no way she could leave now and thought they might enjoy the summer festival. She had never attended the one in town and looked forward to see all the events. Anna took her up on the invitation and they planed to be there within two weeks.

Anna had another reason for coming on this trip. All the family wanted Becky and Frankie to move home with them. After a few days of watching Becky with the other children, it was apparent to Anna that this was her home.

Up rooting either of them now, would be far too hard of an adjustment in their lives and she never brought up the family's request.

During their visit, Anna did ask Becky if she would consider bringing all the children to the farm next summer. Becky told her it would be a wonderful experience for them, but the orphanage would never allow her to take them out even for one night. Then she added how the State would step in and really cause a commotion. She thanked her for such a wonderful invitation, but for now, they would have to stay there and follow the rules even though at times they did not seem fair.

For the first time since Becky had lived there she finally attended the summer festival. Sam's entire family had never missed any back in the surrounding counties of their home and thoroughly enjoyed this one as well. As Frankie road the rides with his uncles, Becky felt so bad that Mother Marie had decided against letting to other children go. She understood Mother Marie's position with the State on her back and any rules broken at this point would cause them to come down even sooner to take away the children. So Becky bought enough cotton candy, candy apples and trinkets to give them a little private party she would plan for the next day. If they could not come to the festival, the festival would come to them, was her way of thinking. She told Anna those very words as she filled a box with her purchases and made several trips back to the house.

The carnival booked for this year's festival supplied the music. Usually the city council members book someone local, but this year they were unable to find a band and it worked out in their advantage. They played country music and people danced on the platform that was set up, but as far as being anything exceptional, you could see by the crowd that their attention focused mainly on the rides and handmade crafts. All the booths set up with their goods from canned items to woodcarvings, were the most spectacular pieces of art Becky had ever seen.

She told Anna, "The time put into their works of truly gifted art, is no where near the prices they are asking. And the quilt you made for me and Sam would have been first prize; right along side these unimaginably crafted pieces."

Anna thanked her for the beautiful compliments on her quilt and said, "To me, it's just a way of sewing pretty scrap pieces of material together with only love in your thoughts as I work. I have made so many over the years its just second nature to me."

"Well Anna!" stated Becky, then, second nature to anyone who can create masterpieces such as these, are blessings from God." Then she asked her if she ever made any to sell. Anna told her she could, but never really thought about selling them.

Becky said, "If you decide you would like to make some to sell, I would like to place an order for ten."

"Ten!" gasped Anna.

"Ten." Becky returned, and then, "I would love to give them to very special friends as gifts. To me they are warm delicate and exquisite pieces of art. And to purchase such a gift in a department store is unheard of."

With that, all Anna could say was, "I guess I'll get started as soon as I get home."

After the festival, Becky sat down at the kitchen table and asked everyone for ideas on her party at the orphanage the next day. Sam's sister, Jennie suggested bobbing for apples and Anna added musical chairs to give out the fun toys Becky had bought. With everyone eager to participate, Becky was sure this would make up for the children having to stay inside. She called Mother Marie to clear her plans and she readily approved. They set time aside in the afternoon when all the little ones were up from their naps and ready to play.

The party was a great success and the children had a ball. Mother Marie laughed so hard when Sister Ruthie volunteered to show the kids how to bob for apples that tears rolled down her face. Then she had to sit down because her sides were so sore. Anna found amazement, by the behavior of so many children in one room together. Each one helped the other and shared so enthusiastically she just cherished every moment. Towards the end of their party time, Mother Marie clapped her hands and every child came to attention. She had them help pick up, which they did without so much as a whimper. When they were finished, they lined up like little soldiers and after they said their thank yous, they were lead to the dorms to wash their faces and hands.

Father Mathew invited Becky and all her family to stay for dinner and they gladly accepted the invitation. Just to be near these children was more joy than they had ever encountered. Anna knew for herself now, why Becky belonged here and the rest of the family knew as well.

While Becky had her company those past two weeks, Sarah had been dating Steven. With all the people in the house, she had not had a moment for any private conversations. Now that Sam's family had gone back to the farm, Becky could finally relax with Sarah and catch up. Becky had noticed, even with a house full of people that something was different about Sarah. Over coffee one very early morning, Becky watched her. The smile on her face radiated a sense of peace, in a way Becky had never seen. Her mind seemed miles away, as if in a deep daydream.

Becky could not help herself and asked, "Sarah? Where are you?" With no response, she snapped her fingers by Sarah's ear.

She looked at Becky and simply said, "I'm in love."

"Who are you in love with? Asked Becky, then, I didn't know you were seeing anyone."

"Steven," Sarah replied.

"Steven?" asked Becky.

Then Sarah went on to say, "We started out with coffee in the teachers lounge, then coffee in the teachers lounge. Taking a dreamy deep breath she continued, and after that lunch, breakfast, a movie, late dinners and."

"O.K!" Becky interrupted; then, I get it, and asked, why didn't you tell me?"

Still in her dreamy hemisphere, Sarah said, "You have been busy with the children and then company, while I have fallen for the most wonderful man in the world. For the first time in so many years, I feel so! I cannot even describe how this feels. It's so strong and light all at the same time."

"Wow!" replied Becky saying in the same breath, You are in love."

Sarah went on, "Everyday is better, happier and more precious than the last."

"How does Steven feel?" asked Becky.

"He's so wonderful!" said Sarah.

Becky laughed then re-asked, "How does Steven feel?"

She answered, "The same."

Frankie stumbled into the kitchen about that time, rubbing his eyes as he climbed into his chair.

"Good morning," said Becky.

He yawned then smiled, letting her know he was ready for his breakfast. Sarah took her coffee out on the back porch and sat quietly listening to the morning sounds of birds doing their early chores as they chirped and flew rapidly about the yard. Becky just smiled and shook her head while she prepared Frankie's meal.

Over the next few months, Becky only saw Sarah as she left for work and heard her return quietly late at night. Merriam was getting pretty much the same from Steven and together they watched as their relationship grew. They were like teenagers in love for the first time and it was exciting for Becky to see her special friend become so happy. Merriam was pleased that Steven had moved on and had found such a wonderful person as Sarah to share his life.

Another year had flown by and Sally came home from college ready to plan a vacation. With little time off, she was ready to have some fun. This year she wanted to pick their trip and Steven asked her if she would mind including Sarah in their plans.

She reminded her father saying, "I'm the one that told you two you should be together. And now that she is a big part of our family, she should do all the things we do."

Steven's son, Phillip and James, liked Sarah right off and they told their father he was a very lucky man to have Sarah in his life.

Sally requested a dream vacation saying, "Let's go somewhere, Beachie!"

After some thought, Steven asked Sally if she had a girlfriend at school that would like to go along.

She asked, "Where are we going, dad?"

"We will go to the beach, just like you requested," he replied.

Two weeks later, Steven had found a house to rent with Sarah's help, right on the beach in California. He rented it for a full month and reserved three rental cars to accommodate everyone. That way they could all come and go as they pleased.

Becky had made her arrangements to fly to Missouri in time to be there for the county fair that Anna had told her about on her last visit. Merriam took on her schedule of seeing the children to their music lessons and Sister Ruthie promised to be her back up in the event something might come up unexpectedly. Oh, how she wished she could take all the children, but that wish she knew was far from reality and she would find other ways of making their world just as special.

She planned to stay three weeks, so Frankie could spend a lot of time getting to know all his family. Anna was busy planning picnics and another reunion, this time including all of both sides of the family. This very proud grandma wanted to show off her talented grandson. To Becky, it seemed like Anna's way of covering her pain, not knowing how to deal with her missing son; she simply transferred her emotions to Frankie, which gave her the comfort she needed desperately to go on.

A few days before Becky was to leave, Mother Marie asked her to join her for tea. They discussed the possibility of the transfer coming and Mother Marie told Becky that Arlin had not found any new information. He had managed to postpone every court date that had come and he promised to do all he could to keep them out of court as long as he could, until they could find a way of settling this problem for the last time. Becky felt relieved about taking this trip and she was very grateful for all the help from so many caring people. Her prayers that evening flowed with praise to the Lord for the blessings He had poured into her life.

Their trip was just as Anna had described, full of fun, family and picnics. Frankie had the best time of his life. They took him fishing and horseback riding every chance they could, in-between all the other activities. Each night after supper, he would play his guitar with his uncles on the front porch until dark.

Anna had given Frankie an outfit of boots and overalls, so he could be just like everyone else on the farm. Becky had to go to town after a few days and purchase another set of overalls after Frankie refused to wear anything else. He was up early every morning eagerly waiting to help with the chores of feeding the chickens and gathering eggs. The after breakfast, he would ride with his grandfather on the tractor to check on the cows.

Anna, watching from the porch screen said one day, "What a little blessing you have Becky."

Cheerfully responding, she answered, "My special gift from God!"

The day they went to the county fair, Anna told everyone she planned to eat there and that she was not going to take the picnic basket this year. It was a special occasion and there would be all kinds of food for them to eat. Frankie was looking forward to the rides and cotton candy his cousins promised to buy for him. Becky took plenty of cash and her camera, with several rolls of film to catch every shot she could, for the album and journal she kept for Sam. Becky prayed continuously, that one day soon, they would be back together and share all kinds of precious memories just like these moments of their son's life.

By the end of the day, everyone was ready to go home and relax. Overstuffed with junk food and still spinning from the rides, Frankie was exhausted. He fell asleep on the drive home and slept until breakfast the next day. The first thing he wanted when he woke up was a candy apple. Becky told him that would not be good and Anna fixed him a big bowl of oatmeal. She did however, cut up some small pieces of apple and put a bit of cinnamon sugar on it to satisfy his craving.

They had many evenings filled with stories of old times and music while their time lasted. Anna said she would visit in the fall before winter set in and asked Becky to plan to stay even longer on her next trip. She promised her she would and asked if a whole month would be too long. Anna was thrilled and said she would count the days until they returned. Then before they went home, Anna gave her four of the quilts she had ordered. Becky gave her five hundred dollars for them and then told her that they were worth far more. Anna, dumbfounded by this, just shook her head in disbelief. She could not comprehend how her hand-sewn quilts were worth so much, but she enjoyed making them for people and if they brought in extra money for the farm, she felt she should not ask any questions and continue to sew.

Settling back to his routine, Frankie found it very difficult to keep his mind off all the times he had helped his grandpa with the farm chores. Becky quickly returned his interest in his music to ease his frustration. But every chance he had, he would tell the other children his version of his fond memories of the trip. It had turned him into a little chatterbox just like his mother and Becky found a lot of joy each time she was able to listen to his tales.

During the time Becky was away, Arlin had several meetings with not only the State officials; he had even met with the Governor. They were long time friends and with his help had managed to postpone the transfers yet again for a period of a few more months. He had come to understand that the State was only trying to use all their resources to find permanent homes for the children. Even with all his gathered information, something was missing, and why they could not just come out and say exactly what the actual problem was, eluded his mind. He did however, through the discussions he had had with one of the social workers; found that the communities involvement with the children's social and academic participation would play an enormous part on the final decisions in their next hearings. Vehemently, he called a meeting at the Church with Father Mathew, Mother Marie, Merriam and Becky, to come up with any ideas to make this happen.

The tension Becky held with this whole situation was wearing her temper thin. She placed her weekly call for any new information concerning her husband and totally lost it with them.

After hearing the same exact response for the past five years, she lashed out with a stern voice to the person on the other end of the line and said, "I really don't believe that you even bother to check into finding any new information! Time after time I call just to hear the same quick answer of, "I'm sorry, Mrs. Malloy, there's no news today! There has to be something. And if you really cared, you would try a bit harder," as she slammed down the receiver, only to call back immediately and apologize for her outburst, as she cried into the phone.

Merriam stood in the kitchen doorway watching Becky's emotional lapse, while Frankie clung to her side with his arms wrapped around her leg in total freight.

When she turned and saw his face, she apologized and told him, "Don't be afraid, Frankie. Mamma is so sorry for getting angry with the man on the phone. I miss daddy so much, that sometimes it's just so hard not to get mad." He ran over to her and leaped into her arms.

Then in his sweet little voice he said, "Its o.k. mamma, daddy is going to come home, you'll see." Merriam, with tears in her eyes and holding back the lump in her throat, stood frozen in place and helpless.

When Steven and Sarah returned from their vacation, Merriam and Arlin filled them in on all that was happening with the orphanage. Arlin requested their presence at the meeting and told them this would be the last resort that he could possibly think of in solving the situation. He went on to tell them, if this did not satisfy the State, with the re-elections coming soon, he would have a difficult time getting the new Governor's support. Because of the fact that his friend would not be running for another term and the upcoming candidates would be much less lenient. Merriam told them about Becky's outburst she had had on the phone, and then told them she did not think Becky could take much more. Sarah knew exactly what she meant and felt her deep concerns as well.

Father Mathew opened the meeting with prayer and then Arlin took the stand and held nothing back as to the outcome if their efforts failed. He knew from experience to lay out the whole truth, that way there would be no questions of why things did not turn out for the lack of total commitment. He wanted Becky to prepare herself emotionally to be able to accept what might have to be.

Everyone gave their inputs of ways to get the community involved. Merriam had on her agenda, all sorts' of ideas on fundraisers to update the orphanage. Steven said he would work on his end through the school to involve the children at the orphanage in the extra curricular activities. In addition, Father Mathew told him that the current transportation of the bus used for their transport was in desperate need of repair. Becky assured him that would no longer be a problem, and then said she would purchase a new bus. Sarah offered her services of tutoring and any other need she could provide. By the end of their meeting, a new enlightened enthusiasm filled their emotions. Just before they adjourned, Becky said, "If it would be alright with you, Father Mathew, I would like to talk with the congregation this Sunday before the end of your service."

He looked at her, thinking and replied, "I think you have a great idea there. I will give my sermon this week that will get everyone's attention to the problems at hand. It will be short, but to the point, and then I will announce that after the service there will be a community meeting, followed by a brunch provided by the Church." With all in favor, Arlin closed the meeting and told everyone to work on their speeches with a fine toothcomb, that with all their good intentions, they were a long way from being out of the woods.

With only two days to prepare for this event, Becky took it upon herself to take some of the pressure off the Nun's by having the brunch catered in. Merriam helped her set the menu and then accompanied her to the caterers. With that done, she could keep up her routine with the children and focus all her spare time to her speech. Alin contacted the State officials and the Governor, requesting their attendance, in hope; they could soften their hearts to the communities' efforts and give their approval.

Merriam, Sarah, Becky and Frankie were shocked when they stepped out the door to head for the Church that morning. There were cars parking everywhere! Father Mathew, along with three other men was guiding people further on the lawn of the park. The word of this event had spread through the church and to other Churches throughout the county. Mother Marie quickly assigned the Nun's to get all the children into the Church, and then she had Merriam, Sarah and Becky take their seats among them so the Nun's could prepare extra food for the overflowing crowd.

Father Mathew gave his sermon, followed by a short service. He started with a heart felt praise to God for the miracle of fellowship that had been brought here on this day. As he spoke, the entire congregation sat in total silence, listening to every word that so gracefully flowed from his lips. Before he gave the stand to Arlin, he had the choir sing Amazing Grace.

Arlin took the stand and his speech took off from Father Mathew's explaining the entire situation and the outcome if the community was unwilling to participate. Merriam was next in line and gave all her ideas about the fundraisers to update the orphanage. Then she turned the stand over to Mother Marie. As she spoke, her eyes made contact with many people throughout the congregation. She had her own alluring way, even in a large crowd to reach individual hearts. When she finished, she introduced Becky with explanations of the many things that she had already done for the children and went on to say that even one person can make a world of difference.

Becky took the stand and for a brief time looked as if she were silently praying, standing with her hands interlocked, clutched under a bowed chin. She began with thanking everyone for coming and went on to speak in a way she thought how the children saw all this. She told them in detailed description how from the first time she helped take care of them, to the individual little things that brought her so much joy. When she finished saying what blessings children are, she raised her fist and said, "We, as God's children can not let these defenseless gifts be taken away!" After a standing ovation, Arlin took the stand once again and asked for volunteers. Holding up a clipboard, he asked the audience to write down all they are willing to do. When Father Mathew dismissed the crowd, everyone gathered in the dining room for brunch.

It was after dark when the crowd had finally gone home. Before the Governor left, he looked over the list of people who had signed up for various tasks. The money offered Arlin counted was well over ten thousand dollars. He left very optimistic that their efforts would succeed and told Arlin to stay in contact with him to keep him up to date.

Two weeks went by and Arlin received notification by the State that they had made an agreement with the Church officials, giving them a three-month trial period. At the end of that time, they would re-evaluate. Giving the news to everyone, Arlin stressed the importance of following to the letter what the community had agreed to do. Because he explained, "This is our last chance and if we can't get all the people to follow through, they will step in and there will be no stopping them." With a new school year starting, Becky became concerned about people becoming so involved with their own lives, that they may forget the promises they had made. Merriam vowed to stay on their back full time so not to let that happen.

With Frankie and all the other children in school now, Becky and Merriam spent those hours planning bake sales and the other fundraisers. The people that had signed up for the after school time as big brothers and sisters to the older children began enthusiastically. At the end of the three months, Becky's fears had begun to take shape. They had slowly started dropping out, giving one excuse after another and time was running out. The money from the fundraisers was more than enough to cover all the expenses, but the special needs of the older children had begun to concern the Church.

Twenty-two children's lives would change drastically very soon if no intervention came forthwith. Merriam planned a dinner, inviting Steven, Stone and Bessie to attend. They divided the boys and girls for more outside activities among themselves. The girls would come to Becky's and they would have sewing and cooking lessons. The boys, bused to Stone and Bessie's home to learn even more music and then afterwards, taken to the park to play baseball.

Arlin came in well after dinner and Steven filled him in on their new plans. After listening with great concentration, he informed them to be prepared for the worst. "The community has let us down. He said, and then, without their support to their word, the officials will have no choice but to do the inevitable."

Becky stood up and said, "I'm not going to let this happen!" I'll go door to door and remind them. And the plans we've made here tonight we will do, starting first thing tomorrow."

Sarah and Merriam became very concerned for Becky. They knew all too well, this would be the last straw, that broke the camels back. With so many tragedies in the last few years, this would take its toll and Becky could loose everything. Sarah decided to take a leave from work and devote all her time to Becky's plans. While doing this she would work on getting Becky's frame of mind stronger and help her emotionally get through yet another troubled time of her life.

Chapter Seven

All the efforts made by the few devoted people had not been enough to satisfy the State. Although the Church felt there had been many improvements, they were defenseless now with Child Welfare. Arlin had received the States final findings and he was to deliver them to the Church. Yet he still could not understand other than the fact they wanted these children adopted out, why they would prefer foster care over all they had through the Church. He pounded his fist on his desk and felt, with all the power he had in his hands, he had failed to bring justice to these innocent kids. Not even knowing how to give this news to Becky, was going to be the hardest verdict he ever in all his years had to give, tore him into pieces.

Sitting in Mother Marie's office as she read the papers, for the first time ever, she broke down and cried. No one had ever seen a glimpse of a tear in her eyes, other than laughter and as hard as it was, Arlin sat facing her, holding back all his emotion. When he got up to leave, she asked if he could stay a while longer. Telling him there was more at stake here than he realized. She wiped her face on her sleeves in her outrage as she stood from her desk. As she paced the room, she started asking questions, "Why is it that the State did this after so many years? Something is not kosher! Please excuse my expression, here! Someone or something is behind all this."

He listened to her accusations with deep interest and after a while started wondering the same things himself. "Why?" he thought, and then, you may be on to something here, Mother!" Going on further he added, I am going to do some private snooping around. Let's just see what their up too. This is an election year, but I do not think that is it. I will find the underlying cause of this just as fast as I can. Right now, I have to be the one who tells Becky."

She told him that Merriam and Sarah were at the house now and they would help any way they could. He stopped at the door and said, "Call me if anything happens, I want to be here to check out who picks up these kids."

Becky knew by the look on Arlin's face, what he had come to say. She ran out the door and down towards the park. Sarah started to follow and Arlin stopped her and said to give her some time alone. He told them about the paperwork he had given Mother Marie, then went on and said both of them just cannot believe why this is happening now.

"What could it be? Sarah asked.

Merriam stood silently listening to every word he said. "After all this time they never said anything when they did their inspections and now suddenly it all just been turned and twisted upside down." He replied.

Breaking her silence, Merriam asked, "How soon are they taking them?"

He answered, "According to the paperwork it will be over the next few weeks. I do not trust anything they say right now. As he left, he said, I've got to go, there are some calls I need to make and I will hire a private investigator if need be."

Sarah looked out the door to see if she could spot Becky and there was no sign of her anywhere. It was dark now and the lights on the gazebo and walkways were bright enough for anyone to see. Sarah's concern deepened and she jumped into her car and drove through town searching. Merriam called Steven to help and then Mother Marie to see if she might be in the Church. After a thorough search, Becky was not to be found. Both Sarah and Steven drove late into the night, calling out into the damp chilling rain. Sarah had to return to the house, she had become frantic with worry and Steven followed behind her. Then it was all he could do to calm Sarah down.

Becky had started running and just could not stop. Then finding herself miles from home in this torrential downpour, she fell to her knees, screaming out her questions to God, "You can't do this!" "Please, I can't take another single loss, not now!" Forgive me for asking so much from other people. I know, you know what's best, but this?" Collapsing to the ground, she continued praying through her sobbing, "If you would bring Sam home, together we could take these awful things away. Alone, I am only half as strong. "Help me Lord!" Help me save these children. I give you my life for Sam, Frankie, all the children and everyone. As she stood to her feet, she ended her prayers, "In Jesus name, Amen." Then she walked towards home.

Sarah was waiting at the door with towels in hand, as Becky appeared through the foggy dimmed lights of the park. Soaked, calm and quiet she entered the house, a sigh of relief rushed through the air. Becky accepted the towel Sarah wrapped around her shoulders, and then continued walking silently to her room.

Sarah made her a cup of hot tea, hoping she would come back and join them. As they sat waiting, Mother Marie told Merriam once again that adoption would be their only answer, but with two or even less weeks, and the last adoption twelve years ago, it would be a miracle if ever she had seen one. Those words Mother Marie had spoke, without her intent, planted a seed for the second time in Merriam.

After a long warming shower, Becky came back into the living room and sat in her rocker. She apologized for worrying them, but explained her need to be alone. Sarah placed the cup into her hands and told her to sip it slowly. Becky looked to Mother Marie and asked, "When will you be telling the children they will be going away?" Her heart sunk to her stomach. The look she saw in Becky's eyes as she asked that question was piercing, cold and unbearably sad all at the same time. She started to cry and felt so guilty, even though she had nothing to do with any of this. Her place was to handle any questions and face all problems with anyone, all day, and everyday.

She reached for Becky's hand and asked, "Would you like to be there when I tell them?"

"Yes. She answered, then, there are so many to hold at one time. Could we take just one child at a time?"

Mother Marie, projecting a slight warming smile answered, "If you feel that would be best, that's what we will do."

"I do, she replied. Then in a bitter voice Becky stated, that way, after twenty two times, I'll hurt enough for all of them." An eerie silence hazed and lingered over the entire room. Nothing more exchanged from anyone.

Mother Marie spent the next several hours on her knees after lighting candles for each child and sending out a special request to comfort Becky's heart. When she ended her prayer session, she turned to find Becky in her daily pew, on her knees and her head down in silence. Sister Ruthie entered through the side door and walked over to Mother Marie. Glancing over to Becky, she asked her how Becky was holding up. All she could do was shake her head and left for her office. Sister Ruthie joined Becky and stayed by her side. When Becky sat back, she put her hand into Sister Ruthie's and they just sat.

Her prayers that morning had been for God to give her words to comfort and a way to answer all their questions, in just the most delicate way they could understand. In her mind, there was no reason why they had to leave. These children are well adjusted, behaved, happy and loved. There needs met more than many. Nothing made sense and she desperately needed Gods words, because she absolutely had none.

That day, Mother Marie cancelled school. Each child followed, one after the other and then taken to another room, until all of them were told. When they were down to the last six, the youngest group, one of the Nun's, called Mother Marie away. She asked Becky to wait until she returned and left the room.

Arlin was waiting for Mother Marie with news as to why this was all happening. After all the efforts and meetings, it had come down to just one simple explanation. When she entered her office, Arlin was sitting at her desk with his feet crossed on top. Now her patience was just about shot and with the look on her face, he quickly stood up at attention, but extended the biggest smile his face could possibly project.

She walked over to the front of the desk and said, "Please tell me you bring good news."

After having her sit down he said, "The simple, simple, simple reason is, there are not enough Nun's for the amount of children! For every five children, one Nun, for six babies two. Then he went on, Becky and the entire community does not count. You're one Nun short for their acceptance."

Mother Marie stood up and started pacing the room, then asked, "If I can bring in another Nun?"

Arlin interrupted her saying, "Yes, one Nun."

"But it still seems to me they will just continue on, looking to find some loophole to take these children," she replied.

"I have talked to the Governor and he has agreed to stop all action, if, the Church will bring on another Nun. He stated and then just unexpectedly, as Merriam had suggested in a private conversation, he blurted out, "The only other alternative is for Becky to adopt the little ones."

Smiling with a new enthusiasm, she said, "That might just be the right way to go. It may be months before I could transfer another Nun."

Then Arlin said, "Let's ask Becky if she is willing to take on this enormous responsibility. She would need to do the adoption while I still have the Governor's support, elections are coming up and another Governor could see things in a whole different prospective." As Mother Marie opened her office door, she caught Sister Ruthie in the hall and asked her to bring Becky to her office at once.

Becky came as soon as Sister Ruthie gave her Mother Marie's request. The first thing she asked when she reached the door was, "What's happened now?"

Arlin asked her to take a seat and went on to say, "We have something extremely important to ask you." Her emotional state had gone from anger to shear exhaustion and she felt numb until Arlin asked, "Becky? Are you willing to adopt the six babies?"

She looked up at him with an astonished look; her eyes welled with tears as she turned to Mother Marie for assurance to what she had just heard. Mother Marie nodding her head saying, "Yes!" Becky's head fell into her lap and with her hands pressed against the sides of her face, she lifted back up, with her fingers now covering her lips, she paused for a moment then asked, "Please, tell me I'm not dreaming that this moment is real. That is not a question! It's a miracle, a wonderful, gracious miraculous gift from God!"

Arlin went over the details with her for the requirements for adoption. With all she had done over the past six years with the orphanage, things could move quit rapidly. He, being the judge for the county and with the governors support, it was a matter of formality and completing all the steps according to the laws. "First," he said, then, I will do background checks on both you and Sam. There will be an inspection of your home with interviews, a psychiatric evaluation, which will not be any problem at all, from whom I have found you to be. And then, two separate court hearings."

When he finished, Becky stood from her chair and said, "Please start these proceedings as soon as possible." Before she left, he told her and Mother Marie not to say a word to anyone until he had finalized all the paperwork.

Becky went back to the room where the younger children had been waiting and then took them home to play with Frankie in the back yard. Mother Marie instructed Sister Ruthie to take the other children to the recreation room for popcorn and games.

As the children played, Becky knew she could now let go of the worries she had carried for so long. She felt a new beginning had come and the peace that flowed through her body was like nothing she had ever experienced. Seven children, she thought to herself, yet not one fear or hesitation ever entered her mind. She new this was God's will for her and she was thankful for His divine intervention. How she would have survived them taken away or if she could have been strong enough, the Lord only knew. She remembered the words that her parents had left of them always watching over her and somehow felt they too had had a part in putting these gifts in her hands.

While the children played, Becky could not keep herself from giving Merriam and Sarah all the news that had transpired that day. She told them what Arlin had said about keeping this under wraps, but she knew how concerned they were and to her it didn't seem fair. They were both ecstatic with happiness, yet relieved at the same time. Becky laughed when she thought about how Sam's face would look when he came home and greeted by his seven children. With puzzled looks from their faces, Becky told them she was thinking of Sam's reaction to his new family. They returned her laughter as she went on describing each child stepping up to welcome their daddy home. Then suddenly realizing she had missed her weekly call, she asked Sarah if she could watch the children and headed straight in to the phone. This time, before she picked up the receiver, she gathered her strength and prayed for patience with the person she would be speaking to on the other end of the line.

Before she could make the call, the doorbell rang and Arlin was there with papers in hand. Looking at the size of his folder she said, "By the looks of all those papers, this is going to take a while. I think I should take the children back home." Then she laughed saying, "I won't have to take them very far, soon to be home." While she gathered the children, she asked if he could stay for dinner and said she would only be about an hour getting them settled. He said that would be fine and he would help start dinner while she was gone.

Walking the children through the Church, she stopped, then bowed her head and asked God's forgiveness, that she would be back in a short while to talk and pray. She had never missed her time on her way in and out to pray, with the exception of the storm and the special meetings with the community. She felt He deserved an explanation as she passed through. Mother Marie and Sister Ruthie tended to the children and sent Becky on, as they knew Arlin was waiting. She took her pew as usual before leaving, even though Arlin was waiting, saying to herself that the Lord comes before anything and anyone else.

After dinner, Sarah and Steven invited Frankie to go with them for ice cream. With Arlin and Becky deep into paperwork, Merriam looked at Frankie with a sad face and her bottom lip stuck out. Frankie just had to ask if she could go too. With everyone laughing, Becky turned from the table and asked, "Frankie!" I think they owe you a double scoop, don't you?"

With the biggest smile and his irresistible dimples he answered, "Yeah!" Then he danced as he led them out the door.

When Arlin had finished explaining his papers and getting Becky's signature on all of them, she had some question she needed him to address. Her biggest concern was the fact that her husband missing in action, and if that would effect the adoption. Arlin answered, "He is missing in action, "Yes", but the status is, he is in the military, in duty and you have his power of attorney over all his matters. Therefore, there is no problem. The background checks should be back within a week to ten days. After that, I will schedule your first hearing. At that time I will require you to have a physical and mental evaluation with physicians appointed by the court," he explained.

Then Becky asked, "How long do you think all this will take?"

He said, "We're looking at maybe ten days on the background checks, then another week for the hearing, that's close to three weeks. The physical should not take more than two weeks to get all the results back and the mental evaluation, about the same. Therefore, we are looking at six to eight weeks in all. And I will push as hard as I possibly can to have this all wrapped up before Christmas."

"What a perfect time to begin our new life together as a family!" stated Becky. Then she asked, "Would it be out of line to ask if I could tell Sam's mother and father what's happening?"

He replied, "I know how much it would mean to you and to them, but we must wait until we complete all the requirements. I just want everything to go as smooth as possible without any clinches to get in our way."

Taking his words to heart, she said, "Well, I suppose your right and I trust that you have our best interests at heart."

Early the next morning, Becky changed her normal routine. After her shower and a quiet cup of coffee, she headed for the Church. Alone with God, she prayed for His guidance, and then waited in silence. Within moments an urge came over her to make her regular call, that had completed slipped her mind. Immediately standing and thanking the Lord, she ran back to the house.

This time when she called, someone put her on hold. Staying focused, she waited and finally the man came back on the line. He explained there had been another unit sent to the same place that reported sighting Sam, except this unit had gone further into the area. Then he said, "Two of our men watching an enemy camp, saw a man fitting your husbands description. He seemed to be well and he had free run inside the compound. After a few days, the camp moved and our unit had to pull back. There will be more men sent into that area, but that is all I can tell you at this time. We will keep you informed as we hear, and please, feel free to call whenever you like."

Becky thanked him and laid down the phone, quietly whispering, "He'll be home soon." With this news, her hope was now stronger than ever.

By Thanksgiving, Becky had had her first hearing. Arlin ordered her physical and mental evaluations and requested the results by no later than the fifteenth of December.

December sixth Becky had her physical with an appointment scheduled for her first visit to the psychiatrist. After three, one-hour sessions, put together in two weeks, Arlin received the result. According to the psychiatrist's findings, his evaluation found her extremely well adjusted, especially with all the tragic happenings over the past few years. On the nineteenth, Becky received notice by mail with the date of her final hearing.

During the week before the last hearing, Arlin had done his interviews with the children. He asked specific questions concerning their feelings towards Becky and Frankie. Each one had given him their own versions of how much they loved them and at times, Arlin had to contain himself from laughing, with all those unique answers and such serious little expressions.

The morning of the final hearing, she called the defense department to see if any more news had come in. They could only tell her the units were on their way and it could take months before they received any additional updates. Becky thanked him and said, "I do apologize for my behavior in the past, and I pray you can forgive me." The man on the other end told her there was nothing to forgive. Under the circumstances, he thought she had been doing quit well.

Mother Marie had told Becky to take off that day saying she and Sister Ruthie would meet her with the children at the courthouse. That gave Becky plenty of time to finish the odds and ends around the house. As she worked, her excitement flowed into Frankie. He followed behind her everywhere like a puppy, very confused, having to take his bath in the morning and not going to school. She washed the extra towels she had purchased and after folding them, carried them upstairs to put them away.

Frankie followed behind and broke his silence with questions, "Mamma? Why do we have all these beds? Why is there no school today? Are grandma and grandpa coming?" Then he announced, thinking he was right about his grandparents coming said, "There's a great big cake in the figerator!" Becky could hardly keep her face straight as he went on and on. "Look, mamma!" Pulling her by the hand into one of the bedrooms, there's a baby bear on all the beds. Who did that?"

She smiled as she looked down at his serious little face with such deep concern and told him, "Well Frankie, I like baby bears." His face softened to a smile and he forgot all his other questions. She wanted him to be just as surprised as all the others when they would realize they would be coming to live with them. It was, to her, extremely important for them to experience the whole ordeal together as a new family. After they dressed and prepared to leave, Frankie started asking his questions again. Becky would just change his directions with, "Did you brush your teeth? Are you ready for a fun day?" Holding the front door open, she distracted him again saying, "Let's go."

It was a closed, private hearing and Frankie became frightened by the stillness of the large courtroom. Quietly the two of them sat as Arlin entered from his chambers, along with the court reporter and three other men. Asking them to stand, Arlin took his chair and said, "Court is now in session." Frankie lightened the atmosphere by waiving at Arlin and all he could do was laugh. After he composed himself, he asked Becky to stand. Calling her name, "Rebecca Malloy", he started, the court has completed the required evaluations, finding you both physically and mentally competent to adopt these children. He asked, "Do you have anything to say at this time?"

"Yes, I do your honor. She replied. Then, I want the court to know; the raising of these children will be good and loving. Adding, God made this day possible and I praise Him for this miracle."

Arlin asked, "Do you, Rebecca Malloy take these children as your own?"

She replied, "Yes, I most certainly do." Arlin leaned down to the bailiff and requested he bring in the children.

Mother Marie walked them in, each holding the others hand in line with Sister Ruthie bringing up the rear. Standing at attention, with their little faces covered in confusion, Arlin walked around to stand in front of them. Frankie whispered to Becky, "Mamma', he's wearing a dress!" Becky softly chuckled and quieted Frankie to listen.

Arlin knelt down and asked, "Do you want Becky to be your mother? Would you like Frankie to be your brother?"

Yeses echoed throughout the room. Frankie stood up saying, "Yes, yes, yes," until Becky had him stop. Mother Marie stood with tears streaming down her cheeks.

He returned to address the court and starting with Nathan, he said, "Nathan!" Your new legal name is now Nathan Azmon Malloy. You may go sit with your mother. Sarah Jane!" Your new name is Sarah Haniel Malloy! You may go to your new mother too. "Kayla!" Your new name is Kayla Elzabad Malloy, and you may go to your mother. "Joseph!" Your new name is Joseph Benhail Malloy! You can go to your new mother. "Christopher!" Your new name is Christopher Darda Malloy! You can go sit with your mother. Last, but not least, "Michael"; your new name is Michael Colhozeh Malloy! Now you may go to your new mother too."

When he finished, Becky had Kayla on her lap, her arm around Sarah and the boys crowding in from both sides to give her a hug. Frankie stood in front of Becky, his face illuminating with joy, without understanding, yet in total acceptance. All the other children with their complete lack of this new concept through the excitement of the moment indulged themselves by absorbing the love they shared with Becky from nearly the beginning of their lives.

It was taking quite some time to settle them down, so Mother Marie clapped her hands twice, bringing them to a full quieted attention. Taking her last control, she instructed them to follow Sister Ruthie to the van and quietly take their seats. She looked over at Frankie, and with a warm loving smile said, "You too Frankie." He quickly took his place in line, but could not resist dancing his way out of the courtroom. Becky told Mother Marie she would be just a few minutes and she told Becky to take her time that they would wait for her in the van.

Becky followed Arlin into his chambers to sign and notarize all the documents. He explained to her, that the copies he gave her today were only temporary and she would receive the originals in the mail within a few weeks time. She invited him to the house for the celebration she had planned and gave him a hug saying, "Thank you so much for all you have done. You are a God sent blessing and I will always be grateful."

Sarah and Merriam were waiting by the van when Becky walked out of the courthouse. After all the congratulations she had received with hugs, Mother Marie told Becky to take her seat in the van and ride with her children. She rode back to the house with Sarah and Merriam waited for Arlin. Becky leaped into the van and as she did, she grabbed Sister Ruthie's hand, giving her a mischievous grin said, "Let's just wait for everyone to leave." Waiving and motioning to Merriam that is was all right to leave them, she waited until they drove away. Then she and Sister Ruthie turned around to the children and Becky asked, "Would you like to have a party when we get home?" The seatbelts could barely contain their enthusiasm and Becky let them hoop and holler all they wanted. Sister Ruthie started singing and they all sang along through the entire ride home.

Pulling into the drive, Frankie asked, "Mamma? Are all those beds for us kids now?

She turned and replied, "You bet they are!"

And he told the children, "Come on, mamma put baby bears on all your beds, too!"

What a celebration they had! Mother Marie had to take over twice by clapping her hands, once for dinner, then again for cake and ice cream. Becky sat back and said to calm Mother Marie, "Today is their day. They can run, play and be just as happy as they want to be."

It took; it seemed, like forever, to settle them into bed that first night. With Merriam and Sarah's help, they finally went down. Becky did her rounds, tucking each one in, finishing off with Frankie. She asked him if he was happy to have them for his family and Frankie asked, "Do we really get to keep them here with us?"

She answered, "They are all ours now, to love and share good times and sometimes some bad times too. When we all take care of each other and say our prayers, we will always be a happy family."

"I love you, mamma, said Frankie, and then, I wish daddy was here too, so we could love him."

Holding back the tears and through the lump in her throat she managed to say, "We will always love daddy and we'll keep saying our prayers for him to come home."

A peaceful quiet filled the house as Becky walked to the kitchen to join Merriam and Sarah. They sat reminiscing over the children's excitement through the day and how

God, gracefully, in only a way He could, ending this chaotic mess. Then Merriam reminded Becky about the rehearsal for the Christmas Eve service and asked her her plans for Christmas. She said she had been giving that some thought and with all the confusion the children had been through, she decided to spend Christmas like they had last year at the orphanage. Sarah thought that would be a great idea and Merriam said she would let Mother Marie know first thing in the morning.

With Christmas just a few days away, Becky would need all the help she could possibly get to finish her shopping, keeping up with music lessons and the Christmas program. Sarah told her not to fret saying, "Sally will be home tomorrow and we will help all we can."

On her knees that night at the side of her bed, after the emotional splendor of the miracle she had received, she told God, "I don't know the words to truly express what you have given me. A thank you and a blessing is all I can think of with everything that is going through my mind. Your love for these children and me more than proves you are a loving God, with far more purpose than I could ever dream. I thank you so much for this love and all your gracious understanding. Stay with me Lord and help me be the mother these children need so desperately and deserve. In Jesus name, I pray, Amen."

Five a.m., Becky woke to find Kayla and Sarah tucked in on each side of her. Even though her day would be hectic, she took the time to cherish these peaceful tender faces. Then after a while, she needed to get herself into action and start their day as well. Gently waking them and climbing over to the floor, she stopped! Joseph was sleeping on the floor, not far from Kayla's side. Becky wondered about their special connection and had a strange feeling these two were in all rights, actually brother and sister. Crawling off to the bottom of the bed, she thought, "Something else to put on my list of, "to do's!" and though the orphanage my not give her or even have that information, she would find someway on her own to settle her question once and for all.

With the kids all out of bed, Becky showed them where to find their clothes in the dressers and closets. She threw herself together and started breakfast. The doorbell rang just as they sat down to eat and when she opened the door, there stood Richard, Dusty and their brand new baby. "What a wonderful surprise!" Becky said and then, come in." She hugged Richard and Dusty handed Richard the baby, then took her turn with a long amative embrace. Releasing each other in tears, they quickly turned their attention to the baby.

Dusty said, "This is little Richie."

Placing him in Becky's arms, Becky looked into his bright little eyes and said, "Well, how do you do little Richie! You are so precious!"

Richard asked, "Where's Frankie?" Becky busted out in laughter and guided them into the kitchen. The look on their faces when they saw seven children at the table, made Becky's day. She introduced the children, and then told them she had adopted them.

Ending with, "This is my family."

Dusty kissed and hugged her again saying, "I'm so happy for you."

About that time, Sister Ruthie came in to help get the children ready to go and rehearse for the Christmas program. She told Becky after practice she would feed them lunch and Merriam would take them for their music lessons. The rest of the afternoon, they could play in the game room. "This", she told Becky, Will give you time to do your shopping and visit with your friends." Becky apologized and introduced Sister Ruthie to Richard and Dusty. Sister Ruthie welcomed them and asked if they would be here for the holidays. Richard said they would and told her he looked forward to seeing the program they were rehearsing.

"The children should be just about ready to go." Said Becky, and then asked, did everybody brush their teeth?"

Answers of, "Yes," came back with smiles from each little face. Richard had to laugh. Sister Ruthie clapped her hands twice and they formed a line to follow her out the door.

Frankie said, "Bye mamma," with six more echoes of the same as they walked through the door.

After cleaning up the dishes, the three of them sat down with a cup of coffee. Both Richard and Dusty could not believe how Becky's life had turned out. They caught up on the past years they had lost very quickly and wound-up with all the activities they planned for this day. Staying with Becky through the holidays would give them more time to visit. Knowing what Becky had left to do, they were eager to get busy and help.

Sarah and Sally joined then for the shopping, so Richard decided to visit the base and let the ladies hit the mall. Not only did Becky have to take care of all the gifts she needed, she had to do her grocery shopping as well. Tomorrow was Christmas Eve and there would be no time for any last minute shopping. She expected to be up all night finishing her wrapping and getting the packages over to the tree in the recreation room before dawn.

A toy store in the mall became the perfect solution for the twenty-four gifts to buy. Sally had a ball! She found great gifts and before long, Becky's list, narrowed down to the groceries, with the exception of one more store. The older children watched television on a small black and white set. She found the biggest color television possible and arranged to have it delivered Christmas Eve night.

Everyone carried in sacks of groceries and gifts in from Sarah's car. Sally asked Becky, "If it is alright with you, I will get these packages wrapped and tagged?"

Then Sarah jumped in and said, "I will help Sally wrap just as soon as we get these groceries put away."

In a bit of a shock, Becky replied, "If you really want to, it's more than fine with me." By the time, Sister Ruthie marched the children home, the wrapping was complete and dinner was cooking on the stove. Sarah had the children entertaining, while Sister Ruthie and Becky packed the gifts over to the orphanage to place them under the tree. Becky was so thankful for all the help and stopped on her way home to pray, thanking God once again for all the people He guided to help her in so many ways.

Breakfast Christmas Eve, Becky and Dusty made banana pancakes in shapes of snowflakes, animals and stars. They had a great time watching how the kids would pick through the stalk for their favorite shapes. Afterwards, she had them washing themselves up from the sticky syrup and changing into their dress clothes for a party at the orphanage.

The party consisted of the Nun's reading and telling the story of Christmas and singing carols the children loved so dearly. They served cookies and punch, then a gift exchange between the children. By eleven they were back home to have a small lunch and a nap before the evening program. Looking over their dress clothes, now stained with the treats from the party, Becky and Dusty had to wash and pressed each outfit. Richard took care of Richie the entire time that Becky and Dusty washed, and then they served dinner and dressed the children for Church. They were all feeling tired, but with the amusement they found just watching the kids, lifted their spirits and kept them going.

Stone and Bessie's program extremely impressed the entire congregation. The candle light service and choir was breathtaking. The children sat like little soldiers during communion and not one peep heard during that time of silence. Ending the service, Father Mathew said, "I'm going to speak for everyone here tonight and say just this!" "We are all blessed far beyond our wildest dreams!" "Amen."

Christmas morning, after breakfast, everyone dressed for Church. After the service, Becky's family and friends joined Father Mathew, all the Nun's and children at the tree to receive their gifts. Then while the children played, everyone else worked in the kitchen to serve the Christmas feast by noon.

By two, the children were home and down for their naps, giving the grown ups time to relax. Dusty and Becky took off their shoes and sat together on the couch with their feet propped up on the coffee table. Richard put Richie down for his nap and took one as well, leaving Becky and Dusty alone for the first time since they arrived to talk. Becky went over the tragic events of her parent's accident, telling Dusty how close they had become and still wondering why it had happened. Pausing to gather her thoughts, she went on to say, that somehow they had a part in her adopting these kids and knew they are always watching over her. In the same breath, she said, "I pray they are with Sam, too." Dusty told her how sorry she was for not being able to be with her during that time of sorrow and vowed between them, to never let the other go through anything like that again alone.

Frankie was down stairs first from his nap, asking as he walked down, "Mamma, can we call grandma and grandpa? I want to tell them Merry Christmas." Over all the confusion of the past few days' events, Becky was pleased that he had brought them to her attention. She had planned to call them when they came home from the courthouse, but lost tract of time. Without hesitation, she immediately dialed the number and handed the phone to Frankie. Calmly he greeted Anna with, "Merry Christmas." Hearing her voice, his enthusiasm grew; talking just as fast as he could, he told her he now had six new brothers and sisters. Then kept up his pace with each of their names and everything he could think of about them. Becky sat listening and laughing with his descriptions. Then as the other children came down stairs, she told them their grandma and grandpa was on the phone and wanted to say hello.

Joseph took the phone next and quietly said, "Hello, my name is Joseph Benhail Malloy, and then he asked, Are you really my grandma?"

Anna, completely baffled, simply answered, Yes."

He quickly handed the phone to Christopher next and he said, "Merry Christmas."

Anna asked, "What is your name?"

Without hesitation he answered, "I am Christopher, and I like to play the banjo."

"Will you play for me sometime?" she asked.

Shyly he said, "Yes, grandma, I will."

Joseph stood beside Kayla when she took her turn and in her meek faint voice whispered, "My name is Kayla."

Joseph took the phone and said, "Her name is Kayla Elzabad Molloy, as he quickly put the receiver back to her ear.

"Well, Hello, Kayla Elzabad!" How are you?" she replied.

Kayla answered, "I'm fine."

When Michael took the phone, he courteously passed it to Sarah. She said with a stern voice, "My name is Sarah and I'm going to be eight years old."

"I'm your grandma." Anna returned, adding, I'm going on sixty years old." Sarah's eyes grew as big as light bulbs and she handed Michael the receiver.

He said, "Merry Christmas. My name is Michael."

Before Anna could answer, Nathan said, "Merry Christmas, too. My name is Nathan and I love you."

Quickly Anna answered, "We love you all too and Merry Christmas."

Nathan handed Becky the phone and she said, "Merry, Merry, Merry, Merry, Merry, Merry, Merry Christmas!"

Still in shock, Anna could only say, "What a wonderful gift of gifts." After a brief time of laughter, Becky collected her thoughts and explained all the events that had happened over the past weeks with the orphanage. She told her this was the only way she would be able to keep them without any more problems occurring. Anna was very happy for her and said they would love them all. Then Becky went on to tell her the news she had received from the defense department. Explaining it would be weeks or even months before she had any more information. Becky invited them to come and visit anytime. Anna told her, the soonest they could come would be in the spring, after the last chance of snow, and then Anna added, "The next time you come here, all the children will be able to come as well. Have they ever been anywhere, other than school away from the orphanage?" she asked.

Becky said, "No, not really, maybe to the doctor. We are going to have many outings and they will have so much fun on the farm! This has been a wonderful Christmas and I am and always will be very grateful." Anna agreed and asked Becky to keep her well informed of everything, and then everyone behind Anna wished her a Merry Christmas.

Richard had spent a lot of time during their visit on the base. One evening, after all the children and the baby were down for the night, He asked Dusty to join him on the patio to discuss something very important. He said, "I need to ask you something. First, where would you like me to be stationed?"

"I thought you were already assigned to San Diego?" she asked.

"Well; he said, I can transfer here or anywhere. My re-enlistment gives me that option. Adding, do you want to stay here near Becky or where we are?"

Catching her completely off guard she answered, "This is a big decision, going on to ask, do we have to choose right away?"

"No, he answered and then, it's just something to think about for our future. I know how much you and Becky enjoy your time together and remembered you telling me about how you would raise your kids to be as close as the two of you were, so I just thought you might like the idea."

Dusty said, "Let's not mention this to Becky unless we do decide to move here." Richard agreed and they came back in the house to find Becky fast asleep in her rocking chair. Dusty gently woke her and they all retired for the night.

Becky's eyelids weighed heavy for deep devotional prayer that night, she knelt down at the side of her bed and thanked the Lord, listing each one of the blessings she had received throughout the years. Her thoughts were stronger than ever on Sam. She asked God to keep him safe and to guide the men looking for him, keeping them out of harms way, bringing them all home to their families.

Richard and Dusty headed home New Years Day and Becky invited them to come back anytime and stay as long as they wanted. Dusty told her their time together had been wonderful and she hoped to be back soon. On their way out, Richard drove by the base and showed Dusty houses for sale. He said he was just showing her some ideas of what might be available.

She said, "You're really serious!" What about our parents?" She asked.

"We have to make our lives, our own. He answered and then, it's a nice place to raise kids and that is something to consider too, that's all."

Dusty changed the subject asking Richard, "Do you think they will find Sam? Or are they just telling Becky, that they might have spotted him, just to put her into a false hope?"

"Hope is good, Dusty, said Richard, adding, no one is giving her false hope. They do not tell someone they might have found someone for no reason. I couldn't find out anything at the base and that leads me to believe, they believe he is out there."

"Becky's hope is mine as well. I hope it is soon," she added sadly.

January second, up early, Becky prepared the children for school. Mother Marie joined in as Becky march them to the bus stop. After their prayer ritual, Mother Marie asked Becky to have tea in the garden, so they could just sit and talk.

They began their discussion with Mother Marie asking her what she thought of the children's middle names.

Becky looked her in the eyes, with a funny smile and said, "You are reading my mind!" Then, I have wanted to ask you about this for some time."

Mother Marie took out a piece of paper she had tucked in her pocket and began. "I have kept this so I would be able to go over them when we had a time, like today. "Nathan Azmon!" she read, then flowing from one to another, Nathan means given and Azmon means strong. Kayla Elzabad; Elzabad is a gift of God. Father Mathew named Christopher Darda, pearl of wisdom. Sarah Haniel! Sarah means princess and Haniel is grace of God. Father Mathew also gave Joseph his middle name, Benhail, which means, increase son of strength. And I named Michael, Michael Colhozeh. Michael meaning, like God and Colhozec meaning, all seeing." As Becky sat listening to each beautiful word she spoke, she had come to realize, all this had come together in the Lords way and His timing. The love and peace she felt at that moment was unlike any she had ever experienced.

Later on Becky said, "I have another question, but I'm not sure if you will be able to answer it or not."

"What's your question?" asked Mother Marie.

"Joseph and Kayla, are they related or maybe twins?"

"You are correct with your first question," stated Mother Marie, and then she added, I could not give you any history on any of the children. All the babies that have come here had nothing, no birth records, note or even clothing. They came wrapped in towels or odd blankets and left at the door. You have seen the bell they ring when a child is left and by the time one of us gets to the door, no one is there but the baby."

Becky sighed and then said, "I just can't understand how a mother could just walk away from such a precious gift."

With compassion Mother Marie said, "There are a number of reasons why they do, I pray for them and the pain they will live with for the rest of their lives. It has to be unbearable for them at birthdays, holidays and seeing someone else happily being a devoted mother. And, you think Joseph and Kayla could be in fact, brother and sister! Well, according to our records, Joseph came a week before Kayla. Even so, there could possibly be a connection between the two.

"Maybe not, replied Becky, then, it's just the way they interact together that gives me these suspicions and it would be helpful to know this information." With unanswered questions, Mother Marie walked with Becky to the side gate and ended their visit with an invitation to share some time again soon.

Chapter Eight

With all the help Sister Ruthie, Merriam and Sarah gave, it seemed to Becky, there had to be a way to organize to make her household more efficient. She thought of many chores she had put off and it was about time for her to get things in gear.

After walking the children to the bus stop, she always stopped to pray. Sister Ruthie, twice a week would accompany her home to help do laundry. Merriam would come in every day, but her time was short with all her club meetings and activities. Sarah would be home in the evenings and weekends, leaving her with very little spare time to spend with Steven. Becky felt they were giving up too much of their lives, for the life she had chosen.

She walked through the house, with pen and notebook in hand, asking herself, what would make this room better or could I put something here, maybe add this or take this out. By the time she was finished, her notebook was full. Realizing these changes and purchases would involve spending a large amount of money, she would need to go over her finances with Sarah.

After dinner while Becky and Sarah cleaned up the kitchen, Becky told her of the ideas for the house, saying, "I want to make a few changes around the house."

Sarah replied, "O.K...." Becky handed her the notebook. She took the notebook, her cup of coffee and headed for the table. Gently anchoring her cup down, she turned to Becky and asked, "Two washers and two dryers?"

"That's a reasonable request when there are nine people in the house, don't you think?" asked Becky. Then Sarah sat and continued. Becky was starting to think she had over indulged, but when Sarah had completed her list, she was all in favor of every item. By the look on Becky's face, she could tell she was eliminating things from that list in her mind and Sarah got such a kick out of this, she hesitated to say anything. Then finally, Becky said, "O.K., I could do without this and maybe even that, but at least this."

Sarah busted out laughing until tears poured from her eyes. Hardly able to stop, she said, "Becky, I'm just kidding around. What you have on this paper would make a world of difference and you deserve them."

"But, can I afford to do all this?" Becky asked.

"Yes, dear!" she answered and then, you have enough for this, plus the biggest item not even on your list. With still much more than you will ever spend."

"What did I leave off?" asked Becky.

"A vehicle, one large enough to seat the children and two adults," Replied Sarah.

Becky said, "That had completely skipped my mind."

"Why don't you call the contractor you used after the storm and get an estimate, and this weekend Steven and I will take you car shopping. Sarah suggested, then, as far as the washers, dryers and all these little items go, we can take care of them after the construction is finished."

Becky thought she would pick back at Sarah a bit and said, "Thank you so much for being such a great husband and friend. I know I couldn't make it without you!"

Sarah smiled and laughed saying, "I had that coming."

She called the contractor the following day and as before came out to the house two days later. Becky explained the reasons for the changes and he gave suggestions, to not only improve their space, but also even give them larger rooms. The boys were currently sharing two rooms. He suggested taking down the walls to three rooms and building in the dressers to save space. "This house, he said, is so big and so well built, there's nothing we can't do." He liked Becky's ideas for the boy's bathroom, with three sinks, three tubs and three stools. The girl's bedroom was to be the largest, with a walk in closet, shelves and their own bathroom with two sinks, but only one tub and stool.

Next would be the laundry room. It had only a single washer and dryer crammed against a short wall going out to the back of the house. She told him she wanted two washers, two dryers and a few shelves. He asked, "Can I take this room and make it into something so fantastic you won't believe your eyes?"

"With the work that I've seen you do, you can have the entire job as your own personal project, she answered. Then she asked, how long will this take?"

In deep thought, he replied, "With my crew, we're looking at three weeks, possibly four. I can do this job, as I did before, with more help and cut the time down to two weeks or possibly three. We do have one problem! It won't be safe around the children and I have to have you out of the house while we do this construction." He gave her an approximate estimate and told her to call when she felt she was ready to get underway.

The following weekend, Sister Ruthie came to the house, while Becky, Sarah and Steven went car shopping. At a large dealership over thirty miles away, with many different vehicles to chose from, they began. Steven was hilarious! He brought out all the salespersons to see how many people would fit comfortably in various cars, vans and even small buses. Everyone was well entertained on that day! They finally agreed on a custom van. It was a special order for someone and then canceled for some reason or another. As luxurious as a van could be, it had a price tag to match. She couldn't bring herself to trade in their van, there were just memories she wanted to hold onto and when Sam came home, that would be a decision he could make.

While the dealership washed and checked out the van, Steven took Sarah and Becky out to eat. Becky thanked them for all their help with this big decision and asked Steven if he would drive the van home. She told him she would rather drive around their small town to get used to its massive size without the traffic. Sarah, knowing how Becky drives, thought that was the greatest idea she had come up with all day. Becky smiled and wrinkled her nose at Sarah and they all laughed.

Later that evening, Sarah looked over the estimate the contractor had left with Becky and was extremely pleased with his price. Becky told her the only problem was, they would have to be out of the house for two to three weeks. With a helpful suggestion, Steven asked, "What about an extended spring break? The kids get ten days, not including the weekends, adding a few more which won't hurt them and there you go, go on a vacation."

"What a great idea!" replied Becky.

Then Sarah said, "There's one problem. Asking, who is going to be able to go with you? We can't take any extra days off."

Becky thought for a minute and asked, "How about Sister Ruthie? Do you think Mother Marie would let her go?"

With a puzzling look on his face, Steven said, "We'll figure something out."

Mother Marie was reluctant at first, but Father Mathew told her it would be a good experience for her and then she agreed. Becky called Anna with her plans and said they would leave in about two weeks. "Everyone will be so happy to see you and all the kids."

Said Anna and then she asked, "Any news, honey?"

Becky replied, "None yet, but it will come."

The next day Becky scheduled the construction to begin the same day they were to leave. Everything was set and she told Sarah, Sister Ruthie, Merriam and Mother Marie, that she was not going to tell the children until they were on their way. She planned to pack while they were in school and have the van ready to pull out right after dismissal.

Those two weeks flew by for Becky and Sister Ruthie. They shopped for clothes, sleeping bags and planned their agenda in between their regular routines. Sister Ruthie also planned to have snacks, sandwiches, water bottles and games to play as they drove. Becky worked out her map with Steven and Sarah the evening before they left. She had never driven on a road trip and Sister Ruthie would be of little help, except to read the map while Becky drove. Sarah wrote every highway change on paper for Sister Ruthie to read and watch for signs.

The day of departure, while the children were in school, they loaded the van early and Becky told Sister Ruthie to take a good nap for the long night ahead. Becky signed over a few checks to Sarah for anything that might come up with the construction and signed a temporary power of attorney.

Unable to sleep or even rest, Becky made her call early to get new information on Sam. With no news, she walked over to the Church. Mother Marie was with a young couple, showing them around. Becky watched from her pew and thought maybe they were there going over how a marriage ceremony went. She fondly remembered her wedding, first in the little Chapel and than again at her parent's home. In her thoughts, she wished them well and then prayed they had the love she and Sam shared. In silent prayer, she focused her thoughts. Mother Marie soon was by her side. When Becky raised her head and realized she was there, they prayed together, as they had on numerous occasions. When it was time to meet the children, they walked to the bus stop discussing her trip. Mother Marie seemed a bit worried and Becky somehow sensed that feeling. She explained that they were not heading out in a rush to get there. Then assured Mother Marie of her concerns and with her mind eased; Becky told her she would call as soon as they arrived.

Lining them up after they emerged from the bus, Becky walked them straight home. She sent them into the house to change into their play clothes and waived goodbye to Mother Marie as she stood in front of the Church looking on. Sister Ruthie was inside rushing them along and Becky waited by the van. When she brought them out of the house, Becky told them they were going for a ride. Sister Ruthie drove first a while and Becky told the children they were going to their grandma and grandpa's farm. With that, that is all she had to say, Frankie took over with all his stories of his last trip.

With all the potty stops, fueling and meal times, they arrived just in time for supper that next night. Becky and Sister Ruthie were beat! Anna took over the children and they unloaded the van. The kids ran and played so hard, Anna had them down for the night by eight. Sister Ruthie loved the farm, walking around to see the animals and the different flowers Anna had planted so beautifully around the house. Becky sat in a rocker on the porch, absorbing the cool evening air and dozing peacefully. By the time, Sister Ruthie and Anna came to join Becky on the porch she was sound asleep. Sister Ruthie gently woke her and they joined the children in one of the largest bedroom. It had two single beds against either wall, with lots of space for the seven sleeping bags cradled about the floor. Anna handed Sister Ruthie a flashlight to guide their way through the room and bid them a good night's sleep before she left them.

At breakfast Frankie asked, "Mom? Do we get to wear those boots and covercalls this time?"

She corrected his word saying, "Overalls, Frankie."

"No, Mom, grandpa said they are covercalls." He repeated.

Anna laughed and said, "He's right!" Grandpa did teach him that. Then she said, you kids put on your jackets today. It is going to get cold. You may get to see it snow in the next few days."

By Tuesday night, six inches of snow had already fallen and the weather bureau was calling for eight inches more by dawn. Unable to play outside, they watched the snow fall from the windows for hours. Frankie was too little to remember his first snow experience, so for all the children it would be a new one together. Becky spent the day reading to them and playing games, while Sister Ruthie helped Anna in the kitchen.

The following day when the weather had cleared, it had left behind a glittering white wonderland. Becky gave Sister Ruthie a camera with several extra rolls of film saying, "We have seven albums to fill, full of all the special memories a book can hold. "So have a blast!" By the time they caught up with grandpa and the kids, there were snow angels everywhere. When Sam's brother showed up they taught the kids how to make snowmen. Sister Ruthie had snapped pictures all day and Anna finally took her in the house. She did not have gloves on and Anna stated she looked like she was freezing to death.

All the family came to meet the kids. They brought in all kinds of food and gathered in the living room, dining room and kitchen. It was far too cold to have a picnic outside, but they made do with the space they had. When they finished eating, grandpa had the kids and uncles get out their instruments and they taught the kids their kind of country music. Grandpa could not believe how fast the kids picked up on the beat and remembered the words. By the end of the day, they took over the music and put on a show for everyone.

Over those two weeks, Sarah had followed Anna's every step. She enjoyed cooking and especially making cookies. Kayla on the other hand, stayed close to Joseph. All the boys stuck together like glue right behind their grandfather all day, everyday. Sister Ruthie said she had never had such a memorable experience in her life and hoped to come again someday.

All the snow had melted and the weather bureau forecasting the possibility of another major storm on its way, Becky thought they had better call Sarah to see how soon the house would be finished. She informed Becky the house had been completed two days ago and what a relief for Becky to be able to get the kids home before the next storm would hit.

Their time had come to an end with no one ready to go home. Anna and Sarah talked Kayla into helping make sandwiches and snacks for the road. Then, for the first time Kayla smiled and enjoyed her time away from the boys. Becky had them carrying their sleeping bags and luggage to the van for Sister Ruthie to arrange. The goodbyes were tearful for the kids, but Becky lifted their spirits saying they would come back maybe in the summer to visit again. The drive home seemed much faster. The kids slept a lot more and they had a few less stops. Sister Ruthie wrote down the directions in reverse order and overall, Becky thought they had done a great job. Anxious to see how the house had turned out, kept Becky's mind occupied while she drove. But one of her first priorities would be to make her call she was now two weeks behind on and for her, even though they may say the same thing, it didn't matter.

Pulling into the driveway late Saturday afternoon, Steven and Sarah were waiting. They had taken Becky's notebook and along with Merriam and Mother Marie's ideas, managed to cover and set up everything on Becky's list. The washers and dryers were in place and ready to use. Hampers were set up for whites, colors and darks. They bought more towels, washrags and bedding. All the bathrooms had colorful throw rugs and the kids clothes neatly placed in their spaces. With nothing left to do on the list, they figured Becky could get some rest from her trip.

The kids were full of energy as they climbed out of the van. Becky put it to good use by letting them help carry their stuff in the house. They were eager to help and it did not take long at all. After they had been to their rooms, they called to Becky to come see. She followed Sister Ruthie up the stairs and everything was perfect! The kids loved their rooms and the colors the contractor had chosen were beautiful, bright and cheery.

Leaving them to settle in, Becky made her way to the laundry room. With Sister Ruthie not far behind, they found the room amazing. It was so spacious, with long folding tables and racks to hang clothes, cabinets for storage and even a separate place for the brooms and mops. Becky turned to Sister Ruthie and said, "This makes me want to do laundry!" The first thing in next morning, she called the contractor and gave him a well-deserved thank you.

Sally was on her break the week after Becky returned and she helped Sister Ruthie put albums together as Becky had the pictures processed. Sister Ruthie had taken so many great shots; Becky ordered extras for her album too. Mother Marie brought over a box to Becky containing folders with medical records and pictures they had taken of the children. All the albums turned out fantastic, with plenty of room to add future special memories.

Very ashamed and feeling like she was loosing her mind, Becky stopped what she was doing and called the defense department. As she dialed the phone, she lectured herself and said she should wear a sign around her neck or even a heavy string that would tighten on its own around her finger. The man on the phone only had information that the units had gone ashore about a week ago. No further information had come into their office. She closed her eyes for a moment and heard his words once again, "I will be back."

Even though those words always stayed with her, she was beginning to contemplate if she would ever see him again. She went out on the back porch, sat alone and cried. Sally watched from the kitchen window, only to cry herself for the pain she could not even imagine over so many years. Sister Ruthie, standing behind Sally said,

"God knows how much Becky needs these children at this time in her life and we must be strong to help her through whatever comes."

"Is Becky strong enough to go on without him if something were to happen, Sister?" asked Sally.

Placing her hands on Sally's shoulders she answered, "Only God can answer that question."

Nearing time for the children's dismissal, Becky came in the house and washed her face. Sally had gone home and Sister Ruthie walked with her to the bus stop. As they waited, Becky started talking, "It's so hard sometimes to hold on, not knowing if he's hurt, suffering or hungry. So many worries enter my mind. I give those to God, yet with time going on and on, I get to the point where I cannot give them to God fast enough before another enters my thoughts. I love my kids and I am very blessed with each one. It's very selfish to say, but I need my partner, the other half of my whole being." Sister Ruthie kept quiet to let her say exactly all she had been keeping inside for so long. Then, "Do these feelings make me a bad Christian?" she asked.

"Not at all, Becky!" stated Sister Ruthie, and then, God knows how you feel and He is doing everything He can right now. Sometimes we have to be patient a lot longer than we feel we should. He knows what He is doing and in the end, we'll look back and say, "Wow", I never would have been able to accomplish what He has brought together."

"You are right!" Said Becky, then, I need to adjust my way of thinking and get a stronger positive attitude. The old Becky needs to emerge and take hold."

While the kids changed their clothes, Becky came up with the perfect way to spend the evening as a family. Sarah called as they were sitting down to dinner and told Becky she would be out late. Becky told her to have a nice time and that she and the kids were going to talk and look at their albums with popcorn and kool-aid in our pajamas. "I'm jealous!" replied Sarah and then, "We haven't had a pajama party in a long time."

They laughed and Becky said, "We better have one soon then."

Shocked and amazed was Becky! When the kids finished their dinner, they all started working together cleaning up the kitchen. Sarah took her chair to the sink and Kayla put the dishtowel over the back of hers and then slid the chair to the sink beside Sarah. The boys collected the plates and silverware, then took them over to Sarah and placed them on the counter. Frankie asked her for the dishrag and started wiping down the table. Joseph served Becky a cup of coffee and Nathan told her, "We want to help you too, like Sister Ruthie, Aunt Sarah and Mrs. Merriam do."

She sat back in her chair just smiling as she watched. When they thought the kitchen was clean, Becky said, "I have the best kids in the whole world."

Before leaving the room, they asked if they could go and play their music. Frankie said, "Mom", you can come too." Following them down the hall, she thanked God for the intervention that filled her heart with so much joy, especially on a day when she could use it the most.

After playing about an hour, Becky told them it was bath time. She said, "After your baths we will have a pajama party."

Sarah asked, "What's a pajama party?"

Becky answered, "You get into your pajamas and we have popcorn and kool-aid, we tell jokes or funny stories and all kinds of stuff like that." They ran upstairs like a herd of spooked rabbit's!

She made popcorn and kool-aid, and then set up napkins and paper plates on the coffee table, while they bathed. After checking them to see if they were clean and rewashing Christopher's face, they all gathered around the table.

"First!" she said, "I have something to give you." "These were put together by Sally and Sister Ruthie for you." She passed out the photo albums, personalized with a special picture on the front and their name. While they looked them over, Becky snapped pictures as they laughed and shared specific memories on the pages.

Later she pulled out her album and they all piled up by her side on the couch, as she showed them pictures of her life. Very slowly, came to the time when Sam came into her life. She told them he is their daddy now and someday he will come home to them. Becky answered many questions that night, but took her time and explained in ways they could understand.

Settling them into bed and tucking them in for the night, she picked up the living room and re-cleaned the kitchen. Then she returned to the couch and started looking through her album once again. When she came up upon the eight by ten photograph of them at the Chapel, she quietly wept, touching his face and then remembering their first kiss.

Over the next few days, she spent some time organizing a place for all her folders and paperwork. She looked through the folders Mother Marie had brought with the medical records of each child. Finding out for herself that Mother Marie was right, there was nothing on any of the children. They were all up to date on their immunizations and she made a chart to keep on the refrigerator door when they would be due again.

Sally stopped by early one morning and joined Becky and the kids for breakfast. They walked them to the bus and then Sally asked Becky if she would like to go with her to the mall. Becky asked, "I have a few things to do before I can go, if you don't mind waiting?"

"I have all day." Sally replied. Becky stopped in at Church as usual, Mother Marie beside her, motioned for Sally to join them. When Becky finally finished, Mother Marie and Sally were waiting outside.

"Sally tells me the two of you are off for a day at the mall," asked Mother Marie.

Becky looked at Sally and said, "I really can't stay the whole day, Sally."

Then Mother Marie told Becky, "We can look after the children until you get back." "I know you would. I really want to be here when they get out of school.

They need to know I will be here and if I can't, they need me to tell them why, ahead of time," explained Becky.

"You're a good mother, Becky," replied Mother Marie and then, you are right in your way of thinking. They do need the security that comes with love and trust."

Sally said, "There are only two stores I need to go in, so we could be back even before two."

"I do want to go to the music store and look at some sheet music. Becky added. Asking, Can we make it back by two if we leave fairly soon?"

With nervous excitement Sally answered, "No problem at all and if we get moving, I'll take you out to lunch."

Stone and Bessie cut the private music lessons down to three times per week. The school band had taken so much of Stone's time and Bessie having more students than ever; she had to spread them out with a new schedule. In addition, on top of all that, they were in charge of the music program for the summer festival. Becky arranged the children's lesson to be at home and helped Bessie all she could. In between the private instructions, they practiced together and all the kids were now playing extremely well. They had not set a theme for the festival and Becky, after hearing the country bluegrass style her brother in laws played, thought she would try to find some sheet music the kids might like to learn.

That day Becky found several songs to work on with the kids. Her favorite was, "The Sunny Side of Life." Bessie looked over the sheet music and she was thrilled and could not wait until Stone saw them too. Her favorite was, "Red Wing." This style of music she thought was unlike any the kids had ever heard. Becky told her about the country music they had learned while on the farm and told her they really enjoyed it. Bessie's suggestion to start them was to play repetitiously on the piano. She said that would initiate the beat into their minds and they would learn very fast. Bessie was so excited she called off the lessons she had scheduled for that day and stayed through the evening playing the pieces with Becky on the piano. She called Stone at school and told him she would be home soon, that Becky had found the music theme they had been searching for, for the festival. In the past years, it was always country music and it was good, but this would really make people dance. Bessie said, "Stone is going to be emphatically delighted. Then added; we have struggled to find something more, more hometown or down home. This music, with practice and special care, would be perfect. Becky? She asked, "Can you find more of this wonderful music?"

Becky replied, "When I found these at the music store, they had all kinds of this style and records too. I'll go back and see, or better yet, could you manage to take a few hours and go with me?" she asked.

Bessie answered, "With the schedule I have now and everything else to do, it would be at least a week before I could take time out."

Therefore, Becky wrote down the amount of copies they would need and Bessie told her to find the sheet music for all the instruments if possible. With her mindset, Becky told her she would go get them first thing in the morning.

Before eleven the next morning, Becky was back in town with records and a stack of sheet music, headed straight for Bessie's house. They sat and listened to several records between Bessie's private students. Nearing time for the children's dismissal, Becky chose two records to take home for the kids to listen too. She left the rest for Bessie to play when Stone came home.

Behind on her household chores, she let them go. As the kids changed into their play clothes, she grabbed snacks of apples, juice and cookies. She called them into the music room and had them line up chairs. Seated with snacks in hand, she quieted them and asked them to listen to the records she had found. Within minutes of starting the record, the snacks were of no interest and Becky watched their expressions of intense concentration.

Before the first side of the record was finished, they were picking up their instruments and figuring out the notes. She picked out one song and played it over, as Bessie had told her to do. Nearing dinnertime, Becky had not even thought about what she was going to prepare. At that moment, the doorbell rang. When she opened the door, Stone and Bessie rushed in with the biggest grins on their faces, bypassing her, as if they were going to put out a fire. Stone found the kids playing by the notes, but having problems coordinating with each other. He and Bessie jumped right in, setting up music stands and picking out through the stack of sheet music for each instrument. Stone turned off the record player, Bessie sat down with Sarah on the piano and he began to conduct them. With each mistake he would motion to keep on going, until they had ran through the entire selection. He turned to Bessie and said, "We're very rough around the edges here, but I see fantastic potential." Returning his focus, he started them again.

It was nearing eight-o-clock when Becky insisted they stop for dinner. While they sat at the table, you could see the music still flowing through their minds. Frankie, Christopher, Nathan and Sarah, were still humming. Michael bobbed up and down, while Joseph and Kayla swayed back and forth. As Stone, Bessie and Becky looked on, He said, "They are going to play the best I've ever heard!"

Kayla calls it, "Happy music." Becky stated.

"It is, replied Stone, and then added, and the best part is, they'll be ready just in time for summer fest. "What a festival we'll have this year!" Your extremely talented children are going to make this year, a year to remember forever."

"You mean you want my kids to play on stage?" Becky asked hesitantly.

"That's right, all seven." Stone firmly replied.

Bessie told Becky, "He has already planned the music from the records you brought over and the ones you have heard tonight."

Stone broke in, "We will start tomorrow, right after school." He stood from the table, told the kids what a good job they had done and before they left, he said, "Our schedules can be rearranged for this event."

After walking Stone and Bessie to the door, Becky returned to the kitchen table and said, "I am calling our first family meeting." The kids sat wide-eyed and silent, giving her their full attention. In a very serious expression she said, "Stone thinks you can be ready to play a whole bunch of these songs we played today, at the festival." With overwhelming excitement, they jumped out of their chairs and began dancing.

They pulled Becky from her seat to join in and Sarah starting a chain reaction of everyone singing out, "happy music", as they danced. Becky's next question was her concern over stage freight, but obviously, she did not need to ask. As they danced, she led them up the stairs to their rooms and held up a pair of pajamas, waiving bye. It took another half an hour that night to get them settled. Once she had tucked them in for the night, she went down stairs and did the chores she had let slide that day.

Merriam came in the next morning before Becky had a chance to make a pot of coffee. She told Becky the town committee for the festival had met the night before and elected her to take charge over the decorating, booths of handmade crafts, food carts and parking. In her loaded enthusiasm, Becky had to quiet her down. Stone had told them they would be practicing after school today and in his excitement, he had forgotten today was Saturday. She wanted the kids to sleep longer this morning, after the night they had had before. Knowing just how hard and long they would practice today, she wanted them to get plenty of rest.

Sitting to take her first sip of coffee, in flew Steven and Sarah. He said, "Stone called this morning. Sarah and I are going to Houston to pick up the harpsichord."

Becky, very unfamiliar with this, asked, "What's a chord?"

Sarah said, "It's a? It's like a piano, only different."

"O.K...." Becky replied.

Then Sarah continued, "Stone told us about the plans for your music and he located the harpsichord through the university. It has a lot to do with a specific sound he wants to achieve."

"Who is going to play this instrument?" asked Becky.

Steven answered, "Either you or little Sarah, Stone told us."

Then Becky stated, "I pray I'm not putting too much on these kids."

Sarah replied, "These kids play exceptionally well. How they have learned so much so fast, is beyond me."

At that moment, Mother Marie walked in hearing Sarah's statement regarding the children and said, "Abandoned children have a desperate need to please people for their love and attention. After all these years, I have watched so many and they will do whatever it takes for the love they long for. Once, a very nice couple adopted a boy, David, and the adoptive father was a professor who taught biology, David is now a marine biologist. I could tell you many other stories. So you see; God gives them talents or gifts to fit a purpose, each and every time."

Becky said, "That is the most loving gift, or should I say treasure from the Lord, any parent could possibly receive."

Steven started towards the door and said, "Well, Sarah, let's get going so we can be back before dark."

"God be with you," prayed Mother Marie.

After Becky had fed the kids, they were asking to play their new music. Knowing Stone would be in later, for hours of practice, she insisted they do their chores and then play outside until Stone and Bessie arrived.

Merriam, Mother Marie and Becky sat down to discuss Merriam's plans. Her first dilemma was the banners that would hang above the street. Each year they would put a banner with, "Summer fest, something?" She was stuck on the something for this year. Nothing they came up with sounded right, so they moved on. Merriam bolded stated, "But we can't move on!" Without our theme, there is no basis to move on too."

"Don't panic, replied Becky, and then, we'll come up with your something and Sarah is the perfect party organizer you'll ever find. She has helped me many times without a moments notice. And she will be here tonight."

Merriam was off to see Arlin, and Mother Marie headed back to the Church. "Mother Marie?" Becky asked, as she walked her to the door, "Could you send Sister Ruthie over for just a little while so I can join you in Church?"

"Of course, she answered, I'll send her right away."

Becky explained, "I have so much to be thankful for and still I am always asking for more."

Mother Marie replied, "You ask for things you truly need, Becky. He knows already what you will ask, but it pleases Him when you come."

By the time, Becky returned to relieve Sister Ruthie; the kids had her in the music room dancing as they played for her. Leaving them to play, Becky asked Sister Ruthie if she would like a cup of tea. While they sat, Becky filled her in on all the new music. She told Sister Ruthie about a song she had run across, asking her if she knew it, "The Sunnyside of Life." She also asked her if she, along with herself and a few others, would be interested in singing that song at the festival.

"Do you know what would really be fun?" jokingly Sister Ruthie asked, then, "Mother Marie has a beautiful voice, what if we could twist her arm into singing along?"

Becky pictured the stage in her mind with Mother Marie up there singing and swaying back and forth with a beautiful smile. Then she laughed and said, "It would be so out of her character, but in good taste. I'm sure God would approve. I have to work on a plan."

When Sister Ruthie left, Becky checked in on the kids and then called Anna to invite them for this special occasion. She had already asked them, but she wanted to make sure they would make a special effort. Anna was very excited and told Becky she would try her hardest to get everyone there. Next, she called Dusty. She informed Becky, they would be there within the next two weeks, saying, "Richard has transferred to Fort Hood. We are moving next week. I was going to just pop in on you, but with all you have going on, it's best to plan ahead."

"This is great!" Stated Becky, then, we will be raising our kids together and maybe in the same neighborhood."

Dusty went on to say, "We are expecting number two and the doctor told us, we're having twins."

"You better be careful, Dusty!" replied Becky, and she added, you could end up with as many or even more than I have."

They both laughed and Dusty said, "The more, the merrier."

Her calls taken care of, she fixed the kids a big meal for lunch and planned an easy dinner of sandwiches after their practice. The kids talked while they ate, about one song or another with so much enthusiasm that Becky just knew this event was going to turn out better than anyone could ever prayed for.

Shortly after lunch, Stone and Bessie arrived. He carried in another banjo, which seemed odd to Becky, because Christopher was playing both guitar and banjo already. They rearranged the music room to give them the atmosphere of the stage. Then Bessie had the children go outside to play for a while, all except Christopher and Frankie. Stone set up two stools, facing each other and had the boys working together on the banjos. Stone would have Christopher play an easy piece, while Frankie watched his fingers. Both boys picked extremely well on guitar, Christopher had been playing the banjo quit some time now, and he knew Frankie would catch on quickly. Sure enough, he did, and by the time, Steven and Sarah brought in the harpsichord; Frankie had played the piece Christopher had been showing him. Bessie sent them out with the other children for a break, while Stone checked the tune of the harpsichord. Bessie brought in little Sarah to show her, her new instrument. It was not even an hour before Sarah had it down.

Stone called all the kids back in and closed them in the music room together. He asked Becky not to bring in anyone during practice for the first week. He wanted their total attention until they were set.

Becky and Sarah listened from the living room and Steven returned the truck he had borrowed and came in later. The sounds from that room were totally, chaotic and went on that way for the first two days. With each day after that, it became more and more pleasant to the ear. In a week's time, just as Stone had said, they had come together and the sounds were beautiful.

Sarah and Merriam worked together on the plan of events, after Bessie told them Stone's theme, "Summer Fest Down Home." The banners were ordered and due to arrive within a few days. Merriam lined up the three woman's clubs in the community to set up booths and displays of homemade items they made for charity. A carnival was booked for rides and games for all the children. The volunteer fire department would have a booth doing blood pressure checks and handling all the emergencies that might arise. Merriam was pleased with all the arrangement now set, until Becky made a statement that she would be making the kids old fashion outfits to complete the down-home theme. Liking her idea, Merriam thought it would really be an event for the entire town to dress also. She immediately made some calls to get this into action.

Two weeks to go and Stone had pushed the kids with practice lasting five hours everyday and eight on the weekends. Not one child ever complaining as the music had become their passion. He realized this when they began pushing him. Before they would begin, Becky had them outside stretching and on every break as well.

During the day, while the kids were in school, Becky sewed Sarah and Kayla's dresses. With the weather being warm, she made them out of lightweight cotton. Full length, with each ruffle slightly overlapping the other, Sarah's dress was pink with white ribbons and Kayla's, white with pink ribbons. For the boys, she bought black dress slacks, short sleeve white cotton shirts and black suspenders and for all their hard work, cowboy boots and hats. Merriam came to help each morning, and then would hurry off to work on her own in the afternoons.

Each morning, Becky tried to convince Mother Marie into singing with her and Sister Ruthie. She would always tell Becky it would not be in good standing for her to sing on a stage. Finally, with Becky's irresistible allure, she said she would discuss it with Father Mathew.

Dusty and Richard arrived the week before the festival and Richard had to report to the base the day after they arrived. Becky had a smaller room fixed up for them and the baby. Not knowing how many to plan on coming with Anna, Sarah planned to stay at Steven's and bunk in with Merriam. They had two other rooms available for Becky's quests and Arlin had his whole house if needed. Becky told Richard and Dusty to wait and find a place after the festival, so she could watch the baby while they settled. This week she told them, was going to be so hectic, that she would need all the help she could get and then some.

Once Richard reported in, his commanding officer gave him another week to find a place. Instead of waiting for Becky, they went ahead and found a place on their own. Only two blocks away from Becky and well within their budget. With Steven and Arlin's help, they moved in and settled in two days.

Father Mathew approved Mother Marie to sing, only because he liked the song. So she came to Becky's, along with Sister Ruthie to practice. Stone had the kid's play, while they worked on the harmony. With Mother Marie's beautiful voice, Sister Ruthie and Becky blended right in tune.

The countdown was with only two days left to prepare. Becky had a dress fitting with the girls and had the boys try on their outfits too. After a few pictures, Becky felt there was still something missing, but just could not put her finger on it. She called Merriam while the girls were still in their dresses and she came over to see what Becky was trying to say. With one look, she told Becky she knew exactly what they needed and she would have them before the festival, and told her it would be a surprise.

On Friday, the day before the festival, Richard and Dusty came over for breakfast; and to help Becky with anything she had left to do. Dusty asked, "What is left on your to do list?"

Becky replied, "After I walk the kids to the bus stop and stop in at Church, I need to call the defense department, and then pick up groceries." Richard told her he would make her call and maybe they would tell him more of what was happening. Becky thought he may be right and gave him the number.

Dusty said, "I'll do the dishes and pick up, while you take the kids. That way, we will be ready to go to the store when you get back."

"Thank you guys, so much, replied Becky, and then, if I miss something, please jump right in there and have a ball!"

With Becky off and running, Dusty started cleaning and Richard made her call. He too was unable to get any further information than she had. There was still no word on the units search. Anna had called while Becky was out and she told Dusty they were on their way. Dusty asked her what time they thought they would arrive and she said about six. She told Anna they would wait dinner and Anna laughed saying, "You'll have to set ten extra places at the table."

Dusty came back with, "If you know Becky!" There will be plenty of food to feed an army."

When all Becky's relatives arrived, the kids were still practicing with Stone. She walked them quietly down the hall to listen without disturbing the beautiful sounds of a waltz named, "Westphalia." The rest of the evening was full of excited confusion. By nine-o-clock, Becky and Anna had the kids down and called it an early night themselves.

Chapter Nine

The big day had finally arrived! Stone was at Becky's door by four a.m., along with Arlin, Steven and Richard, to begin moving and setting up the instruments on stage. Everyone in the house was up and ready to go, with the exception of the children. She let them sleep as long as they could, for the day they had ahead of them.

Anna started them off with a hearty breakfast of bacon, eggs and her famous taters. Afterwards they played out back to relax and kickback, as Becky put it. They needed to unwind from all the practice and be able to play their music and have some fun.

When she finished her chores, she gathered the kids and took them to Church with her to pray. She began by thanking the Lord, "Dear Lord!" How do I begin to give you thanks enough for all the blessings in my life? You have blessed me with so many people, all my children, where can I possibly begin. Your glory, strength and loving grace has no words to describe what you have brought into my life. Bless you Lord, for everything you do. My thanks to you comes from the smallest of fibers of my being. Amen."

Then she had the children follow her in the Lord's Prayer. When they finished, she asked for each one of them, to thank God for everything and everyone He has given them. Joseph and Kayla knelt in quiet prayer and then the other kids followed.

Now this was Becky's second time to experience the summer fest. Last, year's crowd was large, but she had no clue of the number of people that were planning to attend this year's celebration. For the last week, the park had been under intense transformation. A dance floor made of wood completely surrounded the gazebo, and beyond that, rows and rows of chairs. Booths lined in rows, for displays of the crafters art that would come from all across the state. There were food trailers enough to feed the crowds with delights to please any taste. Then, beyond them, the carnival, with rides for all the children and games to play for prizes of stuffed animals and other trinkets. Merriam had hired parking attendants to direct the flow of traffic already lined up and waiting. By the time she walked the kids out of the Church, there were crowds of people everywhere. She had them take each other's hand, and then told them firmly to not let go until they were home.

When they walked into the house, she told them to go take their baths and put on their outfits. Then she said, "After you are all dressed and I fix Sarah and Kayla's hair, we will have a family meeting." She had become intensely concerned for their safety. With so many people and as friendly as the children were, she knew they needed to completely, understand the dangers of talking to strangers and their need to stay together at all times.

Frankie had instigated a plan a few days before, to buy their mother some flowers. They had pooled all the change they had saved to buy them. He had seen so many times, people coming out of the florist shop with beautiful arrangements; and on their faces, he saw the happiest smiles. He wanted to see Becky with one of those smiles from them.

His plan was to sneak out to the florist when no one would notice him being gone. The money weighted down his jean in all his pockets and Becky did not notice as she watched the kids heading up the stairs. Frankie trailed behind slowly, peering back to make his move as soon as she walked out of the room. Then, when he heard her talking to Anna in the kitchen, he snuck out the front door. As he rushed frantically, struggling his way through the crowd, he stopped to check the street for cars before he crossed. There on the corner, stood a man in uniform and he asked Frankie if he was lost. His little face was flushed with the anxiety to complete his venture as quickly as possible, but with the crowd, slowing him down, fear had filled his every thought. He replied to this man, "No sir, I'm not lost. I have to go over there to get my mother some flowers."

The man asked, "What is your name son?"

KAREN MALLORY

Frankie answered, "My name is Frankie Malloy, but I'm not allowed to talk to strangers."

The man said, "I need to buy some flowers too, asking Frankie, Would it be all right if I go with you?"

He replied, "Well sir, you can go, cause you are going there too." Inside the flower shop, Frankie looked over all the flowers and could not make a decision. The shop was crowded, so the clerk did not even notice him or the fact that he needed some assistance. He turned to the stranger and asked, "Can you help me? I have to hurry and get back home. My mom is going to be so mad. I'm not supposed to be here."

The man asked, "What flowers do you have in mind?"

Shrugging his little shoulders, answered, "I don't know." The man looked through the long glass enclosed case full of all sorts of arrangements and found a corsage, made with tiny rose buds that Lady's wear around their wrists. He pulled it out of the case and handed it to Frankie.

"This is very pretty. Said Frankie, and then he asked, how much does it cost?"

"What ever you have should cover it and I'll take care of it so you can get back home before you get into trouble." The man said. Frankie went to the counter, emptied all his pockets as the clerk rang up his purchase and secured the corsage in a box. The stranger winked at the clerk, as he laid down a ten-dollar bill without Frankie's acknowledgement.

He told the man, "Thank you for helping me", and then hurried out the door.

Working his way to cross the street again, the stranger followed along side. He asked Frankie all about his mother and his father. He told the man he had six brothers and sisters and they all lived with their mother and Aunt Sarah. He stopped for a moment just long enough to turn to him and say, "My daddy is coming home soon, mom told us and then we will be very happy. I have to go now, maybe you will see me and my brothers and sisters play our music at the park."

As Frankie tried to run through the crowd, the man said, ""It was nice to meet you, Frankie and I'll be sure to see you soon."

Frankie peeked in the door to make his break for the stairs. When he thought, he had it made, he creped upstairs to his room. There waiting was Becky, with her arms folded and a very angry look upon her face. Hiding the box behind his back he started apologizing, which at this point did him no good whatsoever. She laid into him a lecture like none he would ever forget. She was so upset; she could have canceled the entire day. As he brought around his hand with the boxed corsage, she melted her anger and explained how worried she was with all the strangers in town. She pulled him into her arms and gently squeezed him, and then apologized for not explaining the dangers earlier. He handed her the box and told her that all of them saved their money because they wanted her to have some flowers for today. She called all the kids into the room, giving kisses, hugs, and thank you's. Then she sat them down around the bed and laid down the rules for the day. Explaining what Frankie had done wrong and why she wanted a family meeting. She took in a deep breath and said sternly, "The next time any of you want to do something like Frankie did today, take Sarah, Merriam or someone I know with you." They all promised and she finished by telling Frankie to get ready fast!

Merriam arrived with a handful of dresses and a box for little Sarah and Kayla. She passed out the dresses to Anna, Sam's sisters, Sarah and Becky. Each made out of old dresses she had found at rummage sales and then remade them into beautiful long gowns. Inside the box, were two adorable bonnets, matching the dresses Becky had made. "That is the perfect touch to complete the outfits." Becky said. Merriam instructed all the lady's, to quickly change into her dresses because it was time to go. Sarah's dress was all the colors of a rainbow in tiny little flower patterns, finished off with a long green sash tied around her waist. Anna's dress was a pale peach with white polka dots, the sleeves, in a three quarter length that folded up just above the elbow. Around the waist, Merriam added a thin white belt. Sarah took Anna's hand and they waltz around the living room.

They could not believe how Merriam had done such a perfect job and Sarah asked, "How did you know what our sizes were?" Merriam said she had a good eye, when it comes to fashion and style. Becky came out next, Merriam had taken all the extra material from little Sarah's and Kayla's dresses and blended alternated the pink and white in the exact same overlaid ruffles with the ribbons used to tie long streams that hung down the back. It was the most beautiful compliment of the dresses she had made for her girls. Sam's sisters dresses were both powder blue with white sashes. Merriam embroidered flowers around the necklines and the bottom. She had out done herself on this task and everyone thanked her immensely. Sarah and Merriam took pictures with everyone in their outfits as hugs and thank you'd passed around.

Hand in hand, they walked the children to the park. Becky reminding them of her discussion earlier and telling them not to go anywhere unless one of them was with them. Stone and Bessie were in the gazebo organizing the sheet music to be right at hand for each child to easily access.

The children took their places, Richard and Dusty sat with Anna and her family many rows back from the front of the gazebo, as there were very few chairs left. Stone opened the celebration with, "Redwing" and the crowd gave them a standing applause as they began. Becky, Bessie, Sarah, Mother Marie and Sister Ruthie had chairs placed for them round about in the gazebo. That way, if any of the children needed something, one of them would be right there so not to disrupt the music.

As Becky looked on, one child to the next, she noticed their movements and expressions as they played. Sarah on the harpsichord, would be deep in her concentration, and then would glance up at Christopher or Frankie, smiling and nodding them forward. Kayla with a fixed warm smile looked only at Joseph when her eyes would leave her sheet music. Joseph, matching Kayla's notes precisely, looked stern in his expression as their bows glided across the strings of their fiddles. Moving her eyes to Michael, in her surprise, she found him sitting behind his drums, picking and playing a mandolin, while his foot kept the beat with the base drum. "Stone had found the prefect way to deal with his fidgets," thought Becky. His face beamed as he glanced over the crowd. Nathan moved in the beat of the music, in a standing position, without moving his feet and kept his face turned and fixed on Christopher and Frankie. Christopher, with his lips pressed together firmly, looked as if he was worried he would make a mistake and only took his eyes off his sheet music to check Frankie's fingering. Then, finally reaching Frankie, she smirked and shook her head. His knees bent, tapping his boot, as he swayed with the music. His smile extended from ear to ear, with his tongue curled out around the corner of his mouth, he was thrilled to be up there on that stage. The whole time she looked on, she prayed that her mother and father were there in spirit to witness her very special blessings that only God could have given her. Later, she dreamed of Sam sitting by her side and experiencing this miracle in her life.

After the kids played "Redwing", Stone went on to "Ragtime Annie", and then "Westphalia Waltz", ending their first session with Mother Marie, Sister Ruthie and Becky singing, "The Sunnyside of Life".

Standing up to sing, Mother Marie stood first to sing lead, then Becky in the middle with Sister Ruthie at her side. Starting out, they held hands, and then Mother Marie used hand gestures describing the song. Becky and Sister Ruthie had Mother Marie dancing to the song as she pointed her finger out into the crowd. By the time, they were half way into the song; the entire crowd was standing and clapping their hands with the beat.

With the first session complete and after a long applause, Stone introduced the children to the audience. Afterwards he announced a forty-five minute break with activity announcements, followed by the other singers who had come, and then stating the Malloy's would be back and play again.

Lined up, hand in hand Becky led them through the crowd, back to the house. Anna tucked dish towels as bibs to keep them spot free while they ate their lunch. Becky joined them and told them, "After we are done with all our music, we will team up and go to the carnival. Only if, she insisted, everyone stays together in their team, no matter what!"

With great anticipation on their smiling faces, they shook their heads, "Yes", as they inhaled their lunch to get back to the park.

Back on stage, Stone started their second session with, "Wildwood Flower". While they played, Sister Ruthie came and spoke to Sarah. Sarah left, telling Becky she would be back soon and Sister Ruthie sat down next to Becky. She leaned over towards Sister Ruthie and asked if there was any problem? She replied, "Not that I know of."

Bessie stepped down from the gazebo onto the dance floor where a table was set up for records they would played later for the dance and Becky joined her to stretch her legs for a while. Sarah returned and suggested they look over the list of music for the evening, winking at Bessie without Becky noticing.

Their next selection to play was, "Sally Ann", followed by, "Star of County Down." As the children started into, "Star of County Down", which is a waltz that would bring tears to anyone's eyes, Becky felt a tap on her shoulder from behind. She turned to see who it might be, and there before her, stood Sam, with his hand stretched out, bowing and asking for this dance. She reached with her left hand for his, as her right hand covered her mouth. He took her hand down, giving her a warm smiling with a teary-eyed look and then pulling her into his arms and waltzed her around the floor. She returned his smile with hers, as tears dripped off the sides of her face. Neither, able to continue, they stopped and fell into each other's arms. Suddenly the children stopped playing and looked on at their mother with this strange man. Becky immediately knew the children's fear, took Sam over to the front of the gazebo, and said, "It's alright, Frankie, kids, he, is your daddy!"

Sam looked up at Frankie, winked his eye and said, "Play it again, Frankie," as he took Becky back to the middle of the dance floor.

Frankie changed the selection to "Cripple Creek" and Kayla yelled out, "Happy music!" Sam and Becky showed them their happy dancing, as the children looked over the father they had only seen in pictures. They enjoyed watching them so much, Frankie took charge over Stone's commands and started into, "Midnight on the Water", just to see them waltz again.

As they waltzed, Becky said, "As you can see, I have kept very busy while you have been away, asking him, How do you feel about coming home to find you have seven children?"

He turned her as they danced, so he could look up at them and replied, "There could never be anything more wonderful to top this. I love you so much Becky." Then, continued waltzing, burying his face into Becky's hair to cover his tears of joy.

Stone announced the last song as he glanced over at Frankie, "This one is for your dad, Frankie, "Soldier's Joy". Then he gave Frankie a thumbs up with a big smile.

Before the music had ended, Sam stopped dancing to kiss and hold her tighter in his arms. When he released her slightly, the whole family had gathered around them.

One by one, Becky introduced his children, starting with Frankie, already entangled in his legs. "We met earlier today." Sam stated, looking down at Frankie and then leaning to pick him up into his arms. Then he went on to say, I have waited a very long time to be able to hold you in my arms. I have always loved you and I'm very proud of you for taking such good care of your mom for me."

Frankie replied, "Momma is going to be very happy now and she won't cry anymore."

"We'll make sure of that, won't we buddy?" suggested Sam. Frankie shook his head to agree, and then hugged him. Taking his time with each one of the kids, picking them up and holding them too in his arms, he assured them of his love.

When he had worked his way through the family, greeting them with hugs and hand shacks, followed by Becky and the kids, he turned to Becky, wrapped his arm around her shoulder and relished another kiss, looked over the kids and asked, "Does anyone want to go to the carnival?" Extremely amused by their individual excited reactions, all he could do was bust out laughing.

While the kids rode the rides and they watched their happy faces, Sam had Becky bring him up to date. When she told him about her parent's accident, her tears just ran. He stopped her from continuing further and said, "They would be so proud of you, Becky. And, knowing your dad, we had better show these kids a really good time."

As he wiped her tears away with his handkerchief she said, "Can you just hear dad!" Straighten yourself up young lady; there is no need for this!" They laughed agreeing with her statement and then turned their attentions on the kids.

Dinner consisted of anything they wanted off the food trailers, then off to explore all the games the carnival had to play. With Sam, Richard and his brother's help, all the kids had arms full of stuffed animal and toys to take home. They finished off the evening with ice cream and then danced their way towards home.

Sam helped Becky tuck in the kids that night and then helped carry the instruments back home. With all the family and friends there, it was a short task. All the emotional excitement the day had held, everyone decided to call it a night.

Becky was astonished by the fact that not one child complained of having a tummy ache with all the junk food they had consumed that day. In fact, she did not even notice when they came down stairs dressed for Church. She hurried them through their breakfast and then told them to go get dressed. After she said that, Sarah replied, "But mamma!" We are dressed."

"Me too." Kayla answered.

Then, "Me three." From Frankie, with Nathan, Michael, Christopher and Joseph finishing to seven.

"O.k. then!" Becky replied in a funny sarcastic way, "I'll bet you still need to brush your teeth!" Before she had finished that sentence, they all scattered from the room.

Before Father Mathew started his service that morning, he gave thanks to the Lord for Sam's safe return home to his family. His sermon for the day covered the importance of keeping faith and hope through all circumstances. Telling the congregation that God's purpose involves other people, other events in others lives and all things in His timing, that is far beyond what any human could bring to life. He said, "Asking why or thinking He is not there is such a waste of your own time and needless sorrow. By staying in His word and trusting Him with all your heart, He will bring all situations into a place of peace and joy. And by holding onto that trust you will feel that peace within you through it all."

Sam had a good visit with his family, spending all his time with them while the kids were playing outside, catching up on all he had missed while he was gone. After they went back home, Becky and Sam stayed mostly at home and just enjoyed the kids. They sat looking through the photo albums, with her showing him the fun they had had on the farm and how scared they were when Mother Marie took them to court. He spent a lot of alone time too with those albums over the next several months. Becky sat with him at times, giving him details and sharing the occasional tears.

That fall, he started college and continued his career in the service. Dusty gave birth to twin girls in November and Becky helped her in her spare time with the feedings and household chores. She continued with the children's music lessons, having them learn to play all kinds of music and picking a new theme for the next festival.

Steven and Sarah were married on Valentine's Day. Becky, Sally, Dusty and Merriam attended Sarah in her wedding wearing gorgeous scarlet gowns. Arlin gave Sarah away to Steven and his sons shared the best man seats, with Stone, Sam and Richard.

At their reception, Sam, Richard and the kids played every kind of music, from ballads to good old rock-n-roll. Yet, every time Sam and Becky went to the dance, Frankie would always change the music to a waltz. Just like the day, his daddy came home.

For several years, talent agencies confronted Sam and Becky wanting to make stars of the children. Both of them in agreement, never gave them an inch, saying, "Our children, until they are grown to decide their own careers, will only continue to perform as they do now. For now their music is part of this family and we intend to keep it this way always." They made it perfectly clear, to every agent, that both their spiritual and scholastic education would be their first and utmost priority.

Becky never missed her prayer ritual at her pew and after Sam came home, he was always there to sit by her side and pray as well. Her every prayer had been answered.

Printed in the United States
143819LV00003B/6/P